SECRET OF THE STARS

✴✴✴

T0168779

Baen Books
By Andre Norton

✳ ✳ ✳

SECRET OF THE STARS

* * *

ANDRE NORTON

SECRET OF THE STARS

Secret of the Lost Race copyright © 1959 by Ace Books, Inc.
Star Hunters copyright © 1962 by Andre Norton.

A Baen Books Original

Baen Publishing Enterprises
P.O. Box 1403
Riverdale, NY 10471
www.baen.com

ISBN: 978-1-4767-3674-7

Cover art by Adam Burn

First Baen paperback printing, May 2014

Distributed by Simon & Schuster
1230 Avenue of the Americas
New York, NY 10020

Library of Congress Cataloging-in-Publication Data

Norton, Andre.
 [Novels. Selections]
 Secret of the stars / by Andre Norton.
     pages ; cm
 ISBN 978-1-4767-3674-7 (omni trade pbk.) 1. Science fiction. I. Norton,
Andre. Secret of the lost race. II. Norton, Andre. Star hunter. III. Title.
 PS3527.O632A6 2014
 813'.52--dc23
                        2014002508

Printed in the United States of America

10 9 8 7 6 5 4 3 2 1

＊

CONTENTS

SECRET OF THE LOST RACE

* * *

Confidential: X3457-A-R-
From: Kronfeld, Director, Colonization Project 308
To: Lennox, Commander, Space Scouts, Fifth Sector, Detached Rating
Subject: Service Files
    Require release to this department service files for following:

O-S-S-D 451 Marson, H. Deceased.
O-S-S-D 489 Ksanga, V.T. Deceased.

* * *

Confidential: X3457-A-R- Reply
From: Lennox, Commander, Space Scouts, Fifth Sector, Detached Rating.
To: Kronfeld, Director, Colonization Project 308
Subject: Service Files
    Regret orders forbid release of official records to any department not connected directly with service.

(Message in code from Lennox to Sen Yen Lui, Commander-in-Chief, Fifth Sector, accompanying micros of above)
    What is going on? Who talked and where? Should these files be "lost" for the duration?

(Reply in code from Sen Yen Lui to Lennox)
    Sit tight. We will ask questions of our own. If there is trouble shall contact you at once so you may take proper steps.

* * *

✳ ✳ ✳

Order: 56431-S.S.D.
From: Mahabi Kabali, Space Admiral, Commanding Fifth Sector
To: Sen Yen Lui, Commander-in-Chief, Space Scouts, Fifth Sector
Subject: Service Files

You will herewith order release of records of following (listed below) to be consulted, in accordance with usual procedure, by Kronfeld, Director of Colonization Project 308.

O-S-S-D 451 Marson H. Deceased
O-S-S-D 489 Ksanga, V.T. Deceased

(Coded note accompanying the above)

Sorry. Pressure is on, hard. We cannot sit on this now. Anyway both men are safely dead, and have been for years. And there cannot be any possible leak of the real facts; only suspicions.

(Call on private com-band from Kronfeld to Bryar Morle, Port of N'Yok)

Get your best private investigator on this. We know now that the probable port of entry *was* N'Yok. And there was a child that looked young but was about six or seven. Time of entry approximately fifteen—sixteen years ago. Sure, the trail is cold, and it's getting colder all the time. But this is our first positive lead; it could well be the last. I needn't tell you that this is a category one order. Time is running out. Draw on the Foundation Funds. We can prove our case if we have the evidence. Those boneheads in uniform are already sweating!

(Comment of Bran Hudd, partner in Hudd and Rusto, Private Investigators)

Cold trail? This thing's in space freeze now. What does this joker think we are—miracle men or time travelers? Rusto: He lays down the credits like he grows 'em special in his cellar. So we go through the motion anyway. And a spread of cash can loosen tongues. You have that mock-up of what they think the dame looked like. Shove off and start earning our share.

✳ ✳ ✳

$* \text{\Large ✳} \textbf{1} \text{\Large ✳} *$

JetTown, Port of N'Yok, where strange wares were sold for the amusement, fair or foul, of crewmen out of space, and those who preyed upon them, and the elite who took their cut from the predators in turn. There were circles within circles on the streets, an intricate social organization which would have amazed the city dwellers beyond the rigidly drawn, yet physically unmarked, boundaries of that sinister blot edging out in a triangle, its base fronting on the scarred landing aprons, a narrow tongue licking "uptown."

On the streets a man's life might depend not only on his wits and toughness of body, but also on the development of a sixth sense of impending trouble. Sometimes an uneasy foreboding swept the whole area. That eerie disturbance was alive tonight, though the hour was early and few of the big spots were fully open.

Kern's SunSpot was, but the boast of the SunSpot was that it never closed. The air, tossed about but not in any manner really renewed by the conditioners, was tainted with old smoke, the aroma of weird drinks, and the old, old smell of over-crowded humanity. The big central room was as always with Step and Haggy on duty at the bar. A few of the girls were already drifting in.

Yet the young man, seated alone at the star-and-comet table, his counters in a neat rack before him, the unopened packs of kas-cards at his elbow, checked the highly illegal force-blade in the soft folds of the wide silken sash about his flat middle. His shoulders moved under the loose-sleeved jacket which covered his ruffled shirt as if he were flexing his muscles in prelude to some attack. Trouble—he could taste it, smell it—this was going to be a bad night.

He snapped on the play light above the table. Under that carefully adjusted radiance his thin face was that of a boy, wearing the faint, indecisive cast of adolescence, almost of youthful innocence. That face was worth a lot to his employer. Kern valued Joktar for his face, as well as for the keen brain behind it, and the clever, knowing hands which obeyed that brain. Kern trusted his head star-and-comet dealer as far as he trusted anyone—though that was a limited distance.

Joktar knew that his game was checked at intervals, and that a variety of sly traps had been set for him. A good many dealers in the SunSpot had come to sudden and sometimes messy ends. At least three had been delivered to the Emigration men. Kern had seen to it that all his employees were made fully aware of such object lessons. So far Joktar had run straight, not for any ethical reason since ethics were not learned on the streets, but because playing a straight game with a vip was simply good insurance.

He admired Kern's executive abilities without developing any personal liking for the man. And so far the boss of the SunSpot was the only stable thing Joktar had known in this dangerous world. He had been at the SunSpot most of the life he could remember, which was a short one for he did not even know how old he was. Though strangers always under-calculated his age by a half a dozen years or more.

Since that peculiarity added to his value to Kern, he welcomed it. Though when some buck lost at the tables and turned nasty he was apt to try to take on the "kid" for an easy smash. Accordingly Joktar had acquired a well-known and respected proficiency with a force blade, and had other knowledge of odd forms of personal combat learned from tutors who had picked them up all around the galaxy. As a result Joktar of the SunSpot was now reckoned one of the deadliest infighters on the streets, though he was no call-out man with a ready challenge.

Click, click, the counters with their emblazoned stars, their glittering diamond-paint comets, moved under his slender fingers. He built a small tower, lowered it chip by chip. Every nerve of his was responding to the unseen menace—waiting.

"The E-men are out . . ."

That was a whisper from beyond the table light. Joktar glanced up from his pile of counters. Hudd, the banker from the one-two table, stood there. He was a new man, but too much of a pusher. Joktar gave him another week here, perhaps a day or two more, then he'd push too far, ask one question too many and Kern'd take steps. He wasn't a police plant. So he must be a spotter from one of the other vips; somebody could be planning to pull a climb-up on Kern. Joktar smiled inwardly. How many had tried that game in the past? Almost as many as the counters in his racks. Kern had had a long run and no crack showed yet in his organization.

"They're sweeping?" he asked Hudd as if it did not matter in the least.

"The growl is that they're going to make a big pull."

A big pull. And the news passed to him by Hudd. Joktar added one point to the other. Could this be an oblique warning? Why? Hudd was no friend of his. So why did this newcomer wish to pull any of Kern's men out of an E-net . . . unless he had a future use for him. Only . . . Joktar had not been approached lately with any offer to change allegiance. He always reported such to Kern, knowing that at least half were tests. This a new one?

"Pass the word." He stubbed the light button, swept his card packs and counters into the wide drawer of his table and sealed them there with the pressure of his thumb in the lock slot. He stood up, slim, small, boyish, his cool eyes surveying Hudd with aloof speculation.

The other met that stare with a calculating intentness, as if the younger man was a hand held by a too-lucky player. His lips parted as if he would add to his warning. But Joktar had already turned away with the controlled litheness of a blade man, to cross to the lift which served Kern's private apartment above.

Orrin was on guard aloft. A stocky, solid man, not yet run to seed, trained as a space marine before he left that service under circumstances which made him useful to Kern. Orrin whirled, his blaster half-out of the holster, as Joktar stepped from the anti-grav plate. He laughed a little raggedly, and slapped his weapon back.

"Better sing out on the way up next time, kid. A man can lose half his brain pulling a quiet come-in like that."

"You got the jumps? Well, the signs are up . . . trouble."

Orrin's boots shuffled, his broad face was unusually sober. "Yeah, there's a few! You got a nudge for the boss?"

"Maybe so, maybe no. Call me in."

Orrin snapped the lever of the visa-plate, waved Joktar before it. The whirr of the answering buzzer came as a panel slid into the wall. The dealer flipped the force blade from his sash into Orrin's waiting hand. For anyone to pass Kern's door armed was to face inanimate sentries who eliminated without question. Human guards could make mistakes, Kern's last line of defense never did.

"What's the rumble?"

Kern's lank form sprawled on an eazee-rest. His voice was soft and the tone came from his thin, concave chest. He was dressed in street finery. His lavishly embroidered, brightly colored clothes did not hide the angular lines of his ungainly body. Similarly, his long, curly, gray-brown hair, and the thatch of sideburns that grew to exaggerated points on his sunken cheeks did nothing to soften his sharp features. He pointed and Joktar sat down on a footstool—a concession.

"Nothing as yet," the dealer answered the question.

Kern's silence was an invitation to elaborate.

"I have it that the E-men are on a big pull."

"Yes," Kern yawned. "That would stir up the streets. Who spilled? One of our runners?"

"Hudd."

"Hudd. Well, well, well. Did he make this growl to you personally?"

Joktar smiled, an engaging, boyish expression, until one noted the coolness of his eyes. "He was meant to, wasn't he?"

He fully expected agreement from Kern. Every time he had

spotted one of the boss' checks, Kern admitted readily enough that the test had been his idea. But this time the other shook his head.

"Not my hand, boy."

"Hudd's a plant," Joktar stated firmly.

"Certainly. But for whom, and why? Such small mysteries make life interesting. We'll let him run on the string a little longer until we discover who holds the other end. So he made a point of warning you . . ."

"I haven't had any offers recently." Something in Kern's expression brought that out of Joktar, almost against his will, and he felt self-contempt for offering that avowal.

"I know that. How long have you been here? Fourteen . . . no, it must be fifteen years now. And yet you still look like a dewy-eyed kid. I'd like to learn that trick, it's a neat one for our business. Yes, it was back in '08 that that doll staggered in here with you pulling her along. You were a smart brat even then. I'd like to know where you came from."

An old crawling chill touched Joktar. "You had me psyched, didn't you?"

"Sure. And by a medic who knew his stuff. All he got from you was babble about a big ship and the port here. That doll was queer, too. I sure wish she hadn't died before Doc could run her through the hoops and really learn something. Doc swore you'd been blocked, that you'd never be able to remember more than he got out of you under a talky shot."

"Why did you keep me here, Kern?"

"Well, boy, I like puzzles and you're about the best I've ever got my hands on. You grow a little bigger, but slow, and you keep looking like a kid, yet you've got a brain that ticks fast and straight and you don't get smart ideas. You're about the best dealer I've ever seen spread out the cards. You don't take to dames, nor to rot-gut, nor to happy-smoke. Just you stay the way you are, boy, and we'll rub along without any flarebacks. So, this growl is that the E-men are out? Set up the house warning."

Joktar went to the panel of switches on the far wall, pulled three. Throughout the SunSpot now the general alert would go up. Not that

Kern should have anything to fear from an E-raid, he paid in enough each quarter to equip fifty colonists and that was a matter of official record.

"Could it be Norwold, I wonder? He's been reaching lately. If he's due to get the blast . . ." Kern squirmed out of the soft eazee-rest. "Tip that flutter to Passey, he's our spotman at Norwold's tonight. Tell him to be ready to flit if there's a raid, but also, he's to watch where Norwold plants those two new dolls—we could use 'em here."

"Right." Joktar went out, collecting his blade from Orrin as he passed. He wondered about Kern's guess that Norwold would be netted. You *could* buy your way out of the E-pens, but the price was so high only a vip or a vip's favorite could unpocket enough. The E-men raided to obtain the cheap labor needed to open up a frontier planet. Colonists volunteered, passed rigid tests; emigrants were dispatched by force: neither ever returned. To be caught in an E-raid was the most blighting fear which overhung the streets: processed, drugged, sent out in frozen sleep from which some never awakened, to endure slavery on an alien world.

Colonists were heroes. To be an emigrant one merely had to be alive, reasonably healthy, and in possession of an undamaged body—undamaged that was in the sense that one had the proper number of arms and legs. A good many men on happy-smoke went out in deep freeze. Supposing he was netted, would Kern unpocket to get him out of the pens? He doubted it.

Joktar was on the anti-grav plate when the alarms went, setting up a noiseless vibration which tingled through the flesh, nerves and blood of every man and woman under that roof. *Raid, E-raid—here!* So, Hudd had given him a straight growl after all!

He slammed his hand against the controls of the grav-plate, sending it up instead of down. Too late to try to reach the low runs. There was only the roof way.

But he slowed the plate at the third level. What about Kern? Orrin waved him back when he would have gone to the boss' door.

"Boss says scramble!"

The guard crowded on beside the dealer. Kern, alone, of those in the SunSpot had the power to negotiate with the raiders. But how had his espionage system failed so badly that they had been jumped without any real warning? Was Hudd in E-service? No, he wouldn't have given a warning if that were true. Joktar asked a question of Orrin. He shrugged. "Don't ask me where the snap came, kid. For all I know the boss pulled this flareback himself. He didn't spout any fire when we got the alarm."

Joktar's brain chewed that. He could see no possible cause for Kern to open the SunSpot to raiders. On the other hand the boss had a love for the devious which could be satisfied by this roundabout way of removing some subordinates. Joktar thought of the more prominent employees, trying to pick out any Kern might hold in disfavor.

The plate came to a stop and Joktar's palm flattened on the wall where the heat of his flesh, as well as the patterns on his fingertips, unlocked a door for them. Ahead was a narrow corridor. The tingle of the alarm snuffed out. Orrin snorted.

"They must be close. Let's hope most of the boys made it in time."

At the end of the corridor a series of toe and finger holds led them to a climb-shaft. Topping that they would be directly under the roof. Of course the E-copters would be waiting up there, but the refugees would have fog bombs to handle that situation.

"You got a good lay-up, kid?"

Joktar's sixth sense pricked. Why did Orrin ask that? Every employee of Kern had his own hiding place for the raids.

"Any reason not to try the regular?"

"Dunno," Orrin sounded uneasy. "Just wondered . . . if the boss did set this one off . . . well . . ."

Yes, Kern could have betrayed every bolt hole, every hideout. The trouble was, as Kern's man, he had no choice now. He'd have to follow the set pattern of escape already learned. All other avenues would be the property of Norwold's crowd, or Dander's or Rusanki's and so closed to outsiders.

"Better speed up, they'll be puffing soon," Orrin warned.

Yes, the raiders would loose narcotic gas into the building, following that with the "shake-up" of sonic vibration: an efficient combination to clean out the building. Joktar pulled up to the section where he crawled on hands and knees under the shell of the roof. It was dark here, he would have to locate the fog bombs by touch.

His outstretched hand swept across a row of egg-shaped objects. Joktar wiggled one free and nursed it in his left hand, his other going to the blade in his sash.

He hunched close to the end of the passage, his shoulders now under the trap door. Heaving it up an inch or so he looked out. The glare of raid lights dazzled his eyes. Bringing the small bomb up to that gap he triggered its control and rolled it out.

A second egg followed the first. Then there was a pain twisting at him nerve and muscle: a warning of what would be agony in seconds to come. The sonics were on below.

"Get going!" Orrin shoved him. The fog was curling up from the eggs, cutting down visibility.

"Now!" Orrin's hand at his back half-propelled him through the trapdoor. Apparently, the ex-marine was more sensitive to the vibrator.

Joktar was in the half-crouch of the experienced knife fighter. The fog formed an envelope about them, a mist into which E-men would not dare to blast for fear of shooting their own men.

The dealer made for the far side of the roof. He must swing over, out, and down; a way not to be taken blindly by anyone who had not practiced that maneuver. Then, a short dash to another concealed door and the rest of the escape route tailored to Kern's orders.

Joktar leaped into the whirling blank of the cottony mist. He lighted on solid footing, sped on to the door. There was no sound of Orrin behind, perhaps the guard had not dared to make that jump into nothingness. For a moment, the dealer hesitated, and then the first law of his jungle prevailed: in a raid it was each man for himself.

A panel swung under his hand. He plunged through only to be pinned in a spearhead of brilliant light. Joktar's last coherent thoughts, as he went down under the full impact of a stun ray, was that he must have been included on Kern's list of expendables after all.

Joktar did not open his eyes at once. He let the senses of hearing and smell relay the first information of his new quarters to his brain. He knew he was not alone; a moan, a grunt, a querulous mumble to his left, assured him of company in misfortune. The smell of closely packed and none-too-clean humanity backed up that deduction.

He concentrated on his last clear memory; he had burst through the proper bolt hole, straight into the arms of a reception committee. So, now he must be in the E-pens. For a moment, wild panic shook Joktar's control. Then he forced himself to open his eyes slowly, to lie still, when every inch of him, mind and body, clamored for action. But his first lesson on the streets had been the need for patience— that and the folly of fighting against overwhelming odds blindly and without plan.

Letting his head roll to one side he obtained a floor-level view of his present quarters. Haggy from the SunSpot lay next to him, a drooling thread of saliva spinning from his slack mouth. Haggy, and beyond him was a stranger wearing the grimy skin which spelled happy-smoke addiction.

There were two more, both strangers and drifters, the sort easily swept up in any E-raid. But to find Haggy a fellow captive, that meant that more than one bolt hole of the SunSpot had been tagged. Haggy was not one to linger after the alert was on. Were all of Kern's senior employees here?

Time was one factor which must be reckoned with. Joktar tried to remember whether there had been E-ships waiting in port. But then such a raid usually occurred only when there was a ship ready. No use housing and feeding emigrants at government expense.

A man might escape from a planetside prison. However, as far as Joktar had ever heard, there was no escape except a buy-out from the E-pens. Unless you could prove that you were an honest citizen in good standing with a job. They were careful on that point nowadays, ever since the big stink when they had swept up the son of a councilor who had been doing some sight-seeing on the streets and shipped him off to the stars. Now there was supposed to be a double-check on the status of emigrants and that was when a buy-out could be arranged. But for that a man had to have someone working from the outside.

Kern? Joktar considered the possibility of help from the boss. He thought there was a thin chance, a very thin one, of that. And a man clung to any chance at a time such as this. He had no weapon, they had taken his knife, and the very possession of such a blade would count against him. His hands explored—yes, they'd taken his purse, his other small belongings. But what he wore beneath his shirt, the one thing which he had carried out of his misty childhood, that was still on him.

"Attention!" That impersonal bark out of the air overhead was like a whip-snap. "You will come out through the door immediately!"

✳ ✳ **2** ✳ ✳

As a section of the wall opened, Joktar felt the warning twinge of a vibrator. The captives would leave, all right, or twist in agony. He got to his feet, stooped to shake Haggy. The barman moaned, opened bleared eyes which became terror-stricken as he grew aware of his surroundings. Lurching free of Joktar's hold, he staggered to the door. The dealer followed, to be caught up in the web of a tangle-field. He could still walk, in fact he had to, since he was being drawn down a brightly lighted corridor, but otherwise he could not raise a finger.

The E-men had all the props. But then, why shouldn't they? The Galactic Council was solidly behind this emigration policy which worked two ways. First it got rid of the drifters and those outside the law on the civilized worlds, and second, it helped to open new planets. Thus both problems were settled to the satisfaction of all but the victims, who had no political power anyway.

Haggy had passed through another door ahead; now it was Joktar's turn. The barman was in the process of stripping off his gaudy clothing under the supervision of a bored medic.

"All right, you there," the same man spoke to Joktar, "strip."

Joktar regarded him mutinously. They had relaxed the tangle-field, but if he tried to jump the medic, they would slap it on again and they could tighten those lines of invisible energy to choke the breath out of a man's lungs. No use fighting when there wasn't the smallest chance to win. He dropped his jacket, unwound his belt sash. No chance to palm anything since they must have a spy-spot on him. But, as his shirt followed his jacket, the dealer's hand went to the disc hanging on a chain about his throat.

"Hand that over, you!" the medic was alert.

For the first time since the momentary panic upon his awakening in the pens, Joktar's control came close to snapping. He stood breathing a little raggedly. The medic clasped one hand into a fist and Joktar staggered, bit his lip against an answering cry. That vicious squeeze of the tangle was a warning. He tossed the disc to the medic, who allowed it to fall to the floor and kicked it away spinning.

So he was processed after Haggy, run through the examination machines, his brain busy with escape plans as impossible as they were fleeting. Then, wearing a coverall of coarse red stuff, vividly visible, he was steered into a cell with five others, all strangers.

They were fed from mess kits slid through a wall panel. And there was little talk among them. These were all young, Joktar noted, but of the drifter class, spineless hangers-on such as could be picked up by the hundred in the streets. He squatted back on a bench, the mess tin on his knee.

"Hey!" one of his cellmates sidled down the bench. "You worked for Kern, didn't you?" There was a malicious twist to his half-grin. The gap between his sort and a man who was employed in one of the big spots was an ocean wide.

"Me, I usta run for Lafty 'fore he got wiped off the books," he added in a spurt of half-defiance. "Saw you in the SunSpot layin' 'em out. Think Kern'll unpocket for you now?" His grin grew wider.

Joktar shrugged, chewing methodically at the tasteless mess on his plate.

"Kern got wiped proper," one of the others raised his head to sputter through a full mouth. "Saw four—five of his men being run through here."

That could be true. Though how such a coup could have been managed with runners and spotters planted to prevent just such a catastrophe Joktar did not understand. This report dimmed his one small hope of rescue. Kern himself might be in the pens now. Who was behind it, Norwold?

"Anybody heard where they're fixing to send us?" The thin voice shook a little.

"Ship in port bound for Avar," volunteered the ex-runner.

"Yeah? What's Avar, anybody know?" another of the captives asked.

"Field work," someone answered, but he didn't sound too convincing and Joktar was sure that was a guess. Perhaps because field work could be preferred over labor in a mine.

The ex-runner gave a laugh which was close to a snarl. "Don't matter much, burnout—you goes where you is sent. No pickin' or choosin'. You ain't no colonist. When you lands here your luck is out anyway."

That was only too true. Someone sighed and Joktar finished the last of his food.

"They freezes you, don't they?" the quavering voice asked.

"Sure thing," the ex-runner responded with a ghoulish relish. "No room in an E-ship to have you sittin' round eatin' your fat head off. Stick some needles full of goop in a fella, make him stiff as a board, and bed him down in a hold. He'll keep 'til you get planetside again."

"Only I heard as some don't make it to wake up again."

The ex-runner leaned forward on the bench. "Sure, a man's luck may be run out all the way. They gets enough of 'em through to make a trip pay. Maybe them machines they had us in and out of tell 'em which can make the big jump and live."

"Hey!" One of the others started away from the wall. "I hear someone comin'! Maybe they'll run us out now."

Joktar was on his feet, his mess tin held as if that could serve him in place of his lost force blade. The ex-runner laughed.

"Fixin' for a rumble, kid? You ain't got a chance. Every guard in here carries a tangle. Me, I'd take what they dish out peaceable. No use askin' to be worked over just to prove how big and brave you are."

He was right, but Joktar resented that rightness. His own helplessness was a frightening thing. He had believed he was tough and independent. But he began to realize now that there had always been Kern and the SunSpot between him and the full rawness of the streets. Now he was really alone and he needed time to adjust. He put the tin plate on the bench, seated himself beside it. And the ex-runner, reading his face with the shrewdness of his kind, stopped grinning.

A guard stood in an open panel, surveying them with contempt. His glance fastened on Joktar and he beckoned. The hope which had died a few moments earlier revived. Kern, buying him out? Joktar shoved past the ex-runner, only too willing to obey that summons. The familiar strangle of the tangle fell about him and his spark of hope flickered.

Two more guards closed in at the end of the corridor and one of them spoke to the man escorting the captive.

"Gentlehomo Ericksen wants you at the front office. We're to hold this one until later."

"Why the change?"

"Spaceport police want to ask him some questions."

Spaceport police? Joktar was bewildered. Was this some move of Kern's? The boss had his contacts in the port control, all vips did. But, as the first guard left, the tangle caught with a painful grip about his middle.

"Get going, you!"

The pace they set was close to a run and Joktar sweated, his first uneasiness growing close to fear. These guards had a furtive air, as if they were acting beyond their orders. Yet their attitude toward him did not suggest they were in Kern's pay.

His puzzlement grew as he was hustled into a small room to front a man in the uniform of the port police as well as a young man wearing a tunic Joktar had not seen before. The regular space patrol went in dark blue, this man's garb was silver-gray and sported a badge bearing a glittering constellation, instead of the comet and circle of stars. Joktar blinked. Somewhere—perhaps in that portion of his brain which had been blocked so long ago—a small prick of warning flashed, then spread. He knew that this stranger spelled a deadly danger out of all proportion to their present meeting.

Then he glimpsed what the strange officer was holding and sucked in his breath. The disc he had been forced to abandon in the examination room swung from its chain gripped between the other's forefinger and thumb. Above it the man's face was stark with anger. Yet Joktar was sure he had never seen the other before.

"Well, Gentlehomo," the policeman spoke first, "this one of the scum who jumped you and your friend?"

"If he isn't, he knows them! This proves it, doesn't it? How else would a burnout from the streets get a scout's ident? You—" he added two descriptive expressions which flattened Joktar's lips against his teeth in a tight snarl. Then the dealer rocked under a blow across his face.

"Well? Speak up! Where did you get this ident?" In its way, the policeman's reasonable tone was as deadly as the open brutality of the officer's attack.

"I've always had it." Joktar was startled into the direct truth and knew that they would never believe him.

One of the guards who had brought him there spoke hurriedly:

"Look here, we'll have to make this quick. They've ordered him up to the front office. There's a buy-out waiting."

The officer in the gray tunic stiffened. "Who'd unpocket for this dirt?" he demanded. "Talk you, and straight on orbit! Who burned down Kender last week? And where did you get his ident, you swine?" He swung the disc as a flail and the metal ripped Joktar's already bruised cheek.

When he shook his head, as much to combat dizziness as to deny the charge, they really went to work. He was helpless in the tangle and they battered him until at last, he lay on the floor, trying to hold to the ragged edge of consciousness, still bewildered. There was a bustle at the door.

". . . ordered to get him to the front office. He's been cleared."

Cutting across that came a hot protest from the officer. "He's not going to get away so easy. He's one of the gang who mugged Kender, and he's going to pay for it."

Again the reasonable policeman: "If we hold him legally, we'll have to have more proof than just that ident-disc. He could have bought that from some stumble-bum for the price of a drink. And how do you know he didn't?"

"Wouldn't he have said so? This story about its being his—these things don't just float around in free-fall, you know. One is given to a man when he swears in, and he doesn't lose it easy. Kender was dead when they ripped his off. Why this little scum could trade on that ident anywhere, saying he was on detached duty, and live high!"

"But you'll still have a time proving murder on him."

"I tell you he isn't just going to walk out of here!"

There was an amused chuckle from the policeman. "No, you've seen to that. The boys'll have to carry him."

"Yeah," the guard sounded morose. "We take him upstairs looking this way and there'll be a beef blowing us higher than the first Moon base."

"Look here," a new voice said. "How about this, we're loading 'em in the *Griffin* right this minute. Slip him in with the rest of that bunch and who'll care afterwards? Just a mistake on somebody's part. They can't reach out and grab him out of space, and the front office won't speak up if there's likely to be a stink. He can't do anyone any harm where the *Griffin*'s going."

"And where's that?" demanded the space officer.

"Fenris."

The name meant nothing to Joktar but he detected an appeased note in the other's answer.

"Fenris!" The officer laughed. "That should do for him all right. Can you get him out on that ship?"

"If we hurry him through. And what if he doesn't get all the shots? Who's going to care if he doesn't wake up on the other side?"

The last thing Joktar heard was the judicial reply of the policeman: "Seems like you boys have it all figured out. No, I guess no one is going to worry. This whole thing's off record, remember. And you'll have to cook up a tale to satisfy your front office. Me, I'm not going to be dragged into any hassle with them."

They gathered their victim up from the floor and that pushed him over the border of unconsciousness. When he half-aroused again he had been dumped on a flat surface with force enough to set his body aching.

". . . stupid fools. Bring in this one late . . ." voices ebbed and flowed over him.

"What happened? He looks to me like an accident case."

"You aren't paid to ask questions. Probably a fight in one of the pens and this one started it. They hauled him out to keep the peace. We get enough of those."

Hands were stripping off his coverall. There was a sharp stab of pain, then another. A persistent buzzing, then black and cold—a cold so intense he shriveled, as a man shriveled under a force blade slash.

Joktar did not know or feel when he was rolled from the table into that waiting box with an unhealthy resemblance to a coffin, when the lid of that was made fast in impatient haste with skimped attention to various dials and indicators. A placard was slapped on the top, and the box became one of many in a truck waiting to roll.

Then came the spaceport where the transport waited under the crane projecting from the E-ship's hatch. The jaws of the crane bit into one box after another and they swung up, over into the maw of the cargo hold, each to be pegged down in a niche from which the cargo would eventually be discharged alive or dead as chance willed it. This would be months later in planet time and half the galaxy away in space. The last box was wedged in, the hatch sealed.

Not too long afterwards, the ship trembled to the push of jets, arose on her tail flames, moved out on course.

In the E-station front office, a man waited with a packet of credit notes. He grew impatient, demanded action, at last made a closed com-call to a number which surprised, irritated, and faintly alarmed the man in whose office he waited.

Another man, also equipped with credits, heard a rumor in the waiting room, confirmed it in two surreptitious and hurried interviews, and left the E-station. He debated the necessity of the return of the credits to their proper owner. And, because he was not foolhardy, he went back to the streets, found a hideout and admitted to the man there that certain plans had gone wrong. The man named Kern was disappointed enough to take several steps in the direction of retrieving his own prestige by a few sharp lessons. But once those orders were given, he forgot the whole affair for a while.

A third man in a small, discreet office received a com-call. As a result five men in widely separated points on Terra found themselves embarking on new assignments and three took off by jet for N'Yok.

Two E-guards were questioned, shipped out for Melwambe Port after being warned that if they talked they were going to be given the same processing they had given others. This was done within the month in spite of their protestations. The service could not stand another scandal, not now when there was an alarming new stirring behind scenes. Both E-guards eventually reached a planet named Blore and within the year one died from pal-pest and the other was killed by his fellows for informing on a gang break.

Another man, in the gray uniform of the scouts, went to a jeweler's shop in N'Yok the same hour the *Griffin* lifted. He had an ident-disc forced open. But when he read the name inside he went white under his space brown, remembering certain old stories. He was tempted to drop the disc into the nearest rubbish disposal when he left, but he finally decided to see it destroyed in his ship's atom-break. On his way back to the port, his pocket was picked. When he discovered his loss he was frightened, thoroughly frightened, for the first time in years.

A councilor, making a wide-flung inspection of frontier planet conditions, was scheduled to visit the second planet of the star, Zeta Lupi, in the Wolf Constellation. The name of that world was Loki and its closest neighbor was Fenris. There were hints of trouble on Fenris.

In an outlaw camp on Fenris, a man challenged the mob boss for a blast out. The man was named Samms and had once been an emigrant, now an escapee from the alibite mines. At present he nursed a long-range plan and the call for a blast out was the second move in it. Because the day was an unusually cold one and his opponent had been running a trap line, Samms was a fraction of a second faster and became the leader of the Kortoski mob that night.

* * *

(Report from Hudd and Rusto, N'Yok to B. Morle, redirected to Kronfeld, Director, Colonization Project 308)

Subject was questioned by space scout, disc taken from him, later opened by jeweler. Ident was for Marson, O-S-S-D 451. Scout took disc away from him. Thought subject was responsible for fatal mugging of his partner, Kender, which occurred on streets three weeks ago. Must stress difficulty dealing with E-station. Believe records there purposefully suppressed. Kern also tried to buy-out subject.

(Closed com between Kronfeld and Morle):

Kronfeld: Put men on this space scout. I don't altogether buy this friend-being-mugged story. Might just be something else. The boys in gray are getting upset all along the line. I want a full report on this scout. Will deal with the E people myself. Forget Kern, he's out of the picture now.

(Interdepartmental com)

E-S 59641—7/20

From: E-Service Station, N'Yok Port, Irson, Agent in charge

To: Kronfeld, Director, Colonization Project 308

Subject:

Report concerning emigrant, male, age about eighteen, race, Terran, picked up in raid on SunSpot, fourth day of March. This man shipped out on E-ship *Griffin*, destination planet Fenris for service in alibite mines. Correctly attested "unlawfully employed, unnecessary to the well-being of Terra." Micro of record attached.

(Closed com, Kronfeld to Morle)

K: Are you sure this is the man? Record from E-people way off on age alone.

M: They omitted some facts turned up in his physical, too. This record was edited. Certainly wrong on age, I have witnesses who can prove that. But if you are right there would be such a difference. They're working hard to cover up the irregularity in his ship out. But he was the one sent to Fenris all right. What can you do about that?

K: Nothing until he arrives. I'll alert our agent there. Trouble is that is a critical point just at present. He would land in a place such as that! With luck we may be able to bid him in at the auction. Fenris! It looks as if someone would like to get rid of him just as badly as we want to pull him into the fold. Blast those damn scouts. This was badly muddled straight from the beginning. I hope Thorn and Cullan can roast their tails straight up their spines! Send me everything you can dig up as fast as the boys feed it to you.

(Excerpt from Galactic Guide)

Fenris: Third planet in the system of star Zeta Lupi, Constellation Wolf. With the two other planets in this system, Hel and Loki, it shares a climate and terrain hardly endurable for native Terran stock.

Principle export: alibite and some furs. Traces of earlier native race, now extinct, exist in form of stone work and mounds. Subject to severe storms and nine months of freezing winter weather per solar year. One port: Siwaki. Two towns: Siwaki, Sandi, center of mining territory. Posted by survey as unsuitable for tourist travel. An "A" certificate required from anyone engaging passage to Siwaki.

* * *

At another camp, on the other side of a small mountain range, a spaceman who had been cashiered from the service and only recently had been bought out of a labor gang, listened carefully to the man who had put up the credits for his release. Then he talked himself, describing an event in his own past in detail. His benefactor was thus enabled to fit another piece into a very wide and broken puzzle, rounding out a pattern to please the man in the discreet office on Terra.

But the *Griffin* rode on, snapped into hyper-space, carrying in her cargo the missing element which would influence movements from Terra, to Fenris, to Loki. And an ex-star-and-comet dealer from the streets began the first step towards realizing a bizarre future.

✳ ✴ **3** ✴ ✳

About the Port of Siwaki the landscape was almost lunar in starkness. Only the harshness of the jagged peaks which enclosed the cup of the valley were muffled—one could not say softened—by a thick growth of vegetation on the lower slopes. This vegetation existed in the cold months as odd spongelike skeletons with stem surfaces which could withstand even a tri-steel blade, and was a slate-blue in color.

That blue stain spread up to meet the snow. And always the cold bit deep, through thermo underclothing and furs, through the heated walls of the living domes, stinging inward to a man's bones.

Fenris was alibite. Men went to the mines, ore came back. A fringe of businesses based on that two-way traffic made up Siwaki. And there were a few fools mad enough to try trapping for furs in the river valleys. But they were only a handful, the remnants of men who had pioneered Fenris before the companies fastened their strangleholds on the port and the three-quarters-frozen world.

This morning four of those independents had paused to scan the notice of an E-ship auction posted on the government board. Two of them shrugged, one spat eloquently, but the fourth continued to read on into the fine print of the clipped code of governmental language, until one of his companions tugged at the sleeve of his outer fur coat.

"No use trying to buck that."

The reader's eyes, which were all that showed between the

25

shielding roll of lamby wool about his hood and the frost mask covering nose and mouth, still held to the poster. Although the outdoor garb of Fenris added bulk to the body it covered, there was a hint of youthfulness in the way he shook off his fellow's hold.

"We'll stay," he spoke flatly, the authority of his tone not muffled by his mask. The man with him shrugged, but his mittened hand rested on the second belt about his middle, the one which supported the universal blaster of the frontiersman and a twenty-inch knife in a fur-tufted sheath.

At that moment, the numbed cargo mentioned in the poster was beginning to revive. Joktar, his memories of the E-station very hazy now, heard the muted chorus of mutters, moans, and such other symptoms of distress as he had heard in the N'Yok pens.

"This one's breathing."

He was grabbed, armpits and feet, swung out on a flat surface. Swift jabs of pain, then he was flung back to the misery of full revival. For misery it was, as the torture of returning circulation carried with it a belated realization of where he must be and why.

Sitting up, he blinked at the lights in the room, rubbing his hands over his bare body as if their pressure could relieve the tingling. For some reason he seemed to have recovered more quickly than the rest, for of the twenty men lying along the shelflike projection, he was the first to move freely. Memory supplied a name . . . Fenris. Just a name . . . he had no idea what kind of world lay outside the walls of this room.

"Stir up!" Men appeared in the doorway, wearing coveralls with the symbol of the port service on back and breast. They worked with rough efficiency to rouse the rest of the captives. Joktar sat where he was, a dull hatred seething inside him, wise enough not to resist. But his desire for escape was fast crystallizing into a drive almost as basic as his will to live.

The head guard reached him, gave a half-grin as he surveyed Joktar's slim body.

"The E's must be baby snatching now," he commented. "You'll end up on the bargain counter, sonny."

"All right, all right! On your feet, you dead heads!" The captives were pushed into a ragged line. "Get these on."

A duffel bag was produced and from it the guards pulled small bundles of cloth, tossing one to each man in line. Joktar drew on the pair of shorts, snapped the belt cord about his narrow waist.

"Mess . . ." They were pushed past the door, each handed a pleasantly warm container. Joktar felt real hunger, twisting off the top to swallow down a thick liquid, half-stew, half-soup.

"Now get this!" The head guard mounted a platform at the end of the room. "You're on Fenris. And this is no planet where you can go over the hill and live to get away." He snapped a terse word to his underlings and they put up a video projector. "There's only two places a man can live here. Right at this port, and up at the mines. You try to blast off, and this is what'll happen."

At a second snap of his fingers, a series of vivid video scenes appeared on the wall above his head. If the horrors they pictured had been faked, the creator had had a very morbid imagination. Joktar did not believe that they had been. Every stark detail of what could happen to a runaway was there in three-dimensional color: blanket storms, lamby on the prowl, poison springs, and half a dozen other terrors native to this wolf world. Even breathing without any protection meant that the icy crystals in the winds could bring a quick and fatal lung disorder. As a lesson against escape the show was very forceful. But the pictures did not in the least modify Joktar's private plans to stage a break-out at the first opportunity.

"Now you're going up for auction," the guard told them. "You'll probably be mine fodder. Play along with the rules, don't try any tough stuff, and you can maybe buy your time someday. First ten of you, this way."

By chance, Joktar was numbered among that ten. He was hustled on into a larger room, standing with his group on the platform facing a small audience of perhaps a dozen or so. Most of them were seated at ease, their outer furs slung back. But there were three or four others to the rear of the room who did not look so much at home.

". . . certified fit and able for labor . . ." someone droned. A man in E-service uniform was reading from the ship record.

The Fenrian guards thrust their charges into line again. One by one, they took a man by the shoulders, turned him slowly about for the inspection of the buyers. As they reached him, Joktar heard a voice rise from the bidders.

"What's that kid doing here? Nobody could get a full week's worth out of a skinny little worm like that!"

"I dunno, Lars, those skinny ones sometimes are tougher than you think." Another man arose and came forward to the edge of the platform. "Let's see your paws, kid."

The guard didn't give the Terran time to obey on his own. Clamping a grip on the captive's elbows, he swung his arms out. The bidder stabbed critically at the nearest palm.

"Soft. Well, that'll harden up using a digger. Might make a sorter of him. Only they'd better take a mark down on his price."

Joktar was shoved back into line and his neighbor brought out. The bidding began and, when they reached Joktar once again, he saw one of the men by the doorway move forward.

"Ten skins, prime lamby," the words broke through the monotonous offers of credits. The man who had examined Joktar's hands swung around in his seat, scowling.

"Who let this woods beast in?" he demanded.

The newcomer continued to thread a way between the seats until he stood by the E-officer.

"E-auction, right?" he asked, his tone holding much the same bite as had that of the mine man.

"Yes." The officer was plainly bored by it all.

"No privileged bidders, at least the notice didn't say so."

"No privileged bidders."

"Then I offer ten prime lamby skins." He stood there, his feet in their fur-lined, fur-cuffed boots, slightly apart, his body balanced as if he were about to issue a call out for a blaster meeting.

"Ten prime lamby skins bid," repeated the E-officer.

"Fifty credits!" snapped the challenging company man.

"Fifteen skins."

"One hundred credits!" a second of the miners cut in.

The E-officer waited a moment and then spoke to the other. "You still interested?"

Joktar watched the newcomer glance to his fellows by the door as if in appeal. When there came no answer from them, he shrugged, walked back. A snicker arose from the company men.

"Stay out in your mountain dens and freeze!" called the victorious bidder. Then he turned to the business at hand. "Well, do I get him for a hundred?"

The E-officer nodded and Joktar became the property of one of the companies.

They were sorted out into company groups at the end of the sale, fed, given quarters for the night, and each a suit of thermo clothing. Joktar listened eagerly to the guards, treasuring every scrap of information. He was now owned by the Jard-Nellis Corporation and their holdings were in a newly opened sector edging into the Kamador mountains; he had not been particularly fortunate. He tried to learn something about that other bidder, but discovered only that he was a trapper and that his bid was probably only another move in the old struggle between the companies and the handful of men who had pioneered Fenris on their own.

Early the next morning, the emigrants were loaded into the cargo hold of a crawler bound for the mines. Aircraft was not practical on the wolf world. Freakish storms had brought about too many crashes during the early days of settlement. Now transportation followed the archaic modes of travel, the roads themselves patrolled constantly against washout and storm damage. And against something or someone else, Joktar surmised, when he assessed the number and quality of the weapons carried by an unnecessarily large number of guards riding the crawler.

None of the emigrants were the type to rebel in order to break-out into the highly inhospitable wilderness they had already been indoctrinated to fear. So why the guards? And blasters and needlers were no protection against storms.

The heavy vehicle ground away from the port, but the emigrants in its windowless middle section had no view of the countryside. Fifteen men, drifters from the streets, happy-smokers already sunk in the gloom of a cut-off addict, a couple of bruisers who might have been the personal guards of some vip, shared those cramped quarters. The bruisers Joktar studied until he decided that they were not the stuff from which rebels were made. They might instead, if they survived the initial months of breaking in, serve as guards over their fellows.

As the men in the crawler began to shake down into a gang, he held aloof. Already the muscle men were asserting themselves. Joktar did not fear having to face either of them alone in rough and tumble, he knew too many tricks of infighting. But the two of them together would be a different matter.

The long day ended when the crawler sheltered for the night at a way station and the men were hustled from its warm interior, through a chill which bit like acid, into a dome. It was then that Joktar learned something new about himself. That cold which ate at his fellows, even subdued the bruisers, did not strike at him with the same intensity. His thermo suit was no better than theirs, and he had none of the outer furs of the guards. But to him that change of air was more exhilarating than numbing.

He thought about that as he swallowed the canned stew, remembering one or two other odd happenings out of the past. Those summer days in N'Yok when Kern had rallied him on always appearing cool, he had not been able to understand why others of the SunSpot staff swore at the heat every time they were forced to venture out of the air-conditioned building. And another time, further back when the cook, crazy mad from drinking sar-juice, had locked him, then only a small boy, into the freeze room. The dark cavern of the freeze room had scared him some but not the cold. When Mei-Mei, Kern's current favorite, had found him, she'd been scared, too, but because he had walked out under his own power. At the time he hadn't understood clearly what had excited her so much; now he began to. Suppose he could stand extremes of both hot and cold better than most men?

If that were true, it became a point on which to build an escape plan. He was so intent upon his thoughts that he momentarily forgot his surroundings. Then a foot struck against the knee of one of his outstretched legs.

"You there, bones, pay attention when a man talks."

Joktar glanced up. This would have come sooner or later, he had been resigned to such trouble ever since he had sighted the muscle men in their group. They were making the old, familiar play of the streets. Since he was, to outward appearances, fair game, someone they could belt around as an object lesson, they were going to put on a show. But neither was armed and it looked as if he had only to take one at a time.

A hand pawed at him, fastening thick fingers in the front of his thermo suit. Joktar yielded to that pull with a willingness the other had not expected. What followed was a complete reversal of the attacker's intentions.

The ex-dealer caressed skinned knuckles with the fingers of his other hand, and stepped over one flattened body to meet the snarling rush of his late assailant's partner. But a voice from the door of their lockup startled them both.

"All right you jet-propelled muckers! That does it!"

Joktar didn't need the jerk of a tangle to halt him.

He stood quietly, enveloped by the invisible cords, while the guard crossed to him.

"You," the company man stabbed a finger at Joktar, "over there." His order was enforced by a pull from the tangle. "Since you have so much energy, we'll just make you a load-hop on the jumper." His words meant nothing to his victim, save that the Terran did not doubt they meant a change from the crawler, and so perhaps a thin chance for eventual escape. "The rest of you," the guard used another tangle as a lash, sending them reeling backward, "walk small, or you'll be cut down to size the hard way."

He motioned Joktar ahead, out into an open space where a much smaller copy of the crawler stood.

"Take a good look," he bade his prisoner. "That's a jumper, used to supply the prospectors' holes back in the mountains . . ." He waved to the peaks murkily visible through the dome. "You try to travel outside her belly and—" a click of his gloved fingers, a carefully cultivated sinister expression suggested the deadly pictures they had been shown at the base. "And you won't be wearing one of these," he plucked at his upper layer of furs. "Thermo suit will keep you alive just long enough to load-hop at each point, you work on the double and your driver is kind-hearted. Now, let's see you load."

There was a pile of boxes and duffel bags waiting, and a gaping hole in the jumper's middle in which to stow them. Joktar went to work. Most of the cargo was easy enough to handle. But he sweated over the last box and the guard grinned.

"Not riding your tail flames so high now, are you, fighting man? Wait 'til you have to wrestle that one out at the Halfway Point. We'll have you babbling before you get in."

Joktar finished the job and the man waved him inside with the cargo.

"Stow in, we're going to run now."

The door of the cargo space slammed shut, and the new load-hop hurriedly hunted for anchorage in the dark as the jumper pulsed for a take-off. He discovered that the machine had been well-named, since the progress of the vehicle alternated unevenly between straightforward rumbling on the surface and sudden blind leaps, shaking the passenger painfully back and forth with the cargo.

In this hold, the atmosphere was distinctly colder. Joktar felt his thermo suit adjusting, but not enough to compensate entirely for that drop. But he was not really uncomfortable. And at last the jumper ground to halt.

"Get to it! Dump everything marked in red. Make any mistakes and you'll put 'em back in, slow time!"

The hold door was open and Joktar edged out to be faced by a gust of ice feathered wind. He gasped and choked, then he could breathe again, and shouldered out the first bag. A furred guard, masked, stood with a drawn blaster to one side.

Only that blaster was not on the load-hop, Joktar learned in one quick glance. Rather, the stance of the company man suggested trouble from beyond, where a swirling curtain of fine snow and ice crystals made a moving mist.

Joktar sprinted past the guard, dumped the bag at the side of a small dome and made a second lunge with a box. A pair of smaller bags, and then he could spot no more red marks. He thumped on the roof of the hold and the door closed. The machine rumbled on. Joktar breathed on his hands. He had stripped off his thermo mitts to find that his fingers were stiff, but not numb.

He began to wonder about the jumper. There was a driver somewhere aloft, and very probably a guard. Two men at least and both armed. He was unarmed and locked in between halts. He eyed the cargo about him speculatively. Could the contents of any of these boxes and bags serve his purpose? He investigated, only to discover that with bare hands none of the containers could be forced. Naturally! Who would leave a slave shut in with the raw materials for rebellion?

He'd either have to move during an unloading period, or just wait for some lucky chance. As a gambler he knew the odd pattern of percentages which his kind generally termed luck. There were men, he had seen them in action, who had times when they could call the sequence of cards and be sure they were right. That was a self-confidence he himself had known at intervals. But one could not control that ability at will.

Only could he afford to wait for one of those mysterious waves of luck, hoping to ride to freedom on its crest? He continued to rub his hands together as if limbering his fingers for a very important deal.

The jumper was climbing, her next port of call must be high in the mountains. According to what he had heard at Siwaki, the "holes" of the explorer-prospectors were always in danger. A company man had to be highly paid to venture that far from the safety of the main road and the mine settlement. How many men manned a hole, and how long did each party stay in such isolation? Did they use E labor? To escape from such an outpost must be easier than from the compounds at the mines.

The jumper was slowing down. Another post? No, the machine was reversing.

But not quickly enough!

A hammer blow struck the front end and the vehicle's backward spurt slowed to a feeble crawl. The floor under Joktar tilted at a sharp angle, the crawl became a skid. He tried to dodge the shifting cargo. Then the pace of the skid was fantastically accelerated. His last conscious thought was that the driver had lost control and they were falling down some mountain slope.

Joktar stirred feebly. No light now . . . dark and cold, such cold as he had never before known. He pushed against the obstruction pinning him down, felt a package give until he was able to free his legs. No bones broken; but his body was stiff and bruised.

The jumper was silent, no throb of motor. And the heat of the cargo hold had seeped away. He pounded on the wall in a sudden spurt of panic. There was no answer, just as somehow he had known there would not be. But he must get out of this trap.

Perhaps the machine had been rigged with an emergency exit in expectation of just such an accident. His exploration, conducted by touch, brought him to a panel which yielded. Pushing that up he forced an opening for escape.

4

Snow cascaded through the opening to engulf him. Now he could hear the scream of wind through the broken fangs of the peaks, a shriek of ravening hunger. He fought the snow with his hands, kicked his way out, until he sat on the side of the half-buried jumper.

It had been evening when he loaded that machine back at the road station. Now the sky was gray, he judged the hour early morning. The jumper had been jammed by a slide into a narrow valley, he could sight the scars of its passage down the mountain.

Joktar set to work digging, laboring to uncover the driver's compartment. A half-hour later, breathing hard, he had that wreckage clear. The driver and the guard might have died before the fall, for it was plain from the evidence that the jumper had been first smashed by the wing of an avalanche. From the dead he must take the means of keeping himself alive.

The sun was up, awaking glitter on the snow field, when Joktar inventoried his new wealth, reckoning his supplies as weapons in his fight for survival and freedom.

Over his thermo suit he now wore furs, the coat a little large, as were the warmly lined boots that reached to mid-thigh. The driver's blaster had been crushed, but the guard's weapon was now belted around him. He had found the emergency rations, eaten a full meal.

And now he set about making up a pack of necessities, a force axe, food, a map ripped from the stereo-case of the vehicle.

Among the cargo, there must be other things he could use, but the amount he could pack was strictly limited. Maybe, after he explored and found a base to hole up in, he could return and loot again, if the rescue force from the company had not located the wreck.

Joktar's efforts had kept his mind fully occupied. Only when he had his pack assembled and stood up to search for the best path out of the valley did the full force of his present loneliness strike. In spite of his lack of any close friends on the streets, Joktar had never before been totally removed from the physical presence of human beings. In the pens of the E-station, aboard the jumper, there had always been others, even if he had known them to be inimical.

Now he stood alone, buffeted by a moaning wind. To hunt out his own kind was to choose to return to the very imprisonment he fled. He had to face this as he had always faced any danger, with a core of stubborn determination based upon every ounce of will. With Fenris' wolf's breath at his back, he plunged into the drifts of the valley.

But he was not through the end notch before he began to doubt the wisdom of his course. The sun, shining when he left the wreck, was covered now by a mass of clouds, driving the darkness of twilight down upon the half-buried landscape. Storm! And the horror stories of the port were warning that he must find shelter.

Joktar rounded a mass of boulders imbedded in frozen earth and snow, the debris of an earlier avalanche. Something now showed through the murk, a line of smoke whipped by the wind. His mittened hand went to his blaster, holding the weapon against the thick fur of his new coat. Did that smoke mark another hole? But he was no longer unarmed, and he had to find cover. Joktar floundered on towards that tenuous beacon.

Only no dome showed above the drifts, nothing to suggest any human camp site. And the wind puffed to him a smell ripe with rottenness that lacerated the inner lining of his nostrils and throat. Joktar retched and coughed. Some of that reek had been filtered by his face mask, but he was still sickened by it.

Now he knew how wrong he had been in his guess about the smoke's source. Instead of a human outpost, he had been steadily approaching one of the major perils of Fenris, a poisonous hot spring where the melting snow seeped through porous rock to issue forth again as lethal steam. Men and animals, trapped in such country while seeking warmth, ended as piles of bones to warn off their kind.

Joktar collapsed in the snow as another coughing bout racked him. He tore off his mask, rubbed the white stuff he snatched up in both hands across his gasping mouth. Still on his hands and knees, he crawled away from that whipping banner of steam, plowing head first into a mat of spongelike brush, the very impetus of his charge carrying him over the initial rubbery resistance.

So he tumbled head first into a deep crease in the floor of the valley. Brush snapped back over his head, roofing out the snow and most of the fury of the wind. After some moments he realized that by blind chance alone he had found the shelter he needed as the storm hit with a hammer blow.

The wild rage overhead was deafening, beating out coherent thought, the power to do anything except endure for the length of the fury. Joktar squirmed against the hard earth, drew up his legs and arms into the loose folds of his outer furs, rolling ballwise. The shriek of the wind began a throb in his head, a beat in his blood. This was beyond anything he had ever known, and at last he retreated numbly into unconsciousness.

His rousing was as dazed as the process of revival at the port. He stretched cramped limbs, felt the pain of renewed circulation. And he had no idea that he was the first man since the Terrans had landed on Fenris to survive a blanket storm in the open. A subconscious will to live continued to direct his struggles. In spite of the brush roof, a quantity of snow had drifted around him and he beat free of this covering.

Sitting up in the hollow the twisting and turning of his body had made, Joktar fumbled with his pack, found food in the form of a self-heating can of stew. The top fell from his shaking fingers, some of the contents slopped across the back of his hand. But he ate, and the warmth of that specially prepared nourishment soothed mouth and throat, gathered comfortably in his middle. He had resolution enough to cap the container before he finished the ration. Then, as he chewed on a wafer of concentrates, he hunted for a thin section in the brush wall. The howl of the wind had died, only the rustle of his furs, and the creak of snow under him could be heard.

To break through the brush was so difficult he was tempted to use his blaster as a cutter. Only the knowledge that he did not have an extra charge was a deterrent, and the same was true for the force axe which must provide him with a reserve weapon. A last bull's rush, his arms protectively over his face, carried him out.

Overhead the sky was gray, but there were no thick clouds. He could see with sharp clarity the barriers of cliff walls making a girdle about the valley. Believing it must be close to evening he began a hunt for better shelter.

Underfoot the snow creaked. The eerie stillness was somehow more nerve-twisting than the onslaught of the storm. He was one small living thing in that white cup where only the poisonous flag of steam waved. And that quiet brought down on him once more the sensation of loneliness. Were there no birds, no animals, nothing else alive here?

The temptation to return to the wreck pulled at him so strongly that he started back. As he gained the foot of the break leading into the smaller valley sound rent the air, a rumble as of thunder, magnified and echoed from the peaks.

Out of the narrow cut he had been about to enter, puffed a cloud of white as the roar died away. Avalanche! Another snow slide that built in seconds a wall between him and the jumper.

Shaking his head dazedly, Joktar retreated down valley, no goal in mind now. There was the brush masked cut, but he wanted no more of that. His head ached, his snow-caked boots and coat weighed him down. He headed for the cliff to his left.

Another rumble back in the peaks. Tons of snow and earth must have cascaded down that time. Perhaps the jumper was now completely buried. He was sobbing a little as he wavered along, reeling against a pinnacle of rock half-detached from the parent cliff.

Steadying himself with one hand, Joktar blinked at what that stone sentry guarded, a black break in the wall. Maybe it was a cave!

The Terran lurched toward the pocket of dark, his free hand out to it in a gesture close to supplication, his other gripping the blaster. And because he had that weapon ready, he did not die.

For, without any sound of warning, hideous death launched from the cave, aiming for his head and shoulders. Sheer instinct brought the barrel of his blaster up, set his finger to the firing button, as a slavering weight bowled him back through a crusted reef of snow.

Claws caught and tore with convulsive jerks at the loose folds of fur, and the excess material protecting his body. For the thing which attacked him was dead before they hit the ground together, the stench of its burned fur and scorched flesh marking the success of his blaster bolt. He lay under the weight of the beast, too shaken to struggle free, hardly daring to believe that he was not seriously injured.

When he did throw off the mangled carcass, he examined it. This was no "lamby," the evil-tempered ruminant which was certainly no "lamb" to its hunters, though its fine, velvety fur with the tightly curled overcoat was accepted as legal tender on Fenris. This fur was not lamby; where it was still unblackened, it was white with an undercoat of faint blue, a perfect match in shade to the snow drifts. There were no hooves, but large paws on all four limbs, which were heavily furred and had retractable claws. The width of those feet suggested their owner could prowl over crusts that another might break through. The head was wide, showing a double row of fangs; the mark of a meat eater. And above that blunt muzzle were set two oversized eyes which Joktar studied closely.

They did not resemble any proper animal eyes he had known, for the balls were collections of myriad lenses, each equipped with a minute lid of its own; some were now closed, others wide open, as if the beast could use all or just a fraction of its seeing apparatus, as it pleased. And in contrast to the size of the eyes, the ears were unusually small and well-hidden in the thick fur. A cat, or a bear? Anyway it was sudden death on four feet.

Joktar stood up, trying to pull his tattered fur coat into place. The rank smell of the creature filled the air. With caution he approached the hole from which it had sprung to attack. Dropping to one knee, he snapped the blaster on to a wave pattern and aimed it into the cave. There was an answering puff of fire, from the bedding of the beast he discovered when he at last crawled in to kick out the noisome smoldering mass.

Using his belt knife, he tore at the brush for firewood, dragging a mound of the stuff back to the cave. The scorched smell still hung about the stiffening carcass of the cat-bear, but now he no longer found that odor revolting. Instead he turned upon the body, knife in hand.

Hacking off the loose hide he found a layer of yellow fat and haggled that free in chunks, his untutored butchery a messy job. But Joktar got what he wanted, fresh meat, which appealed to him more than the concentrates and scientifically balanced rations of the emergency supplies.

The chunks of meat he spitted and tried to roast were charred rather than cooked, but he chewed them down avidly. The animal's fat answered some inner craving and he gorged on it. Washing his hands and face with snow, he huddled back into the cave to total up assets and debits with the cool caution born of his past employment at the gaming tables.

He was alive, in spite of some narrow escapes. He was armed, though he would have to conserve the voltage clip of the blaster. There were the supplies he had looted from the jumper. Also, the map.

Joktar unfolded that in the flickering light of the fire. The thick mark, curling between wavering lines which must represent mountains, could be the road from the spaceport to the mines. And the smaller, dotted lines should be trails to the holes. A red cross on one suggested it was the outpost where he had unloaded cargo. But he could not be sure. There was a second red cross, only they had never reached this second stop on their trip. Perhaps somewhere between those two marks the jumper had gone over the cliff. He shrugged, this was all just guessing.

The glaring truth which he had to face was that there could be no shelter on Fenris for off-worlders except at the port or the mines. And if he ventured into either he would betray himself. Yet he was also sure he could not continue to live off the country.

Suppose he struck due west to the main road. But, he could only follow that to Siwaki and there a newcomer in a small community would be a marked man. The port, the mines, the road stations—all traps for the escapee. But what about the prospectors' holes? He was handicapped by his lack of knowledge. How many men to a hole? How often were they visited by supply jumpers? What form of communication with the mines did they have? And could he even hope to locate one of them in this white wilderness?

As he curled up behind his barrier of fire, Joktar knew a certain renewal of confidence, perhaps induced by his full stomach and the fact that so far he had managed to beat the odds. There was tomorrow in which to act, and he was still alive.

The night was not quiet, for the half-butchered carcass proved bait for other inhabitants of Fenris. There were weird cries of protest and warning, snarls of battle, eyes gleaming across the flames at him. At last he sat up, blaster on his knee, straining his eyes in an effort to make out the forms he sensed waited out there for his fire to die.

When the morning dawned the calm held, not even a cat's paw of wind dabbed across the snow dunes. Joktar shrugged on his pack and tried to pick out a goal. The jumper lay to the north, at least he believed that the choked valley which held its wreckage lay to the north. He began to walk in that direction.

The banners of poisonous steam ascended unruffled, marking a stretch of bare rock mottled with yellowish encrustations. But his path away from there was not easy. The snow had been sculptured into banks as desert sand is driven into dunes, each bank given a knife-sharp coating. To venture would leave him thigh- or waist-deep in soft snow. So he wove a trail back and forth.

In all the white immensity, he was the only moving creature. No bird quartered the sky, and if any animal skulked there, Joktar could not spot it. Loneliness ate into him and he redoubled his struggles to reach the cliffs. Right beyond a single barrier might lie the road which the jumper had traveled.

He paused, fought for control. To venture further down that path of thought was to end pounding at the door of some mine dome begging to be taken into its slave gang! More than just the active horrors the emigrants had been shown at the port might keep a man fast in bondage, the stark emptiness of Fenris itself worked for the companies.

Joktar reached the cliffs, squatted in the lee of a boulder to eat of the fat he had seared in his morning fire; he followed those greasy mouthfuls with a concentrate tablet. Weariness weighed on him like an extra pack on his shoulders, but his determination to keep going set him to climbing.

He dragged himself up on a plateau where the wind had swept away the snow which so encumbered the valley. To reach the other edge of that table land and see the new valley below was relatively easy. There was one thing about this snow-buried country, when the wind was dead there was no way to hide a trail. And below he could see one.

Trees here were much taller than the stunted brush which had sheltered him from the storm. And into a grove of them wound that trail, coming out again and striking off at right angles.

Those tracks drew Joktar. He fought, he crawled, he staggered on until he reached those two smoothly packed strips which hinted at a vehicle of some kind, the spoor running between them which might mark a man's passing. He trailed it among the trees, out into the open, turned northward again toward the crags.

The pale sun was well-down, evening was closing in. Joktar tried to quicken pace. The tracks led into another narrow valley. He guessed that he was perilously near the end of his strength. His body ached, his breath came in sharp, panting gasps and the snow slope before him dimmed and brightened in rhythm to the pounding of his heart.

Lurching from side to side, unable to keep his feet, he crashed against a wall, clung there, staring blearily ahead. This trail could have been made any time since the end of the last storm, the traveler could be a day or more ahead.

Here was no cave, but he hollowed out a small burrow in the shelter of a bush and choked down food. Tonight he must sleep. And once more rolled into a ball, Joktar met the cold and the dark as he had met the fury of the storm.

Sound broke the silence of the mountains. Joktar started up. But that had been no roar of avalanche. He blinked at sun on the snow, stirred sluggishly. What had awakened him? A man's shout? An animal cry?

He hunted for food, realized that his supplies were now low. The last can of self-heating stew had been finished the night before. Now the trail in the snow was his only hope of being guided to shelter or more food. Once more he shambled into the open, and began to trudge on.

A new fear arose to haunt his mind. What if he were traveling in the wrong direction? Had the traveler been bound the other way? He could not backtrack now, only trust that he had chosen rightly. His shamble became a wavering trot. Rounding a bend in the valley wall he came upon the unmistakable evidence of a camp.

The stranger had sheltered better than he; a windbreak of boulders had charred sticks of a fire laid before it. Joktar drew off his mitten, poked his fingers into that ashy pile. One fear dissolved, warmth still clung there. He had a blaster, was equipped to fight for what he had to have. Now all that mattered was catching up with the other.

Doggedly the Terran cut down his pace to preserve his strength. But time wore on and he could see no signs of his gaining on the other. A noon-time camp and he squatted in the same spot hours later, wondering if he could make contact before nightfall.

The day was graying into dusk when the valley became a narrow slit, a gate way.

"Arrrh . . ."

That was certainly no human word, echoing hollowly like a beast's roar between the walls. The sound stopped Joktar short. He reached for his blaster, memories of the cat-bear well to the fore.

No animal erupted from a pool of shadow to attack. Instead he caught another noise, the sharp, unforgettable crack of a blaster bolt. Six feet ahead a boulder smoked, the stone blackened by that stroke of man-made lightning.

There was no mistaking the warning in that. Joktar threw himself to the left, skidded painfully across the bare gravel which floored the cut, brought up against the cliff, an altogether too small pile of stones providing him with very inadequate refuge.

"You, get out!"

That voice was certainly human, the words Terran, and the order clear. But Joktar, instead of obeying, dug his mittens into the gravel and flattened himself as well as he could.

✳ ✳ **5** ✳ ✳

"I said blast out of here, snooper!"

The words boomed from rock to rock, distorted by the walls of the cliffs. They were reinforced by a second bolt from the blaster. Gravel smoked less than a yard away as Joktar tried to claw into the iron hard earth.

He was over the first shock and was thinking fast. Such an ambush suggested that the unseen behind that blaster was expecting trouble. Would a company man on a lawful prospecting trip be so wary?

Those guards on the crawlers and jumpers carried a weight of armament through the wilderness. Were the companies facing some other challenge besides an occasional lamby or cat-bear? He remembered suddenly the man in Siwaki who had bid for him with an offer of lamby skins.

But there was no time to wonder. A third crack of the blaster delivered a flash almost in his eyes. He was sure he smelt the singe of fur that time. And he knew he was licked. So he made the only move possible.

Joktar stood up, walked out into the main cut of the valley, his hands up, mittened palms out. Before him nothing moved, he could not spot the other's lurking place.

"All right, the deal's yours."

"No deals, snooper. No deals with any company man."

45

For the first time, Joktar remembered that his looted furs must carry, breast and back, the company insignia.

"I'm no company man . . ." his words tripped over each other in his eagerness. "I got this coat from—" But he never had a chance to finish his explanation.

"You're just asking for a burn-down, snooper," commented that echoing voice. "Drop your blaster, toss it over by that red rock and then get back down that valley and *fast!*"

A flick of dazzling light not two inches from his right boot underlined that order. With his hands shaking more from frustrated anger than fear, Joktar unbuckled his weapon belt and tossed it with the still-holstered blaster at the red rock. He turned glumly and went back, his face taut and hard. Now he had to outthink the man in ambush, if only to win back the weapon which would mean the difference between life and death in this wilderness.

Not sure whether the other would trail him, Joktar slogged back as far as the point where the stranger had halted that noon. Night was close, he couldn't go any farther. At that moment, he ceased to care whether a sharpshooter with a blaster crouched behind every rock, he was done.

But he made an effort to grub up brush for a fire. And when that was kindled he sat, allowing the warmth to seep through his torn furs, and ease a little of the weariness of his body. A drop of moisture on his cheek drew his attention to a drift of fine snow particles. The dead calm which had followed the storm was gone. He could hear the call of the rising wind in the peaks.

So he looked about him for cover. A torch improvised from a twist of brush stems gave him light to survey the cliff. And the wind puffed that flame to display a shadowy pockmark.

The crevice was round and large enough to allow him to insert two fingers. And that hole was only one in a line marching straight up the rock. Some were mere depressions almost filled with a deposit of wind-blown sand and grit. But Joktar did not think they were natural, the borings were too round, the line too straight. Some intelligent mind had fashioned them, and since the labor had been difficult, the reason behind their borings must have been important.

Save that the holes were in a straight line he might have deemed them an aid to a climber, a primitive ladder. A ladder! Suppose one used rungs planted in each hole, pieces of suitably trimmed wood to be fitted and withdrawn at will.

With such equipment one could reach a secret trail along the heights, paralleling the valley, and such a trail would round that ambush.

Roused out of a lethargy induced by fatigue, Joktar smiled, without any gentleness in that sardonic curve of lip. This suggested escape from the valley appealed strongly. Only there was nothing to do at present but wait out the night. He found a boulder-walled nook and slept in snatches while the wind wailed aloft, the snow shifted down to hide the trail he had traced earlier.

In the next day's light, he began his hunt for branches strong enough to serve in such a stair. And by noon he had enough hacked lengths to make his attempt. The light of day had shown him that the procession of holes did not, after all, reach to the top of the cliff, but ended in a shadow line about three-quarters of the way up from the valley floor, a line he would not have otherwise noted. That must mark a hidden ledge, the road he sought.

With the first three of his rungs pounded into the waiting holes, Joktar proceeded to the more delicate task of setting the rest while balanced on precarious support. The business required nerve but he kept to it, testing each wooden spike as well as he could before trusting his weight upon it.

How long he crept up that stone surface, he could never afterwards guess. In the end his groping fingers closed on the edge of the ledge and he heaved up, to lie gasping in a wedge-shaped groove cut back into the cliff.

The wind puffed snow in his face and he licked the moisture from his cracked lips. If he stood there would be no head room in that opening, but he crouched on his hands and knees, to draw up his supply bag, wriggle free and add to his equipment all the spindles he could reach. The force axe was now tied to his belt in place of the missing blaster.

Jerking the pack behind him, Joktar crawled along that hidden ledge. Now he could mark the ancient tool signs on the weathered surface of the stone. Someone, with incredible effort, had chiseled out this road, which must be concealed from the valley below. But, as he progressed, his first elation dwindled. He couldn't cover miles on his hands and knees. The original fashioners of this passage had either been dwarfs or the discomfort of four-footed progress had not bothered them.

"Four-footed progress," he repeated aloud.

Terrans had been exploring the galaxy now for little less than three centuries. And on more than one world they had discovered traces of other civilizations, ones which had budded, flowered, and faded all in the far past, until even the life forms which had conceived and built them had vanished. Four intelligent alien races had been discovered, two of them humanoid. And the planets which housed those had been quarantined, since none had achieved space flight save in their own systems.

Some explorers believed that once there had been another space-roving breed, and that traces of their far flung empire had been found on widely separated worlds in different systems. The one idea which did register was that the Terrans had come late into an old, old field where life was flickering to extinction, where deserted worlds held only the ancient remains of their former fecundity, and where intelligent life was now the exception rather than the rule.

Joktar had listened to the talk of spacemen for years, had heard queer tales spun by men who had prowled the rim until they had lost touch with their own kind. He had seen video shots of strange buildings on long-dead worlds, with races pictured on the walls, not even vaguely human in appearance.

So here he might be using a road made by "men" who were not akin to his species. That he could accept. But suddenly the wedge opened out, he was able to get to his feet. Making better time, he pushed forward, pausing now and then to glance below for landmarks.

The red rock loomed up at last. And now he crept again, having no desire to alert any sentry. But the narrow throat of the valley spread out into an oval basin where the sun glinted on the mirror of an ice-sheathed lake rimmed by a respectable grove of trees.

Flanking the lake was a mound, surely the work of intelligent beings. And the labor which had gone into its erection was awe-inspiring. Great boulders or blocks of stone, taller than a man, surfaced its sides. Crudely cut but fitted together with an engineer's skill, they rose in graduated tiers of stone slabs, the last row forming a thick wall. It was a crude fort, a place of refuge in a hostile land. And it was very old for the base row of blocks were half-buried in a rising tide of soil. Also the place was occupied.

That was smoke, not steam from deadly hot springs, curling up from the scattering of hovels constructed of brush and stone. Joktar could see figures moving about. But, save that they were dressed in the furs of Fenrian winter clothing he could not identify them.

The huts on the mound-fort had nothing in common with the domes of the mining companies. In fact the whole camp appeared an impermanent affair used for the same reason that its unknown builders had first intended, a shelter in a hostile country. Were 'copters or sweep-ships in use on Fenris, those men could have had no defense against attack. A single spraying of nerve gas, a vibrator stationed overhead and every defender might be shaken loose. But here where there was no air transport, they were reasonably safe and Joktar did not doubt now that these were no friends to the companies.

Somewhere on that untidy lump of earth and stone must be the man who had ambushed him. And he wanted his blaster back, as well as to learn the motives which had established such a hideout.

Dusk was drawing in, the red points of fires on the mound promised not only warmth but food, also the presence of Joktar's own kind. Only he believed that to try to climb that artificial hillock would bring a rough and perhaps fatal greeting. He went on along the wedge trail, passing the fort, following the cliff back as the outward curve of the wall widened, hoping to find a place to camp for the night.

The valley was larger than he had thought and he was well-away from the vicinity of the mound when he discovered what he was seeking as the trail sloped down into a funnel.

Joktar lay belly-down and felt below for what he hoped would be the holes necessary to the climbing pins. There they were! He pressed into service again the handful of pegs he had brought, to dangle from the last of those and drop into a cave slit.

He dared make no fire, and his dreams were haunted with terrifying climbs up walls as blaster bolts spit and crackled about him. He awoke, gasping, crawled to the mouth of the cave to look out upon a clear white night. Fenris' large moon awoke a faint glitter along the ridges of snow banks and visibility was excellent.

The Terran studied the landscape, marking cover which would take him closer to the fort. If he could reach the grove of trees from here without leaving a betraying track on the snow, he might make the foot of the mound undetected. While he was assessing the possibilities of such a move he heard a sound. Was it the creak of snow crushed by a boot? On the air an indistinguishable murmur of voices. Men were coming towards him.

A black shape emerged from the grove, then turned to call back. Joktar saw, sharply outlined against the snow, a tell-tale silhouette: the fellow was armed with a vorp-rod! Another man, another vorp! These strangers weren't playing. The deadliest weapons known: ones strictly forbidden except to be used by special permission of the patrol. A third and a fourth man, the last dragging a flat sled. And all four of them wore fittings over their boots which enabled them to cross the crusts on the drifts without breaking through.

"... a good report ..."

"Teach 'em to spread those filthy holes of theirs west! Smear off a couple and they'll learn. Those guards aren't going to nose out hunting *us.*"

One of the squad laughed. "How true! Roose'll lay a trail after we're through that'll leave 'em pop-eyed before their first rest break, they try to follow it. That trick of his using zazaar paws on his boots is enough to panic those dome hounds. They don't like to get far away from their precious roads anyway."

"What about the one Merrick discovered coming up the valley?" The new speaker did not sound as carefree as his companions.

"Merrick is going to gather him in today. He only wanted to let him run a little to soften him up. When he brings that snooper in we'll hear the digger sing some pretty songs before we take the usual steps."

"I don't see how a stranger got in this far without being spotted."

"Merrick thinks he's a stray. Perhaps from some jumper caught in the last blanket. If his machine broke down the dim-wit might just be stupid enough to wander about hunting the road again. We'll learn what happened when Merrick produces him."

"Anyway, we've other business now."

"Sure, a hole to scoop. We ought to hit about dawn. We'll get the diggers out with some wake-up fireworks they'll remember."

Joktar watched the small party swing to the right, hidden again by trees. He hesitated for a moment and then made a gambler's decision, to move after the raiders into the night.

Well past dawn, Joktar lay on the crest of a crag. Somewhere below him the raiding party was stationed; the light colored furs of their outerwear blending in with the snow. A track pressed by jumper treads formed a half-loop about a small dome, the interior sun lamp there was a-wink in the half-gloom.

Bit by bit he had built up his own explanation for the excursion he had dogged. The companies on Fenris were not supreme. There existed at least one outlaw organization, able to live off the bleak land and operate in the wilderness, who dared to challenge the monopoly. And who were those outlaws? Escapees from E-gangs, such as himself? That they were Terrans or men of some off-world breed he was certain.

There had been stories told back in the SunSpot of rebels on thinly colonized planets. Some men turned against civilization because they were born wanderers, impatient of any restraint, others were cashiered spacemen, criminals a few jumps ahead of the patrol. Fenris with its largely unexplored wilderness, in spite of its forbidding climate, could offer excellent asylum for such.

Joktar tensed. The raiders had parked their sled just below the crag on which he crouched, and now someone was coming back to it. He squirmed forward. One of the outlaws was shucking off his furs, standing up dressed only in a thermo suit and boots. He unrolled and proceeded to don another fur coat, wrapping a face scarf tightly about chin and mouth before he pulled the hood up over his dark thatch of hair. On the new garment were vividly colored patches of company insignia.

So disguised the raider walked briskly back to the jumper trail. Once out on the road his gait altered, he began to stagger as he circled toward the dome, falling to his knees, struggling up again. Joktar watched the performance critically. The act was good, for all the men in the dome could guess this was the survivor of some road wreck. And from his own position he could see the two vorpmen stationed in concealment on either side of the dome entrance.

The counterfeit wayfarer flopped realistically into a drift and lay there for a long moment before making feeble efforts to rise. He managed that drastic tumble so well that Joktar was certain this was not the first time he had played such a role. Two men issued from the dome running. They wore thermo suits and boots, but no furs. A raider arose to the left, the fourth man Joktar had not been able to spot. Now he skimmed to the door and whipped inside, slamming the cold lock behind him.

Just as the first of the company men reached the man in the drift, he moved with a quick sidewise flip Joktar recognized. One of his unsuspecting prey went off balance, reeling back into the wet embrace of the drift. The attack startled his companion into a momentary pause. In the dome, lights blinked three times. Now the vorpmen came into the open, the black noses of their weapons trained on the company men.

"Freeze! You've had it, diggers!"

No one argued with a vorp, not if he were sane. While the company men obediently "froze" the raider arose and slapped the evidence of drift-wallowing from his furs.

"Woods beasts!" spat the company man on the ground.

The man he had come to aid laughed. "Want your mouth scrubbed out, little man?" he inquired genially. "You make that sound like a naughty word. We're free Fenris woods runners, and don't forget it." His tone, light on the surface, held a bite.

"Wearing a company coat!" The other refused to be intimidated.

The raider smoothed down his furs with one hand as if admiring their fit.

"Good workmanship," he admired. "I'll send Naolas a micro sometime and tell him so. They do you diggers proud. That's why we come to you for help when we need to stock up on supplies. All right, boys, move in and clean out the place."

The whole party entered the dome, raiders and prisoners together. Joktar came to life. His own target was the sled below. Not that he had any hope of finding a weapon there. But there were several bags on it and he had thoughts of adding to his supplies. Only he was not given time to loot. A man came from the dome and Joktar dropped behind a bush.

Peering through a screen which seemed very tenuous, indeed, he saw that the other had holstered his weapon. Apparently the raider feared no more trouble here. Joktar pulled his feet under him, studied the man and the terrain doubtfully. Before he could slam through the bush, the other, if he were any marksman at all, could easily burn him down. He had only the force axe as a counter. Now he felt the tiny throb in the haft as he pressed the button to release the pure energy which served as a blade.

The man picked up the sled cord, gave a sharp jerk to free the runners from the hold of the snow. He dragged it back to the dome, leaving Joktar bitterly disappointed. Caution, engrained in him during his years on the streets, had won.

Frustrated he watched the man re-enter the dome. To get to the sled now, he would have to cross the open and he was wearing a company coat.

It was then, through the earth under him, that he had advance notice of new arrivals. For a moment he did not connect that faint *thud-thud* with trouble. Then he recalled his own ride in a jumper. The dome was about to have some legitimate visitors and the raiders might well be trapped inside.

Joktar sat back on his heels and stared absently at the structure and the waiting sled. Suppose he was to dash down the road, flag the advancing jumper, and warn its crew? The ignominious defeat of the company men could be turned into a victory. And what might he expect in the way of gratitude from the new victors?

As matters stood, he had no cause to favor either party. To reveal himself to the company employees could send him straight back to the labor gangs. On the other hand the outlaws had already taken his blaster and had some rather sinister future plans for him. Perhaps it was to his own advantage just to wait and see if these two parties cancelled each other out. Having so logically and prudently balanced one scheme of action against the other, Joktar went to work to do the direct opposite of what good sense dictated.

✳ ✳ **6** ✳ ✳

Almost independently of his thoughts, Joktar's hands moved, scraping up snow, packing the stuff with his fingers into a tight, hard ball. Joktar, who had never had a normal childhood, was instinctively fashioning a weapon known to Terran children far back into the mists of earth-bound time. He cradled the ball, tossed the sphere from one hand to the other. And then he threw with the skill of a practiced knife man.

The missile smashed against the dome with a crack almost as forceful as a blaster bolt. One of the raiders, complete with vorp, burst from the door, took refuge behind the sled, awaiting action.

Now more than vibration through the ground advertised the coming of the jumper. The crunch of its treads on ice and snow could be heard above the purr of an engine laboring to bore ahead. The man in ambush behind the sled whistled shrilly, and the second vorpman came out, crossed the clearing about the dome in a zig-zag rush. It seemed plain that the raiders were preparing to fight rather than run, a decision which surprised Joktar.

A third outlaw emerged and took cover. To all outward appearances the dome was as always when the jumper crawled into view. In the doorway of the dome stood a waiting figure, blaze of company badge on his chest, as one of the jumper's crew climbed out of the control cabin.

Perhaps the sight of the sled alerted the newcomer. He cried out and his hand went to his blaster. Then he spun around and went down in the snow, picked off by a marksman in hiding. The chain lightning which was a vorp in action raked along the jumper just above ground level, leaving fused metal, turning the machine into scrap. Then the same fire struck across the control cabin fusing in turn a nose gun just sliding out to return fire.

Joktar admired the competence of the raiders. In the few minutes since his ball had struck the dome, they had rendered useless the enemy transportation and added its crew to their bag of prisoners. He waited eagerly for their next move.

The man who had been clipped by the blaster was collected, his partner ordered out of the jumper, both hustled inside the dome. There appeared to be no load-up on this trip. When the vorpmen explored the cargo they brought out two boxes to be dumped on the sled.

Joktar watched the raider in the company coat. The man stood on tiptoe to touch the smear of snow left by the Terran's warning before he turned to study the landscape, sighting for the probable line of flight. Joktar dropped flat, feeling as if the other could spot him out. Instead they went about the business of looting the dome, adding their choice of goods to the sled.

The sun was well up to a mid-morning position before the job was finished, and the captives were brought out to stand by the impotent jumper. Stripped of their furs, the company men were tied to that vehicle, their coats dumped beyond reach. Then the vorpmen turned upon the dome, slicing the surface with the full force of their beams, cutting the tough substance into bits. As the jumper, the hole shelter would have to be written off the company books.

"By rights, diggers," the raid leader's voice carried easily to Joktar, "we ought to blast you. You'd burn us quick enough if the situation were reversed. But we'll give you a chance. Pick yourselves free, and you can slog back to the next hole, if that's still in existence by the time you make it. And you can tell Anson Burg that there won't be any more holes left east of the mountain soon."

There was an inarticulate growl in answer to that. Two of the raiders, flanked by the vorpmen, picked up the draw lines of the sled and headed toward Joktar's hiding place.

He had waited too long to retreat. Now his body, numbed by the cold of which he was not entirely conscious, betrayed him. Trying to slip out of sight, he lurched into brush. Instantly a vorp beam snapped in answer.

The fact that his fur coat was too large saved him, as it had when he encountered the cat-bear. Dazedly he tumbled backward, aware of a burning agony spreading down his arm and across his chest from a point on his shoulder. He rolled in the snow, striving to ease that fire, and plunged back into empty space.

There was shouting, the crackle of dry brush. Joktar gave a small, animal whimper as the fire in his shoulder blazed, making him sick. He struggled to get to his feet, peering around with misty eyes to find that he was entrapped in a pocket beneath a broken crust of snow.

His left arm, his whole left side was useless. But with his right hand he pawed for the force axe. Overhead a furred arm swept back brush. Joktar, his lips tight against his teeth in a snarl of animal rage, swung up the axe to make a last stand.

"Here he is!"

He brought up the axe another fraction of an inch, caught his breath at the answering flash of pain across his chest. Then he threw the weapon, saw it whirl out, knock the blaster from the other's hand.

Joktar leaned against the wall of the pocket. His groping hand found snow, smeared it across his face, hoping the cold wet would aid him to fight off the waves of weakness which blurred his eyes and pushed him close to a black out.

"Another digger?" The shadow of a vorp barrel fell across his face and body. "Let's get him out for a look."

They got him out right enough. Joktar bit his lips against a scream of pain as they lifted him. But he fought to keep on his feet when he was out of the pocket. One of the men facing him wore the disguise of the company coat, but only his eyes were to be seen between the overhang of hood and the breathing mask.

"No, I don't think he's one of this gang. You'll find his tracks back there. He's been trailing us all along."

"Why?" demanded the vorpman.

"That's what we'll have to find out. We'll take him back with us."

"But—" the protest was interrupted as the leader spoke directly to Joktar.

"Did you throw that ball to warn us?"

"Yes," somehow Joktar got the answer out as he sagged forward to his knees, writhed at the pull of the torn and singed furs across his body as the other caught his coat to keep him from falling back into the snow pocket. That last punishment was too much, he blacked out completely.

He lay on his back and yet his body moved, sometimes with a jerk which racked through his side. He opened his eyes to discover that he lay on the sled, lashed there with the rest of the cargo.

"Awake, digger?" The shadow of the speaker fell across Joktar's face and he turned his head, to look up at the raider who still wore the company coat.

"I'm not from the mines," he faltered. Somehow it was very important to make that point clear.

"Then you're wearing the wrong coat, digger."

"So are you!" mocked Joktar, the Terran's voice stronger and more steady this time.

"Hmmm . . ." The man broke step and then matched his stride once more to the glide of the sled.

"You one of Skene's crowd? Or Kortoski's? If so, you're way out of your territory."

"I'm out," Joktar said deliberately, "of the cargo hold of a jumper where I was load-hop. I'm an emigrant."

"And what happened to the jumper?" A note in that demanded proof for such a preposterous statement.

"Caught in an avalanche. The driver and guard were both dead when I got out. This coat belonged to the guard."

"Nice story. Since when have they been shipping youngsters out in E-ships?" He reached down to pull Joktar's hood well away from his face, inspecting the other with cold and unbelieving eyes.

"I'm older than I look. And when did the E-men worry about the catch in their nets? Jard-Nedlis bought my time at Siwaki all right."

"If you're talking straight, fella, you've pulled off a neat jump of your own. What planet did you emigrate from?"

Joktar's eyes closed wearily. Talking required more effort than he could now find. "Terra," he answered weakly. His eyes were tightly shut so he could not read the astonishment mirrored in those of his captor.

Then, suddenly it was warm and he no longer rode on the sled. There was artificial light in this place, the glow of an atom bulb. Joktar lay not far from a wall of piled stones slovenly chinked with straggles of moss. And the roof over his head was a mat of brush battened down. He shifted on the pallet, enjoying the warmth, to discover that he could not move his left arm, though the worst of the pain was gone out of his shoulder.

A hand appeared, drew a fur robe back over his bandaged chest. Joktar looked up. No hood or mask hid this man's thin face, and the Terran recognized the badge of that deep brown skin, the brand of deep space worn by the crewmen of star ships. But what was a spaceman doing here?

"They tell me you claim to be from Terra," the stranger said abruptly. "What port? Melwambe? Chein-Ho? Warramura? N'Yok?"

"N'Yok."

"JetTown?" Joktar knew by the faint inflection in that tone that this man must know the streets.

He tested the spaceman's knowledge in turn. "I was a dealer for Kern." Had he ever faced this man across a table at the SunSpot? He didn't think so.

"The SunSpot."

He had been right. This man knew JetTown.

"Star-and-comet, three-worlds-wild, nigs-and-naughts."

"Star-and-comet."

"Rather young to spread 'em out on that table, weren't you?"

Absurdly irritated, Joktar replied with a heat he instantly regretted. "I've dealt for five years, spacer. And if you know Kern's you know no fumbler could keep a table going for him that long!"

To his surprise the other laughed. "You can always touch a man on the raw when you needle his professional pride," he commented.

"Yes, I know Kern's reputation, so I'll concede you were a three-point-down man at the tables. As for your age," he rubbed a thumb back and forth under his lower lip and surveyed Joktar measuringly. "There've always been precocious brats in every business. What's your name, dealer?"

"Joktar."

The thumb was still, the measurement became a fixed stare.

"Just Joktar?" As the other pronounced it, the name now had an unfamiliar lilt. "Where did you get a name like that?"

"I don't know. Where did you get yours?"

But the other was smiling again. "Not from the Ffallian, that's certain. Gwyfl sanzu korg a llywun."

That collection of sounds made no sense, yet their cadence fell into a pattern which pricked at the Terran's mind. Was their meaning behind that wall in his brain where Kern's psych-medic had forever erased his past? Joktar struggled up on his elbow to demand:

"What language is that? What did you say?"

The eagerness went out of the spaceman's face. He was cold-eyed now. "If you don't know, then it means nothing to you. You were picked up on a regular E-raid?"

Disappointed, Joktar nodded as he dropped back on the pallet. Now the interrogator proceeded to draw out of him all the details of his life since he had come out of the deep-freeze in Siwaki. When the Terran finished the spaceman shook his head.

"You're covered with luck."

"You believe everything I told you?" mocked Joktar, his patience worn to a very fine thread.

The other laughed. "Boy, you couldn't give me a wrong answer if you wanted to. You had a sniff of ver-talk before you came around."

Joktar's good fist clamped on the fur robe over him. "Don't take any chances, do you?" he asked in a voice which was even enough, but his eyes were less well-controlled.

"On Fenris, you don't. Not if you want to keep out of the companies' claws. You might have been a plant."

Joktar had to accept the truth of that. But the thought of being drugged before he was questioned rankled.

"Who are you?" he shot back.

"My name's Rysdyke, not that that would mean anything to you."

A spark of anger dictated Joktar's reply.

"Erased the rolls?" he asked casually, watching the other to see if that shot took effect. And he was avenged in measure by seeing a dark stain spread under the other's deep tan. However, if that question had stabbed deep in a hidden tender spot, Rysdyke did not permit the jab to rattle him.

"Erased the rolls," he agreed. Then he stood up. "Get yourself some bunk time. The chief'll be in to see you later."

He turned down the atom lamp and went out. But Joktar did not sleep. Instead he reached back into his memory as far as he could, shuffling and dealing out in patterns all the scraps of recollection, as he might have dealt kas-cards, hoping for a winning hand. Only nothing fell properly into place, there were no brilliants on which to bet.

Dim, very dim, pictures of a big ship. Of a woman who crooned to herself, or spoke to him, urging always that they must take care, that they were in danger, that men in uniform personified that danger.

Men in uniform! What uniform? The police? He had never shrunk from them, just known the wariness of the lawless against the law. Spacemen? He had faced hundreds of them across his table with only a general interest in the yarns they could spin, and a slight contempt for their inept playing of a highly skilled game of chance.

There was the officer in gray, the one who had questioned him at the E-station. Perhaps that sniff of ver-talk had heightened his powers of recall, sparked some hidden memory. Yes, it was a gray tunic he hated. He must fear gray tunics, but why?

If he could only force past that mental curtain the long-ago conditioning had left in his mind! Rysdyke must know something. What was so odd about his name? And who were the Ffallian? Who spoke that language which had dripped so liquidly from the spaceman's tongue?

True, most of the men he knew had two names. But on the streets nicknames were accepted; admittedly, Joktar was unlike any other he had ever heard. Joktar . . . Ffallian . . . his thoughts began to spin fantastic patterns as he drifted into sleep.

Rysdyke did not return to the hut for the next two days where Joktar, his disappointment and frustration growing, waited to pin him down for an explanation. His nurse, caring for him brusquely but with some experience, was a taciturn man who commented now and then on the state of the weather and carried with him a none-too-pleasant aroma of half-cured skins. He only became animated when Joktar chanced to mention the cat-bear, and then he would favor his patient with a lecture on the habits and natures of various animals to be found in the Fenrian wilderness, pouring forth a flood of facts the Terran found to be interesting after all.

And the more he heard from Roose, the more Joktar began to realize that his own trek across this territory was in the nature of a fabulous exploit. For someone green to Fenris to survive both blanket storm and an attack from a zazaar was astonishing to Roose.

"You did as good as a regular woods-runner, boy," he commented. "You'd be able to run a prime trap line. Wait 'til you get that burn of yours scarred over good and you 'n' me'll head out into the breaks and get us some real hunting."

"But I thought you people were in the business of raiding company holes," Joktar hoped to draw out more information.

"Sure, we do that. But we run fur traps, too. Can't get all the grub and supplies we need raiding. 'Bout a dozen of the fellas have lines out and have regular hunting sections up back . . ." He jerked a thumb toward the forepart of the hut. "The chief, he was a trader, he knows how to sell our stuff to smugglers."

"Thank you for the recommendation, Roose."

Joktar recognized the voice, though he had not seen before the face of the man who now entered the hut. This was the raider who had led the attack on the mine hole wearing the livery of the company.

He was as tall as Roose, having the advantage of Rysdyke by several inches. But unlike the ursine trapper, this man was slender and moved lithely. Now he squatted down by the Terran's pallet.

"So you plan to hit the hills with Roose?"

"Ah, chief, the kid's good! He'd have to be, or he couldn't get him a zazaar and last out a blanket."

The other nodded. "Exactly, Roose. In fact he's so good he bothers me. But there are a lot of surprises in the universe, and by this time we should be used to bombs out of a blue, yellow, or pink sky. Kauto fflywryl orta . . ."

Again the words meant nothing, yet pried at Joktar's memory.

"I don't understand . . ."

The other sighed. "No, you don't. Which is a pity. But maybe time'll solve that problem. You were handy with that snowball back at the hole. I gather you have a dislike for the companies."

"Wouldn't you, under the circumstances?"

"Maybe. But you could have warned them and been given free status."

"Would I?" Joktar returned dryly.

He answered with a smile. "No, probably not. You've guessed rightly just how far their gratitude would reach."

"I know the streets."

"And you're lucky. About one man in a thousand ever escapes, and out of that number, one in five hundred lasts out his first week of freedom."

"You get your recruits the hard way."

"We have exactly two escaped emigrants in this mob. The rest of us are free trappers and a few who do not explain their past occupations."

"But you all hate the companies."

"Not the companies," the other corrected him. "Fenris would be a deserted hell hole without the mines. But we are at war with their methods and their deliberate hogging of this planet. The alibite mines occupy a few pimples on this continent, the companies exploit them and that's that. They will do nothing to build up trade or import any goods save the supplies they themselves need. They won't sell passage on their ships to free men, but they bring in their bonded employees and emigrants they can control utterly. The freeze-out is on and has been for two years. Not a single free trader can get field clearance at

Siwaki. No ship save a company one or a patrol cruiser can set down here. They think they have Fenris sewn up tight and they want to keep it that way.

"If free man can establish independent holdings on this world the companies can't hold their emigrant gangs without triple the number of guards they now employ or other expensive safety devices. Now the country itself is a barrier against escape, with settlements it wouldn't be.

"They want alibite only. We want other things. Sure, this climate is grim, almost six months of winter, or what seems winter to Terrans. But second-generation settlers from Kanbod, or Nord, or Aesir could live well here. Men can adapt, you're an example."

Of what? Joktar wanted to ask when the chief was hailed from outside the hut.

✳ ✳ ✳

(Closed com between Kronfeld and Morle)

M: Scouts aren't on to our man. The one who took the disc really thought subject had helped mug his partner. He's shipped out since. Serves in the Third Sector, no contact with critical Fifth in the past. Doesn't know Lennox as far as I can learn. So that angle can be washed out.

K: It's pleasant to be able to eliminate *one* small factor anyway. Did your man get to Kern?

M: We're trying. Kern's a vip on the streets. Even the port authorities are touchy about pushing him.

K: Why was he raided then?

M: Funny thing about that. The word around is that Kern arranged that bit of action himself, to get rid of some underlings he didn't trust. And the E-men exceeded their instructions, making a clean sweep. I know he never intended *our* man to be held and he unpocketed for ten others who were pulled in. Hudd did discover that Kern took in the woman and child. Woman died soon after. She was ill when she arrived. He can now establish that the child was our subject. What about the Fenris angle, any word from there?

K: One of Thom's agents tried to bid him in at the auction, but didn't make it; couldn't press that without blowing his cover. He'll pass the word in the outlands. There's a brawl cooking up there and maybe we can spring them during the trouble. But if our information is correct, this lad can take worse than Fenris and still come up fighting. We have to have him. I'd cheerfully fry those service fanatics if I could get these two hands on them and had a hot enough fire handy.

(Report to home office, Harband Mining Company, Project 65, Fenris)

Prospect Hole, Blue Mountain district destroyed by local outlaw group. Request permission to go all out against these woods-runners. May we appeal to the patrol for assistance?

(Reply from home office)

Do nothing. Committee on way to investigate situation. Ramifications reach beyond Fenris. Must be no trouble. Repeat, no trouble while Councilor Cullan is on Loki.

✳ ✳ ✳

* ✳ **7** ✳ *

"Samms is going to move. Since he's had the blast out with Raymark and made himself top man in the Kortoski mob, everything's been quiet. Now he wants a general council."

Joktar stood within the slightly open hut door. The major portion of the men housed on the mound-fort were gathered outside listening to a report from a man dressed in full trail kit.

"His runner's going through the Five Peak district. They want us and Ebers' crowd. Samms aims to make it a bit parley. Swears he has a major chance for all of us now—"

Rysdyke interrupted. "This could be the break we've been waiting for, Hogan. Raymark was no good to deal with; he wanted our sections kept separate so we wouldn't have to share any good loot. Samms may be a different sort."

"Samms and Ebers," the chief repeated thoughtfully. "Well, a meet won't do any harm. We can listen to what they have to offer but we don't have to commit ourselves. That is, if this is on a straight orbit. Suppose we say we'll meet them at the River Island," he glanced at the sky, "and, since the signs look promising for a quiet weather spell, make that three days from now. You can tell that to this runner, Marco. Then you take two of the boys with vorps and full supplies. I just want to make sure that no one is planning an incident."

Several of the listening men grinned wolfishly. Joktar gathered that one's trust in one's fellow men did not spread any further on Fenris than it had in the streets. The company broke apart and only Rysdyke and the chief remained before Joktar's hut.

"What do you make of this?" the ex-spaceman wanted to know.

The other's answer was cryptic. "Perks supported Samms just before he called Raymark out."

"Perks? But he turned yellow-belly, sold out to the companies. He doesn't dare leave the Harband compound; he'd be shot on sight after what happened to his squad in that ambush. Oh, do you think Samms might be following the same flight pattern? That why you sent the vorps ahead?"

"Might be." There was a lazy, teasing note in that answer. "Joktar!" He had not turned his head, but he spoke the eavesdropper's name with certainty. The quasi-prisoner opened the makeshift door of the hut.

"Here's the problem, boy," Hogan continued. "You should know it's like from the streets. The Kortoski mob—they range north of here—had Raymark for their boss. He wasn't too bright when it came to planning capers, but he was a good fighter and had what it took to keep his boys in hand, an old time trapper. Then his mob picked up an escapee last year. He'd had luck about as spectacular as yours. Seems Samms is a third-generation Martian colonist and so adapts better to this god-forsaken climate.

"Samms began to pick up a following of his own inside the mob, among them one very bright boy, Perks. Perks had furnished a lot of the brains behind Raymark before then. He can plan but he's no leader; most of the mob hate his guts. Then, about four months ago, Perks apparently got fed up. He and a squad he was leading were captured in a quite obvious trap. And since then Perks has fared well at company hands."

"Sold out his own men!" Rysdyke exploded.

"So it appears. Then, a very short time ago, Samms called Raymark to a blast out. Raymark was erased, and Samms is top man. Now," Hogan glanced at Joktar for the first time, "give me *your* unvarnished appraisal of the situation."

"I'd say Samms was planted."

"Where, by whom, for what?" Hogan inquired in that lazy voice.

"On the surface by the companies, maybe to do just what he did, climb to the top in some mob then to take it out of running, or use it to cut down some of the other independents."

"And Perks?"

"Was his runner."

"But you said 'on the surface.' What could lie under that surface?"

"That Samms is straight and the Perks situation is in reverse. Perks has been planted on the company by Samms. When he's rooted there solid, Samms moves to take over the mob. Maybe Perks got news to him to spark that jump."

Hogan laughed. Rysdyke's scowl faded as he chewed on that.

"So speaks a man who knows the streets. That the way a vip such as Kern would move?"

Joktar shrugged, bit his lip as that gesture pulled his sore shoulder.

"With variations. Both are pretty simple set-ups for a man like Kern." He gave credit where it was due. Kern, the intriguer, had been fascinating to watch in operation, and Kern's plans had always worked with the precision of well-tended machinery.

"Then this hot news Samms wants to share with us—" Rysdyke began.

"Could conceivably be the real goods. So we'll attend Samms' council with our own precautions laid down in advance. My young friend," he spoke again directly to Joktar, "the criminal mind is sometimes a distinct asset. I think you should meet Samms, your private estimation of him and his proposal may be enlightening. Suppose you set yourself to the business of getting on your feet in time to accompany us."

The party which left on the third day was a small, select one. As yet Joktar knew only a small portion of the mob. Most of them had been trappers, individuals who had pioneered in the Fenrian backlands before the companies took over. One or two had been prospectors frozen out by the monopolies. The two major exceptions were Rysdyke, a cashiered spaceman, and the chief, Hogan, who had once been a trader in Siwaki, losing his business when the companies closed the port to free ships.

Now Hogan, Rysdyke, Roose, and another trapper named Tolkus, with Joktar in tow, left for the council. But the Terran believed that others had gone before them more secretly.

The day was a fine one with no wind and Joktar stripped off his face mask, having learned that he could do as well without that added covering. Their trail wove into the grove and the Terran tried to picture this country as it was when the big thaw was in progress. Fenris must be a totally different world then. Another track joined the trail they followed. Roose pointed to it.

"Lamby bull, and big!"

"How long ago?" The trapper dropped to one knee, inspected the indentations in the snow with his nose only a few inches above the markings.

"Maybe an hour, could be less."

"The boys went along here two hours ago, and they'd keep an eye on their back trail," Rysdyke offered.

But Roose was troubled. "Bull following a man trail, that way means he has a real mad on. Might even have been creased by some soft head who didn't hunt him down for the real kill. Those cracked guards along the road take shots at everything moving, and a lamby can travel pretty far with a crease to stir him up. A wounded bull is a hard risk any way you look at it."

"Well, you know the drill, Roose. We'll make this your party. And, Tolkus, start weaving. This is no time for any of us to get mixed up with a lamby that wants to chew up a human."

Roose quickened pace, keeping to the trail, while Tolkus wove a new path first to the right, and then to the left, investigating all thick strands of brush or clumps of trees.

"Why did they ever name those devils 'lambys' in the first place?" Rysdyke wondered.

"Someone with an infernal sense of humor pulled that," Hogan remarked. "Anything *less* like a lamb would be hard to find. Only maybe it's the texture of the fur which gave them that designation."

"Just a tourist guide at heart, aren't you?" Rysdyke laughed. "Not that we ever have any tourists to guide, though I'd like to introduce some of the company vips to a lamby. Those bulls are always mean. You get one really mad and he's going to wipe the earth with you or the nearest thing which looks, smells, and moves like you. A lamby will trail a man for miles, hide in the bush along a path, and spike his horns into the first traveler who passes. And since he makes about as much noise as a feather floating in air, he usually wins the first round. Then, if the traveler has had any companions, the lamby will get his in return."

"But does that satisfy the first victim?" asked Joktar. "Lots of little surprises on this world, aren't there?" He remembered his own sudden entanglement with the zazaar.

"Quite true," Hogan agreed. "So try always to make your first attack the last and in your own favor. Yes, this is not what you might term a pleasant world for a restful vacation."

"But it could be a halfway decent one for men to live on," the ex-spaceman defended the wasteland.

"To what other end do we labor?" The lazy note was back in Hogan's voice. "Break the companies' hold, free Fenris, then comes the millennium."

Rysdyke laughed half-angrily. "Don't you believe in anything?"

"Oh, the power of words is well known. And maybe we can badger the companies into recognizing a few rights besides those they sit upon for themselves. But Fenris will never be a garden spot, and men are never going to quit grabbing all they can reach with their grubby fingers. Sweep away the companies here and the vacuum left will be speedily filled. We'll then have master trappers, big traders crowding in, eating up the smaller men, building a kingdom in their turn. And some day the last lamby will be skinned, the last zazaar tracked and denuded of its pelt. Then new deposits of alibite, or something similar will be located, the companies will come back." He rubbed the back of his hand across his mask. "History will repeat itself. That is what is so fatiguing about history, it's so repetitious. Personalities change, the pattern never. Nothing but the same boring mistakes, rises and falls, catastrophes and achievements, balancing each other without end. If man were offered something else—"

Hogan's eyes lifted from the trail, to the sky behind the ragged mountain peaks, "he probably wouldn't dare to take it. No, we'll go on and on in our own twisted way until we're finished like the others before us."

"Those who built your mound-fort?" asked Joktar.

"Yes. Doubtless that was thrown together by some company who had the blah-blah concession here and was determined to hold it against a band of miserable, dirty outlaws. This is a wolf-head planet now, and it always has been. The very climate pulls men into its pattern. Whoever did grub up that artificial mountain must have had a major enemy breathing down their necks. The situation must have been the same: greed, defense of one's treasure, probably eventual loss to other and stronger attackers. Ah—"

A crack of sound, carrying sharply through the air, put the three into action before its echoes had died away. Joktar, favoring his tender shoulder, shoved sideways, squatting behind the best protection he could find, a tree bole surrounded by a draggle of underbrush. And Rysdyke and Hogan disappeared so skillfully and completely that they might have been permanently removed from the landscape by one of the primitive atomic explosions of Terra's past.

Joktar had not been provided with a blaster and he was wondering how he was expected to defend himself. There was a wisp of smoke curling into the air from a heat-shriveled twig. That bit of branch had caught the outer edge of a blaster beam, and it hung only a pace or so beyond where they would have been in another short moment. Since none of them in the least resembled a lamby bull, there was reason to think they had been selected for elimination. Joktar froze, no use provoking another shot from that hidden marksman.

Was someone in Hogan's own organization getting ambitious, wanting to move up as Samms had done, but not willing to risk the face down of a call out where his chief would have an equal chance? Joktar frowned. This was quite like the streets, treachery against treachery, the most cunning player to sweep the board.

Were Hogan and Rysdyke pinned down now as he was, or using

their superior knowledge of woodcraft to scout around behind the man in ambush? He would swear there was nothing moving about.

Snow creaked. Joktar turned his head with infinite stealth, feeling that perhaps the lurking menace might be able to catch the whisper of his hood furs as he moved. But what he saw was not a man.

Matted fur? Hair? Wool? Blue-gray in color, so close in shade to the branches which framed it that the actual outlines were blurred. Sprouting from that mat of hair were two sharp, upward-pointing horns, a third centering a broad toad's snout. And all three of those horns were sticky with red clots, clots which had dribbled down to the fur. A drip of mucous from the nose flaps was also discolored with that tell-tale scarlet. This thing had gored to kill and recently.

The eyes, deep-set in that stained fur, blinked. Joktar pressed against his tree, feeling that trunk had suddenly become transparent.

Again that creak of snow. The head pushed forward, bringing into visibility thickly maned shoulders, forefeet with sharply split hooves as dreadfully bedabbled as the horns. Slowly, with caution but no fear, the lamby bull came out into the open path, head up, nostril flaps open to the full.

Those first few steps brought the beast almost level with Joktar. The Terran expected every second to see that head swing in his direction. And for the first time in his life, he knew a wave of the kind of fear which saps wits, weakens muscle, makes a man wait supinely for death. He fought against that as the lamby minced almost delicately past his tree. And he could not at first believe the creature was not hunting him.

There came a rush, but not in his direction. The beast leaped along the trail, making an impetuous dive, carrying on into a brush wall between two trees. Crack of blaster bolt. A thin, high wail which could come from an animal or a man. Another crack of blaster, then an inhuman scream of agony.

The stench of burned flesh and hair hung foul on a rising wind. Joktar pulled away from the tree, stumbled into a run which took him along the lamby's route. Why he was impelled to trace that charge he could not have said. But he knew he would find death before him.

He ploughed through the break in the underbrush to a scene of butchery. The lamby, most of its head charred away, lay on the human body it had been trampling. And working to free the latter were Roose and Hogan. A moment later Rysdyke crashed into the small clearing from the other side.

"Tolkus?"

Hogan caught a fragment of torn hood, tugged at it until the head it had once protected rolled limply to display the features of the dead. To Joktar the man was a stranger.

"Who?" Rysdyke's question was half-protest. Roose's breath puffed out in a thin white cloud through his mask.

"Never saw this one before, chief." He shoved at the carcass of the lamby, forcing it off the body. The rent and bloodied fur of the stranger's coat bore no company badge.

"Now I wonder," Hogan considered the corpse impersonally. "Could he have been an envoy from Samms or Ebers? Or is someone in our mob ambitious enough to set up a swap."

"That just isn't so!" Roose spun around in the stained snow to stare indignantly up at his leader. "You know that none of the boys'd stand for a swap on you, chief. Never!"

"So I had thought," Hogan commented lazily. "But there can always be sudden changes in the wind of policy. We, or I, was set up for this one. Whether the lamby was part of the original scheme, an extemporaneous last-minute double-check which failed, or just a coincidence which worked to save the skins of the righteous, we'll never know. In the meantime, I propose we push the pace a little. It would never do for us to be late to the meeting now."

"No," Rysdyke was breathing a little hard. "I want to see who looks surprised when we do arrive."

"Yes, that point has also occurred to me. Joktar, suppose you carry this." Hogan picked up the blaster which had been the property of the dead sniper and tossed it over.

The rock island Hogan had designated for the meeting proved to be another of the remains left by the forgotten earlier inhabitants of Fenris. Once there had been an island in the middle of a now ice-bound river . . . or perhaps there had only been the projection of a reef. But based on that limited foundation was a circular wall of blocks, fitted together with fine skill, supporting now, well above water level, a hollow cone. Smoke ascended from the broken top of the cone, to be tattered by the wind.

"Somebody's there," Rysdyke observed.

But Roose was more intent upon the mountains beyond and Joktar, ignorant as he was of the Fenrian weather signs, could note those banks of gathering clouds in a thick roll to the northeast.

"Weather's not holding," the trapper pointed to the sky. "There's a blanket building."

"Right," Hogan's voice was clipped, urgent. "Tolkus," he ordered the man who had joined them just as they left the forest clearing, "you circle and warn all our boys. Tell them to hunt shelter—quick!"

"But—" Rysdyke began to protest.

"We're not the only ones to see those clouds," Hogan replied. "No one is going to start trouble with a blanket coming. If we do have to face a show down, the action will come after the storm clouds. And the sooner we all get to cover the better!"

The ice covering the river was patterned with the tracks of men and sleds. The sleds themselves were staked out at a break in the cone wall. Hogan made a sharp turn to the left at the point and Joktar, copying him, found a narrow flight of stairs set in the wall itself, the tread stones projecting only inches. The passage was a funnel and the Terran's imagination provided him with a picture of what would happen should a rock be hurled down that grade to meet upward bound traffic.

"Hulllloo!" Hogan's call, echoing eerily up that stair, announced them and they were met by a dozen or so men. In the cone top there were traces of partitions, remains of small cells about the walls, floored with frozen earth. And in the center space a fire blazed while piles of wood filled several of the wall cells.

Even in the short time it had taken them to cross the river and climb the inner stair, the clouds had blotted out most of the daylight, stretching in oily black tongues from the peaks.

"Coming up a regular bury-in," commented one of those awaiting Hogan. His speech was underlined by a blast of wind screaming across the broken top of the cone.

And with the wind came a whirling wall of snow. The men were fast at work. Smaller fires were kindled closer to the overhang of the outer walls. And with such fires before them and the solid blocks of the ancient stone at their backs, they prepared as best they could to wait out the fury of the blanket.

In the open, such a storm could bury the unfortunate. But here the ruins afforded almost as much protection as a company dome. The fire in the center hissed out under a dump of snow. Only the constant roaring of the wind was a growing torment to the ears, making it impossible for a man to hear the voice of even the neighbors he crowded against.

✳ ✳ **8** ✳ ✳

Joktar leaned his forehead against his knees. Under and around him he could feel the shudder of the cone. There came a crash to be heard even above the boom of the wind. A portion of the ancient stonework gave, was swept inward. Joktar felt the man beside him stir, hitch away. Under the shrilling of the storm, there sounded a thin screaming. He began to crawl after his neighbor.

The moment they ventured away from the wall, wind and snow lashed. They clawed over one of the small cell partitions, came to the mass of rubble which half-buried a man. Together they pulled apart the debris, blinded by snow, deafened by the wind, blundering awkwardly because their sense of touch was numbed. Finally they drew the man free, as he screamed again and went limp.

Somehow they got him back to the wall, to the warmth of their own share of fire. Joktar, his shoulder aching cruelly, half-collapsed against that stone support while his companion tried to aid the injured. Until the storm passed there was little they could do for him.

Time moved by no normal measure. Hours . . . half a day . . . Joktar became aware that there were longer and longer pauses in the blasts overhead, that the snow was allowing a window on the open sky once again. As the storm died, men shook free of small drifts, looked about dazedly, not quite sure they had once more beaten Fenris.

"So Gagly got it." One of the white-powdered figures hunched forward to peer into the face of the man they had dragged from the cave-in.

"Gagly?" Hogan stripped off his mitten to push questing fingers into the throat opening of the other's furs. "Yes, he's gone. You're going to miss Gagly, Samms . . . a pilot . . ."

"So, we'll miss him." Wide shoulders moved under the furs of one of the others in a shrug which was close to perfunctory. Above the scarf mask, Samms' eyes were pale and shallow like mirrors to reflect an outside world, rather than reveal the emotions of the man who wore them in his skull.

He turned away from his dead follower to call: "Ebers, over here!"

One of the men brushing snow from his furs, stamping numb feet, raised his head, but made no move to obey that brusque summons.

"Ride out, Samms." His voice was a slow drawl, carrying a measure of authority. "We'll chew out your proposition when we're ready."

Above the face mask those pale gray eyes did not change, but Samms' hand twitched, and was quickly checked. That twitch had been toward his blaster; Joktar had not been alone in noting that. Rysdyke, standing to one side, slid his feet a little apart as if bracing his body before calling for a blast out.

Some time passed before the center fire was rebuilt and they gathered around it to share provisions from their trailbags. They were still eating when the leader of the Kortoski mob arose, strode back and forth in the firelight as if his impatience goaded him into at least that counterfeit of action.

"They've leveled a new landing field in the Harband company," he announced. "Plan to deliver supplies there straight without setting down at Siwaki. Just another move towards closing the regular port entirely. When all the fields are located in company areas, we can never hope to bring free traders in here again."

"And what countermeasures do you propose?" That was Hogan sounding disinterested, almost languid. Samms came around quickly as if he had been challenged.

"Not to sit on our tails and wait!"

Joktar, watching narrowly, noting the unchanging shallowness of those gray eyes, revised his first judgment of Samms. On the surface, judged by his speech, his attitude, the outlaw was a hot-tempered brawler, ready to use weapon or fist to bull his way to what he wanted. A type readily understood by the trappers he sought to rule.

Only those eyes belied such a first reading. And Joktar chose to believe the eyes. Samms had the subtle signs of a gambler who had long ago graduated from a star-and-comet table to games played without the aid of kas-cards or counters. The Terran longed to know what series of events had brought Samms to Fenris as an emigrant. And he marked the other down as dangerous.

"So you don't believe in waiting," Hogan continued calmly. "May we ask what sort of action you are urging on us?"

"They are going to bring in a private ship on the Harband field. Two company vips, six in the crew. What if they found a reception committee ready to scoop the lot. We could dicker with Harband if we had their vips parked up here."

"How did you comb out this information, Samms?" Ebers' drawl came from the other side of the fire.

"Oh, Samms has his lines of information. Pretty effective they are too, it would seem. Perks is really delivering," Hogan returned.

"Perks was planted," the other agreed readily. "When the time comes, he'll give us more help than just information!"

"And just how did Perks make himself so solid with the companies that he can give us all this help? Wasn't he the only survivor of a squad who got theirs on the Lizard Back?"

Hogan answered for Samms. "He was. Too bad, Samms, these awkward questions are bound to be asked. They're doubly awkward for you because that squad were mostly loyal to Raymark, weren't they? How *did* Perks make such a fine impression on his new employers? Use a judicious sellout as an introduction?"

A low mutter ran around the circle, growing to a growl. But Samms showed no signs of discomfiture.

"Perks was jumped. Then he was bright enough to take his chances with a good story when they pulled him in. He had one ready."

"Always be prepared for capture as well as other eventualities," remarked Hogan.

"Now," Ebers struck in again, "we are being offered some tempting bait and invited to come close and take a sniff. Three mobs able to take this new field! Expect us to swallow that!"

"I would say that the taking of the field would only be a temporary move," Hogan spoke directly to Ebers. "Samms has suggested kidnapping. We scoop up the vips, keep them while we dicker with the company until Harband and the rest promise us the wherewithal to make life merrier here in the wilderness. That it, Samms?"

"Sure, sure," Ebers snarled his interruption. "We button up these vips, Harband yells and the patrol comes running. Those lads could cut us off in the breaks and starve us out. And where could we park the vips to have them ready and yet able to breathe and walk?"

"Yes, another small problem. To establish any kind of a semi-permanent base is to invite immediate investigation from the patrol. Move around and we expose our prisoners to the elements and lose them before we can prove their value."

"Not if we take them off-planet!"

That one sentence from Samms might have been the opening blast of a second blanket the way it silenced his listeners. Joktar caught the new note in the other's voice. Samms was getting close to his serious play now.

Hogan plucked at his mask. "Well, well. Do I detect some thoughts of Councilor Cullan and his visit to Loki?"

Again that tiny movement toward the blaster. All of Samms' impatience could not be an act. And Hogan was deliberately applying pressure.

"What's this Cullan got to do with it? He one of the vips?" Ebers wanted to know.

"At present he's a member of the Supreme Council, and he's anti-company, doesn't believe in the monopolies on frontier planets. He's argued the subject for years, now he's beginning to get backing, big backing. And the vips are worrying. Three years ago there was a serious shake-up in the Colonization Section. A man named Kronfeld got in as one of the project directors. He's no political hack, but came up through the technical side. He's talked Alvarn Thomlistos into supporting some of his ideas. And the Great Thorn has established a new foundation, backed by the net profits from the Alban Freight, the Orsfo-Kol Mining Corporation and a few other such organizations."

Joktar was startled. The net profits of the companies Hogan listed were enough to make a man slightly breathless when he tried to reckon the amounts of credits involved.

"I don't think I need point out that the Great Thorn has friends on a great many different government levels. So Cullan sat down with Kronfeld and listened, *really* listened, to some truths. With Thom backing the spread of these ideas there's going to be a lot of activity around the galaxy. About two months from now Cullan will be on Loki, gathering material for an assault on the company set-up as it is at present. Suppose a shipload of Harband vips, together with some spokesmen from our own select group, were to land there about the same time. Our arrival couldn't be hushed up so that Cullan wouldn't hear of it, and the subject matter could be just his meat. That is what you have in mind, isn't it, Samms?"

If he were aware Hogan had taken over, Samms made no sign of either recognizing that or admitting defeat now.

"You are correct and amazingly well-informed."

"And with Gagly dead, you'll need the services of a pilot. Rysdyke now has the distinction of being the only free one on Fenris. Perhaps you had him in mind all along; Gagly had been out of space for five years. Now . . . when do you suggest we make this try to take over the Harband Field?"

"You mean you're willing to go along with this crazy scheme, Hogan?" Ebers sounded incredulous.

"I think it has a number of possibilities."

"Enough to get us all killed!" Ebers shot back. It was Samms who answered that.

"Would you rather rot out here? We have to make some definite move against the companies soon and I don't mean just knocking off a hole in the mountains! We really have to cut into their cruising orbits or we're outclassed and through. The free men on Fenris either climb to the top now or they cease to be free!"

"He's right, you know, Ebers. We've dragged on here for two years now with a closed port. Our trade's been finished entirely for six months. We're three mobs, and a scattering of loners; we're all that are left. And how many new recruits do you get? Not enough to take the places of the men we lose, let alone build up our strength. I give us just about another six months of this life and we *will* be finished."

Again the mutter ran about the fire-lit circle. Ebers took up the argument.

"And *you* think, Hogan," he accented the "you" in a way Joktar guessed was intended to needle Samms, "that this plan does have a chance?"

"Oh, the odds against its success are high enough. But would you rather finish really blasting Harband where it will hurt, or let company guards, bad weather and luck whittle you down to nothing out here? And there is a slim chance we may be able to pull it off. Samms has Perks planted, remember?"

"I dunno," Ebers answered slowly, but his protest was not so sharp.

Samms jerked a thumb at the body rolled against the wall of the cone. "We lost one man here today. You don't know how many more might have been caught in the blanket. Better for a man to go down fighting than this way."

"I have two raiding parties out. I'll have to recall those. And there are maybe some loners who'd join with us. Roughly, maybe fifty. But I won't take any but volunteers."

"Good enough. And I ought to do as well. You, Samms?"

"Thirty—forty—if I can talk some of the loners in," he spoke absently, as if his mind were on another problem.

"Suppose we capture this ship and Rysdyke is able to fly her off-world. Who goes along to meet Cullan? We can't load all our men on board."

"A committee, I'd say," Hogan replied. "The rest of our combined forces should hold the company compound if we're successful. Those who stay can arm some of the emigrants. They may not be of use in the open, but they can help defend the domes."

"For how long would we have to hold the compound?" Ebers wanted to know.

Hogan stood up. "This whole scheme is a matter of ifs, ands, and buts. But I agree, Samms has a point. We'd better risk a big gamble now than drift along as we have been doing. This ship combined with Cullan's visit to Loki furnishes us with a chance. Even if we fail, Harband can't sit on the news of our attack, and rumors alone could make things uncomfortable for the companies."

"A lot of good that would do men already dead," Ebers commented sourly. "Only maybe you're right, this is a chance we won't have again. Sounds like a mighty thin one though."

"History is made up of thin chances which have succeeded." Hogan slung his supply bag over his shoulder. "Has Perks given you any idea, Samms, when we should start moving?"

"Soon. You'd better call in your raiding parties."

"Will do." Hogan, Rysdyke, Roose and Joktar left the cone. When they were across the river and heading to the back trail, Hogan spoke to the Terran.

"What do you think of Samms?"

"Just now he isn't very happy."

"Why?"

"Because you're playing the hand he picked."

Hogan laughed. "Yes, I fear I spoiled his original plan somewhat."

"But you backed him, otherwise Ebers would have walked out!" Rysdyke objected.

"He took over," Joktar corrected. With great daring he added a question of his own. "Are you Cullan's man?"

"You've an active imagination, son," was Hogan's only reply.

Fenris' moon, brighter, yet in its way more cold and stark than Terra's, rode a cloudless sky. Below the fluff of brush on the mountain slopes were the clustered domes of the Harband holdings, covering the mouths of the galleries running back into the mountains. There were lights in those domes, and sweeping spotlights outside to cover the land lying within the sonic barrier. These kept off outlaw and beast alike. To Joktar their own expedition seemed increasingly foolhardy.

Hogan might have been reading his mind when, after rising on one knee to use a pair of vision lenses, he said, "There's this in our favor, they won't be expecting any attack."

"From what I see, they won't have to. How can anyone get across those spot paths? And what happens if the sonic barrier isn't cut before we reach it?"

"Ifs, ands, maybes, and buts again. Perks is to take the barrier out."

"And will he?" queried Rysdyke.

Hogan laughed. "How pessimistic we are tonight. Well, the charge hasn't been sounded as yet. You have a chance to withdraw in good order, heroes."

"There *is* a ship!" Rysdyke crowded up closer, his hand reaching past Hogan to point at that slim shape caught momentarily in one of the spots: a silver needle aimed at the cold heavens.

"So that much is true." Hogan's glasses were aimed, not at the ship, but at the domes with their wreaths of colored lights.

Another of the mob crawled up under the cover of the brush.

"Jumper on the road," he reported. "Our boys in it, they flashed the signal."

Close to sunset, hours before, the first move in their attack had been made when they overran the nearest road station. The personnel found there were imprisoned, their broadcasting equipment smashed, and a jumper and a crawler seized. The machines were now coming along and if, with their cargos of armed men, they could get through the sonic gates, the forces they carried could hold those entrances open for their fellows.

The smaller vehicle proceeded at the odd leaping gait peculiar to its kind and behind it the crawler emerged from around a bend. Hogan loosened his mask, gave a high carrying whistle. Shadows arose, to flit from cover. Joktar heard that whistle picked up, relayed. A pattern of lights winked on the nearest dome, was answered by a beam from the driver's cabin on the jumper.

"Let's hope," Rysdyke breathed as his shoulder rubbed Joktar's in their forward creep, "that we do have the right recognition signals."

The sonic barrier was invisible. The driver maneuvering the jumper along the rutted road would never know he had crossed it successfully until he reached the domes, or doubled up in agony of wrenched nerves and muscles.

On the jumper surged, rolled, surged again. The machine was in the open and the beam of a spot caught and held it for a moment before flicking on. The crawler trailed. If neither vehicle were expected at the compound, there would be questions and perhaps an alarm. Joktar's fingers tightened on the blaster as he watched that all too slow advance.

The spot was halfway through a sweep across the landing field when its funnel of light jerked skywards.

"That's it!"

Perks' moves were coming on schedule. Now the men in hiding went into action as jumper and crawler halted, discharging their cargos in a boil of outlaws dashing on to the domes. The crackle of blaster fire and the shriller explosion of vorps bolts broke the silence of the night as the weird lightning of blaster fire crossed or met in the air.

Joktar ran forward, part of the first wave headed by Hogan. He saw Roose put on a burst of speed, turn to the right. Rysdyke peeled off after the trapper, and Joktar made a third. There would be a guard on the ship but the crew would normally be quartered at the domes. Whether or not this watchman could close the ship in time depended upon the quality of his vigilance and their own rate of speed. Roose went to one knee, fired, while Rysdyke darted on.

A tracer of fire illuminated for a moment the dark mouth of the hatch in the needle's side. A figure writhed, fell out to the scorched ground beneath. Rysdyke reached the crew ladder, was climbing.

Joktar caught the ladder below the ascending pilot, well aware of what an excellent target he must make against the side of the ship. Rysdyke was in the air lock now, a moment or so later Joktar made the same haven.

The lock was empty. Roose was on the ladder below, the pilot was heading with single-minded determination for the control cabin. Joktar came out in a short corridor. His only knowledge of the geography of the ship had been the points drilled into him by Rysdyke back in camp, and the ex-pilot had been only guessing at the type of spacer this might be.

For all they knew, members of the crew might be in any of the closed cabins, but their time table allowed no time now for a search. Roose came through, closed the lock. And that shut out the wild clamor of the fight. Now all they could hear was the soft thud of their boots on the stair treads.

Three levels and then they were in the control cabin. Rysdyke had already seated himself in one of the web slung seats, his fingers flickering from button to lever to stud. Roose wriggled through the well opening of the stair, locked down its cover. Joktar relaxed, they could not be easily routed now and Rysdyke had before him the controls governing the ship.

"About now," Roose caught the back on one of the other seats, "they must be trying to raise Siwaki and the patrol on their dome coms." But he did not seem at all alarmed at that thought.

"The only way they can get at us is to try to fry us out with a cruiser's tail flames," Rysdyke returned. "And they've no reason to make this a suicide mission. Well, here goes for the second step, boys."

* * 9 * *

He triggered a last lever. "Now we're in business!"

Joktar hoped that the opposition realized that those open ports just above the tail fins had been noted and their threat understood. This ship had been adapted for passenger use from an outer rim scouting craft, and it was still equipped with armament designed to protect explorers landing on newly discovered and perhaps hostile worlds.

"Gonna tickle 'em up now?" Roose asked, highly interested.

"Oh, we'll give 'em a shot, to impress. Joktar, press that white stud . . . the one to the left of the four-lever plate."

As the Terran did just that, a vision plate, topping one of the control panels, came to life. Rysdyke gave more instructions and suddenly the domes appeared clearly on that square. Flashes of blaster and vorp fire still rent the night about them.

The pilot read dials, made some minute corrections, and then pressed a button.

In the air, well above the dome bubbles, burst a small core of light, light which spread in waves, shooting skyward in angry brilliance. Both blaster and vorp fire were swallowed up in a poisonous green radiance.

"Quite a show," commented Roose. "Where do you plant the next shot?"

"On the crag, over that way." Again Rysdyke made adjustments and fired.

A second ball of angry green glowed on an outjut of the heights behind the domes. The fire continued as if feeding upon the substance of the rock, waves spreading from it for an area of yards. Then the glow died, and where that outjut had been there was nothing but a softly glowing hole eaten into the mountain's skin, a hole which Joktar knew would go on, deeper and deeper, until the charge of the bolt was completely exhausted.

"Now they *should* have been watching that one!" Roose laughed. "Might even bite into one of their precious mine galleries and bust it wide open." He moved closer to the vision plate. "You know, fellas, that wouldn't be a bad idea, let's just chew their mine to pieces."

"It's a thought," Rysdyke was grinning. "But I'm afraid we'll have to wait and see if they'll tail-up first. That's orders."

Now as the glow of the initial shots faded, they could catch sight of blaster explosions once more. But it was very evident that the exchange of small fire was not nearly so spirited.

"Calling ship . . . calling ship . . ." a disembodied, metallic voice startled them. Joktar and Roose put back their blasters, smiling sheepishly at each other, while Rysdyke drew the mike of the com to him.

"Ship here. Who calls?"

"This is Waigh. What are you trying to do, you fool, burn us out?"

"That's up to you, Waigh. The range will be corrected one notch for every two minutes you continue your opposition."

There was a startled and baffled silence, before the dome com called again.

"This is Waigh, Cowan, Waigh! You're on range for the domes!"

"Correction," Rysdyke was plainly enjoying the exchange. "This is not Cowan, but Rysdyke, commanding officer, ship. We have taken over in the name of Fenrian Free Men. And I am well aware we are on range for your domes, that is our intention."

"That gives him a tough strip to chew on," Roose remarked.

"First time in years anyone's warmed Waigh's tail hot enough to really sting him."

"The blaster fire's stopped." Joktar had been studying the scene on the vision plate.

Rysdyke held the mike closer, counting into it. "Ten, nine, eight, seven, six, five, four, three, correction one notch now being made. We mean what we say, Waigh. One!"

He pressed the firing button. A second flower of light appeared on the rock face of the mountain to spread in ripples.

"If the first one didn't eat into one of their galleries, this one certainly will," Roose observed. "Waigh's as stubborn as a lamby, though."

"He may be the top Harband man on Fenris, but he has some visiting vips in there, remember? Hogan's betting the off-worlders won't take kindly seeing good ore disintegrated."

"Ship, this is Sa Kim," the voice coming from the com was distorted, but still more remote in tone than Waigh's bellow. "I speak for Harband. What are your terms?"

"Contact the Free Men ground force. They're prepared to state terms," Rysdyke answered briskly.

The center dome on the vision plate flashed white. Rysdyke put down the mike.

"Well, our move worked. This Sa Kim is ready to talk."

Roose stretched. "As neat a job as I ever had a hand in. The chief might have been taking company compounds all his life."

Rysdyke stirred. "He might just have to take over more than this compound."

Joktar leaned back, his slung seat swayed a little. "Trouble with Samms?"

"Yes." With an overflow of furs, Roose fitted his bulk into another of the cabin seats. "I kinda thought Samms was shaping up into a lord-high-what-have-you, but, again, he isn't too solid with his own mob. The Perks deal still smells as far as some of the boys are concerned. I'd say if our chief raised his finger and said, 'Boys, I'm taking over, as of here and now,' Samms could only ask for a blast out to settle it. Then he'd have as much chance as a snowball in a vorp beam. The chief moves slow when he's not being snarled at, but I've seen him take two call-outs against top men. He's alive: they aren't."

"Who *is* Hogan?" Joktar asked impulsively.

Rysdyke's voice was chill. "We don't ask a man here on Fenris what he was off-world. Hogan was a trader in Siwaki. When the trade was pinched off, he turned woods-runner."

"Sure," Roose nodded. "Only me, I don't think he was ever trader, or hunter. He gets a big kick out of blasting the companies where it hurts the most. But he knows a lot about what's going on off-world. You heard how he spouted off at the meeting. I think he's an undercover man for someone big—"

"Ship!"

This time they all recognized the voice. Rysdyke caught for the mike eagerly.

"Ship here."

"This is Hogan. The deal's complete, visitors coming, be ready to open ports."

"That we will, chief."

Roose sent his seat bobbing with a stir. "Wonder what kind of a deal they made. Might circulate a little and find out."

"We stick here. Too easy for someone to sneak in and take over, the same way we did." Rysdyke put down the mike.

"When do you take off for Loki?" Roose wanted to know.

The pilot shrugged. "It'll have to be soon. Hogan wants to planet before Cullan arrives."

"Loki. Fenris is cold, Hel hot, and Loki bare of rock and water. This is a damn twister of a system."

"You chose to come here."

"Sure, but then me, I'm second-generation from Westlund. We're used to cold there. It's not as bad as Fenris, but still cold. I came here for the first alibite rush. Staked me a good claim down on the Frater. That was before the companies rigged registration. I was doing pretty good ten years ago, then they started the freeze-out. My stamper broke down in a cold clip, couldn't get me a new one through their shipping regulations. So . . ." he spread out his mittened hands,

"I lost time on the claim, couldn't deliver my tax quota and they took over. They did the same with all the early boys—those who weren't burned trying to fight it out.

"Well, I'd done some lamby hunting on the side, so I made a fresh start that way, dealing through the chief. When they tried to stamp him flat, we both hit the outlands together. I figure the companies owe me about eight years' living. Maybe now I can collect some of that."

"Party coming." Joktar had been watching the plate.

Roose squinted at the view of the outside. "Yeah, the chief's leading them. I'll go down and open the door."

Joktar lay on a narrow bunk, pressure straps anchoring him. The ship strained now to break the planetary bounds of gravity. Had he felt this before?

Those hazy memories which could not be recaptured, yet existed far inside his brain, answered yes.

Weight crushed him, lay heavy on his bones, lungs, flesh. He fought back in his own way, striving to relax nerve and muscle. They were heading out from Fenris. Slowly, he turned his head to glance at the other occupant of the small cabin.

Hogan lay still, his eyes closed. He must still be anesthetized by the take-off shot. Joktar's private wonder grew. Why hadn't he, himself, succumbed to that anodyne which eased passengers and crew alike, save for the pilot, through the discomfort of the first upward thrust? In these small ships, the break shot was mandatory and he had thought it always worked.

The vibrations reaching him through the walls, the bunk on which he lay, the very air of the cabin was not the punishment he had feared, but rather something more—an energizing revitalizer. He was more alert and alive in spite of the pressure than he had ever remembered being before. It was as if this environment was for him the normal and rational one.

As the pressure lessened, he wanted out of the confines of the cabin. He unfastened the buckles of the straps, sat up on the bunk. The magnetic soles of his looted crew boots anchored him. He took four steps out of the cabin to the ladder. There he paused, making a new discovery. This too was familiar, yet he was no spaceman.

Joktar went to the control cabin. Rysdyke half-lay, half-sat in the pilot's chair, within finger reach of the manual controls. The ship was on auto, but any slip must be instantly rectified by human training and intelligence.

The Terran dropped into the matching seat before the com-unit, watching the vision plate. There was Fenris covering three-quarters of the screen, silver, dark blue, as cold to the sight as it was to all the other senses of the men who battled its forbidding land masses. Joktar closed his eyes, reopened them. That blue and silver ball . . . the color was wrong . . . some long-repressed memory shouted so vigorously that he stirred uneasily.

"Gold," he murmured, unaware that the spoke aloud, "a golden world . . ."

Rysdyke was relaxed in the embrace of his chair, the strain of take-off beginning to fade from his young-old face.

"A golden world," he repeated softly. "There is one golden world, or so they say. The Ffallian know . . ." Again he slid into that other unknown tongue with its singing lilt, "Ffal, yruktar llyumn, Ris syuarktur mann . . ."

To Joktar, the sounds sang, he could almost make sense of them. But because he could not break the barrier within himself, a small spark of rage glowed. He was being deprived of something truly his own, and until he regained that lost treasure he could not live as did other men.

"Who are the Ffallian and where is the golden world?" His demand was as sharp as a blaster bolt.

Rysdyke answered the second part of his question: "Not on any map of ours."

"Why?"

"Because when it was offered to us, we threw it away. Or rather it was thrown away for us." The frustration in Rysdyke's answer matched the bitterness Joktar knew.

"Why?"

"Because," the pilot brought his fist down upon the edge of the control panel as if he were beating against a firmly closed door, "our vips will not admit that we have superiors in space!"

"But the Kandas, the Thas, the Zaft," Joktar told the roll of the planet civilizations the Terrans had found, "none of them have galactic ships, and only the Tlolen are free in their own solar system."

"Yes, those who are not to our own level, we can acknowledge them," Rysdyke sneered. "But you haven't heard of the Ffallian, have you, nor of the others . . . those who claim the golden world? We knew . . . we in the service. I myself saw a video tape and heard . . ." his voice softened. "And I tried to go out there. That's why they blasted me out of space! Proper scouts see nothing, hear nothing, and never tell anything which is not covered by regulations!"

"Scouts?"

"Those in exploration service. But that had its Bluebeard chambers. You stayed in the limits of your assigned sector; some sectors were off-limits altogether. I found a beacon on an asteroid. The signal called me in. And I wasn't the first who had answered. There was a scout ship anchored there, an obsolete type. And in it was a message tape; I ran it for reading, against orders. Then I wanted to go, too."

"To go where?"

"To where the beacon gave a course, as the other scout had before me. Only I'd signaled in when I first found the beacon and the patrol was after me before I could relay to the Others that I was waiting."

"Waiting for what?"

"For those who set the beacon. It was all down there on the tape. We knew of the Ffallian, we'd seen their ships. The patrol had tried to blast them, only they can't touch them. But the Ffallian are only the messengers—guides—the helping hands we slapped away. For learning that, I was cashiered and sent to Hel in a labor battalion. Hogan got me out because he had need for a pilot. I think he was planning to run an old tramp bucket in here for trading. But he knows about the Ffallian, too, and he doesn't believe in the quarantine."

"What about the scout in the ship you found?"

"He was lucky, he went out there. Quite a few scouts have over the years."

"Perhaps they were captured."

"No!" Rysdyke's answer was emphatic. "Those tapes . . . they were the real thing. There's no reason to fear the Ffallian. Why, they've tried over and over to make contact with us peacefully. And one of our scouts came back and he was shot by command of his own officer."

"Why?"

"Because he had been out there, because he could prove it was all true. He was reported on the records as having been killed by the Others. But you can't shut up a whole post personnel and there was talk. Yes, Marson had been with the Ffallian, and the Others . . . those who roam the stars we have never explored. And he came back."

"Why?"

"He brought a concrete offer from them."

"Why don't the services want anything to do with these aliens?"

"Because they are afraid, the vips are anyway. Those Others have what we do not—immortality." Rysdyke stared at the vision plate as if he saw there something other than the harsh disc of Fenris. "Mortals and immortals. The mortals fear and hate the Others for the futures we do not have. We made contact years ago and the vips were frightened, frustrated, felt like children trying to be men. They lashed out, killed, withdrew our forces. But the war has been on our side only."

"Very true. Except that the Others are not immortal."

Hogan emerged from the stairwell. Wearing the tunic of a ship's officer, he had become a man who might pass unnoticed in the trade section of N'Yok itself.

"No, they are not immortal. That is one thing we *have* learned, and the truth has been concealed by those of our kind who must build monsters to hold their own power. The aliens only have a longer life span."

"But why?"

Hogan dropped into the third seat. "Oh, it's all of a piece. We made our first contact fifty years ago. Some men had the facts— Morre, Ksanga, Thom (the Great Thom's grandfather), Marson . . ."

"Morre?" repeated Joktar. Morre was long-dead, his star empire built upon his personal charm and brilliance had collapsed speedily.

"Just so Morre was a fanatic, a dangerous one. He was outraged by what he learned at the first contact. The superiority upon which his whole nature was secured was threatened. To him, the aliens were a horrible threat, not only to mankind at large, but to him personally, which was worse. So he took steps. Reports were faked, distorted. We were told stories, such as Thom was spaced and murdered by the Others. There were atrocity tales spread among the services, if not the public. Morre had the power to do it. Over a period of a very few years, he produced the monsters he believed in. And even after his death, the faked evidence stood. In his way, Morre was a genius, but we have to suffer for his sins."

"So we fought them," Rysdyke's voice was tired and bleak.

"Yes, in a one-sided way. The Ffallian understood. They withdrew for their own safety—which for at least one reason is more precious than we knew until recently. But they never gave up their hope for a meeting between our species and the aliens they represent. They set up beacons, subtly tuned to attract only men with whom they could establish contact. So men did disappear . . . traders, scouts. Only the Ffallian are not *our* problem. We have plans to make for Loki!"

"To meet Cullan . . ."

Hogan sat quietly, there was a peculiar quality to his silence. He was making up his mind, Joktar believed, being hurried into a decision he would have liked to consider more leisurely.

"On the surface Cullan . . ."

"On the surface?" It was Joktar who applied the prod.

"We have Sa and Minta on board. Their proposition is to see Cullan with them. He will stay at the Seven Stars in Nornes. I'll be with them and so will Samms. And we'll all be under surveillance every moment of the time. So we'll keep one line free. You," he turned to Joktar, "are going to have some more trouble with that shoulder of yours. Let's have a look at it now."

Joktar unsealed his tunic and stripped it off. His undershirt followed. As far as he himself could judge, the new pink skin looked healthy enough. He would bear a scar but the burn was well on the way to healing and it was only tender now to direct pressure. Hogan inspected the wound frowningly.

"Looks too good," he commented. "But we can touch it up some. And see that you run a temperature. When we set down on Loki, you're to be sent to the clinic."

"Why?"

"Because I want one of us in position to move without being tailed. And secondly, I want to be sure of keeping you."

Joktar pulled up his shirt. "I'm not likely to try to ship out without papers or credits."

"Ship out, no; *be* shipped out, maybe." Hogan was, he saw, entirely serious.

"You mean the patrol would pick me up as an emigrant escapee?"

"Listen," Hogan stood before him, hands on hips, scowling a little, "if what I think is true, you have more than the patrol to fear now, boy."

Rysdyke's eyes were narrowed, he nodded in agreement.

"But what have I got to do with your quarrel with the companies on Fenris?"

"Fenris! Fenris is the first, but perhaps the least of our objectives. We're snarled up in half a dozen webs, all being spun by some busy spiders working for opposite ends and with the stickiest means they can manufacture out of their devious minds. If we come through the next week or so and take away even one one-hundredth of the stakes on the table, there'll be action to rock more than one system. Freedom for Fenris . . . great nebulae! We're fighting for freedom for a whole species—our own!"

✳ ✴ **10** ✴ ✳

Hogan stood looking down at his own hands, broad hands, pale-skinned through lack of exposure, but strong and tough. His fingers moved. Almost, Joktar decided, as if he were gathering up a hand of kas-cards and spreading out those narrow strips to assess their potential value.

"When do we planet?" he asked.

Rysdyke patted the edge of the panel. "With this little beauty . . . a week, space time. She's built for speed and I'll push her."

"A week . . ." Hogan repeated, but his tone suggested that he desired to cut that in half.

"Our passengers happy?"

"They hadn't come out of break-off sleep when I looked in on them," Hogan answered absently. "Sa is the one to watch. Minta's a bull-headed man but Sa's subtle. He gave in at once when we jumped the compound. His retreat is no sure victory for us."

"What about Samms?"

Hogan grinned. "Samms is busy spinning plans, probably damn good ones. Give that boy another five years and a free hand on Fenris, and perhaps even Sa would have second thoughts about backing him."

"Samms wants Fenris."

"Samms is apt to want a lot of things. Whether he'll be moderately successful in getting them is another matter."

Joktar made his first contribution. "He's dangerous."

"You rate him that?" Hogan favored him with full attention. "Now that's interesting. But there's one thing about Samms, his appetite is bigger than his capacity. He may not be far from discovering that himself the hard way. Now, my wounded hero," Hogan's hand closed upon Joktar's fit shoulder, "you are coming with me to begin languishing in your cabin with a serious relapse. And I warn you, this isn't going to be just an act, it will be a very uncomfortable fact!"

There Hogan was correct. Aided by supplies from the ship's dispensary and a proficiency in their use, which led Joktar to believe that this was not the first time such a program had been in force, the outlaw leader produced results which were lamentable as far as his victim was concerned. By the time they set down on Loki, Joktar was almost oblivious of everything save his own discomfort. Shortly after Rysdyke had brought them in for a perfect three-fin landing, Hogan stood over his bunk to deliver a series of last-minute instructions in a voice which pierced all sick self-preoccupation.

"We're taking off now and you're being sent straight to the clinic. They have orders to put you in isolation. Roll with the beam; you'll hear from us later."

So Joktar's first sight of Nornes was necessarily limited as he was bundled out of the ship into an air scooter, and flown across the maze of islands linked together to form the semi-stable base for the major city of Loki. The buildings were all low, not more than four or five stories high, and the sea beat eternally about the scraps of rock they occupied, making a ceaseless murmur which Joktar found lulling once he was established in a room near the top of one of those structures.

He sat up in bed as the door in the opposite wall became a shimmer of force and then snapped out of existence. The medic who entered was the same who had seen him safely installed in that bed only a short time earlier, but this time he moved with a hint of urgency and the face he turned to his patient was sober.

"What's Hogan's game?" The demand held a hint of hostility.

"Game?" repeated Joktar, the fever artificially induced on board ship still slowed his thinking.

"I agreed to take you in," the medic continued. "I didn't agree to stick my neck out for the big brass to take a swing at."

Joktar's incomprehension must have been mirrored on his face, for the medic paused and then laughed, harshly and without humor. "This is a typical Hogan play. Apparently, he didn't brief you either. But it begins to look, fella, as if you're playing bait and the trap's about to be sprung before Hogan expects it—the wrong way."

"I don't understand . . ."

The medic produced a capsule. Dropping it into Joktar's hand he ordered: "Bite that and wake up a little. You'll need a clear head."

Joktar bit. The sharp sting of the enclosed drop of liquid spread through his mouth and, in some odd fashion, up into his head, clearing away the haze which had hung a curtain between him and the world.

"You have visitors. The wrong kind, if I'm any judge."

What had gone wrong? The Terran was alerted now with that old uneasy feeling which had preceded terror in the streets. Had controls slipped from Hogan's grasp?

"What visitors?"

There was a sharp buzz. The medic pressed Joktar back into the enfolding embrace of the foam plast-bed. Obediently, the Terran relaxed, allowed his head to roll to one side in what he hoped was a realistic pose of weakness, watching the door warily through slits beneath drooping eyelids.

Again the shimmer of a force fading. Another medic stood there. And behind him a spaceman, slight, deeply browned, wearing a gray tunic with a constellation badge. The gleam of stars on his shoulders drew Joktar's notice. A sub-sector commander at least!

From those stars, Joktar's eyes arose to the brown face, to the other's eyes. His shoulder hurt as muscles tensed. He had faced enmity of his own kind before, the dull hatred of the streets, the wild malice of a smoke-drinker on a binge, the stupid but dangerous brutality of a bully. But what he read now was so chilling that his hand moved under the covers in a frantic, subconscious search for a weapon he no longer possessed. The medic standing beside the bed had gripped the Terran's other wrist and that hold tightened in a quick squeeze which could be a warning. He was not facing direct and open anger, but an emotion beyond that; it was cold, lasting, and completely deadly. The spaceman was regarding him as if he were not really human.

"He's the one," the identification was delivered in a monotone. As the officer raised his hand, two more uniformed figures began to move in.

The medic by the bed spoke over his shoulder. "I protest this intrusion. This man is suspected of fungoid fever."

The advance on the bed halted. Fungoid fever was not only highly contagious, it was one of the most terrifying specters of the spaceways.

"This is an isolation ward, preserved by force fields—" the medic continued, and his colleague broke in:

"I have already warned Commander Lennox, sir. He has a Class A warrant."

The medic dropped Joktar's wrist and turned to face the officer squarely.

"I don't care," he paced his words slowly and with emphasis, "if you have the whole patrol below to back you up, Commander. A patient suspected of fungoid is not going to be released from isolation until we are sure, and I have the backing of the Council on that. Shaw," he spoke to the other medic, "take these men down to Unit C and see that each one of them has the full course of preventive shots . . . they've been inside the door. Now get out of here!"

Somehow, the force of his authority sent them away and the door shimmered into place. Joktar sat up. The medic rubbed his hand down his face, he was smiling a little.

"That will give them something to think about," he commented with satisfaction. "Preventive shots will busy them for about four hours and they don't dare refuse them. This is only a temporary respite, you know. If you don't produce fungoid patches in ten hours, Lennox can lift you right out of here. We'll have to make some other move before that time limit. Lennox's no fool, he'll have every inch of this building staked out expecting an escape try. Why is he gunning for you?"

"I honestly don't know. As far as I can remember, I never saw him before." *But he wears a gray coat,* Joktar's thoughts drummed, *and that gray tunic is trouble for me.* Why? If he only knew why!

"Hogan! I wish that man would do a little straight talking once in a while. This leaving people in the dark makes for complications."

"Can you get in touch with him?"

"My dear Gentlehomo," the medic's irritation was rooted in very apparent exasperation, "I have been trying to reach Hogan for over an hour. He isn't to be found at any of the three contacts he gave me."

"Picked up?" Joktar asked. Having swept up Hogan, the authorities might now be gathering in all his followers in a general sweep. Though it was difficult to fit Commander Lennox into a routine police roundup.

"No. We would have been warned of that. Meanwhile, we have to think you out of here, and into hiding somewhere else. And with the guards outside that is going to be a star-class problem."

Joktar, his head clear now, was perfectly willing to tackle what seemed to him not unlike setting up a bolt hole from the SunSpot. But time would pressure them and he had no map of the district in his mind. The islands were connected by bridges and these bridges would be discouragingly easy to close.

"Air transport?" he asked and the medic shook his head.

"The scooters are all powered by beam broadcast. They need only snap that off and every machine would be grounded on the nearest landing surface. And that would be one of their first moves."

"Hogan's supposed to be at the Seven Seas. Where is that in relation to this clinic?"

The medic produced a small hand-video cast, centered its beam on the nearest wall. Instantly a small, clear map snapped into view, each detail vivid.

"We're here. The Seven Stars is the plush hostelry for vips, second island to the left and up, that one which is roughly triangular. The building covers almost the whole island, except for a garden strip to the west, makes it easier to guard. It's a full city within itself; they've got shops, cafes, theaters, everything. Most of the visiting vips never leave it until they are ready to return to the spacefield. A series of conferences can be booked for meetings."

"Who could get in without any questions?"

"The staff are all recorded on ident tapes. It would require an operation and too long a time to let you impersonate any one of them. Most of the guests are taped, too."

Joktar was startled. "With their consent?"

"Oh, most of them agree when it is presented to them as a protective measure. Loki is a central meeting place, not only for this system, but for the planets of Beta Lupi and Alpha Lupi as well. There are some big deals put over under the roof of the Seven Stars and a good many of the visitors are sensitive about personal safety."

Joktar began to feel at home; the situation was quite like that of the streets.

"So, staff impersonation is out and guests are taped. Wouldn't anyone at all get in without a recorded checking?"

"Patrol and our friends, the scouts."

"Patrol is out."

"Yes, with their inner ident we couldn't possibly plant one of those in you. And the first patrolman you met would have you under control when you didn't respond. On the other hand, the scouts aren't so equipped. The only trouble is there are fewer of them and those few are now out for you."

Joktar got out of bed. He stood before the map, studying, impressing details upon his memory. "Got any skin dye," he held up his too-pale hands.

"That could be the least of your worries. I can't produce a uniform."

"No. I'll have to handle that. What time is it? And how long until dark?"

"Dark? They'll keep the big light on the islands tonight. You won't have much dark for a cover. What are you going to do?"

Joktar shook his head. "Just give me a plan of this building and some skin stain, that's all I want. What you don't know, you can't spill later under any talk-shot."

"Entirely correct." The medic became all business. "Your force field is sealed to open only to me or my assistant. I'll be back with what you need as soon as I can. Your 'dark' is due in about an hour."

Joktar paced back and forth across the small room. Whatever drug the medic had given him had finished the fever Hogan had earlier induced, and he was fast regaining his strength. Now he was trying to think his way off the island to the Seven Stars. To wear a scout uniform as his means of entrance there was to court trouble, but that was the simplest and quickest answer to his problem. And if the scouts were few, there would be just that many less to threaten his masquerade.

He throttled his impatience until the medic returned and then went to work with swift efficiency. Liquid applied to his face, neck and hands, gave him a brown skin that could not be distinguished from the heavy tan of the spacemen. And the medic had brought, in addition, a drab set of breeches, seal tunic, and soft boots.

"Maintenance man's suit," he informed Joktar. "You can use the grav-drop at the end of this corridor straight to the first undersurface level and be in the maintenance quarters."

Joktar spread out the rough sketch of the clinic the other had supplied.

"How many undersurface levels?" he asked abruptly. Since his mishap on the roofs of JetTown, he was inclined to try for escape underground.

"Four. Level one is utilities; level two, staff quarters; level three, records and storage; level four, power."

"Outside entrances to any?"

For the first time since he returned, the medic smiled. "You may just have something. Here," he tapped level two, "there was some enlarging done this year and there is a blind corridor going this way," he traced it on the sketch. "They expect to add a half-dozen more rooms along there sometimes in the future. I have a small suite there, myself."

"That runs close to the edge of the island."

"Right. That's why they didn't add living space here . . . or here. But this last room on this side is empty and see how it lies in relation to the outside?"

Joktar saw. "It must be almost under the bridge."

"Yes. Now here on level one," he made another quick dab at the sketch, "is stored emergency bore equipment. You find a portable chewer and bring it down to cut through just below the bridge . . . well, that's as safe a path as I can see."

"What about you? They'll know I had inside help."

"What they think and what they can prove may be two different things. For some reason the scouts aren't parading their reason for wanting to pick you up. And the minute you leave here, we'll have another patient in this room, one with every symptom of fungoid fever. As even your own mother couldn't recognize you once the swelling starts, they won't be able to prove for several days that he isn't you. And if you can get to Hogan tonight you'll be all right . . . unless he has been picked up. If that has happened you'll have to manage on your own anyway."

The medic snapped the force field button and Joktar went into the hall. The pale green walls were blank, though they must conceal other doors. He found the grav-plate at the end of the corridor and pressed the controls to take him to the service level. When he stepped off into another corridor five floors down, he caught the murmur of voices and flattened against the wall to listen intently.

According to the sketch, he had a hall, a large room, and another hall, to transverse. Then came a door which could be unlocked by a small cone he cupped in his hand. From the racked equipment on the other side of that, he must take a chewer and with it get down to the next level, through a maze of living quarters, to the room where he could use the stolen machine. So much depended upon how well-populated these lower regions were, though the time for the evening meal was close and most of those off duty would be in the dining rooms.

The murmur of voices died, Joktar strode on, halting again just inside the large room. Two chairs were occupied by a man wearing a drab tunic akin to his own and a girl. They were intent upon a video screen, a tray of drinks and dishes on a table beside them. Could he cross unnoticed? He must, for by all indications they were settled for some time. The video picture switched to a fantastic display of no-weight ballet and under the floor of the accompanying off-beat rhythm, Joktar forced himself to walk at an ordinary pace to the far door. Once there, he glanced back. Neither of the viewers had moved, he was safe so far.

Breathing a little faster, he sprinted down the hall to bring up against the door panel he wanted, wasting no time in digging the point of the cone into the lock hole. The panel moved, and he dodged inside.

Racks of machines faced him in bewildering profusion as he hurried along the shelves in search of the one the medic had described. But when he found it he was dismayed. It could be termed portable, but certainly one could not conceal it. And remembering the distance he had to transport it, Joktar was uneasy.

He explored the room, hoping for some inspiration, and so came upon the cart, already hung with a creeper floor polisher and two dust suckers. To unbolt the former required time he hated to spare, but at length he was able to trundle the compact machine back into hiding under one of the shelves and shove the chewer into its place.

Pushing the cart before him, Joktar left the room, relocking the door panel. Now everything depended on whether he could pass through the service and personnel quarters without awaking suspicion. And that was a gamble he had to take. He looked into the lounge once again. The shrill *thump-thump* of the ballet still rang out there. As all devotees of that particular skull-wracking rhythm, the two watchers apparently liked reception at maximum. Joktar had never cared for no-weight ballet, but at the moment, he recognized its worth. Masked by the video clamor he got the cart to the other side of the room.

The hall again . . . then the grav-plate. He thumped the descent button and sighed. So far, so good. Though he mustn't relax now; there was still the personnel quarters to be transversed and the chances of meeting others here were ten to one against them.

As the grav-plate halted, Joktar tugged the cart forward again. Through the third door, to the left, down a corridor, then straight right to the end and right again. He was sure of his path even if he wasn't sure of having it all to himself. He would simply have to move along it as if he were employed on some legitimate errand and the medic had made a suggestion or two which could help him there.

More voices. He had just time to jerk the cart away from the corridor door when two young men wearing the tunic insignia of junior interns entered. They were arguing some point and the first never noticed Joktar, but the second gave him a glance and then asked: "Aren't you behind time coming down here now?"

"Yes, Gentlehomo. Special job; the aquarium in the sea lounge, it is leaking." To his heartfelt relief, it looked as if that excuse was going to get by.

"That thing's been cracked for a week; *now* they send someone to look at it!" grumbled the other intern.

Joktar shoved the cart through the door, allowing himself the faster pace of a man on his way to deal with a leaking aquarium.

✳ ✳ **11** ✳ ✳

JOKTAR HUNCHED OVER THE CART, trotting, dreading a challenge, already half-able to feel the sizzling agony of a blaster bolt against the area of skin above his mid-spine. Yard by yard, he won his way past closed doors, half-open doors, doors from which came the sound of voices, of laughter, of music, of video casts. If the personnel had been summoned to an evening meal, either most of the inhabitants of his level were dilatory or they disliked the food.

He made the first turn and saw two more open doors to pass. Now he could no longer give his repair excuse, for the lounge lay in the opposite direction. Exerting a force of will which left him almost physically weak, the Terran kept to an even pace.

Another corridor end, now into the last turn of all. Before him all the doors were closed. This was the newly opened section and there was only one permanent resident: the medic who had given him his directions. He had only to reach the last room and turn the chewer loose on its wall.

Joktar bolted, slamming the cart ahead of him. The door resisted and he pounded until the latch gave stiffly. He wheeled the cart inside the bare room and leaned against the wall, his eyes already seeking the most likely spot on which to work with the chewer.

With the door panel closed, the cart wedged against it as an additional safeguard, Joktar unloaded the machine, turning its dial

106

to the highest frequency. He centered the blunt nose on the point he had selected and pressed the button.

Its low wailing whine tormented the ears; its vibration jarred through his body and set his half-healed shoulder to throbbing. On the wall there was a point of white light. Joktar closed his eyes against the glare, stiffened his body against the beat of the machine. Warmth grew, feeding back to his middle, spreading upward to his shoulders, down his thighs. The warmth was becoming heat, punishing heat. He held fast as that heat scorched until he could smell the fabric of his tunic charring. When he could stand it no longer he leaped back, raised his finger from the control button.

Safe in a far corner of the room, Joktar dared to open his eyes. The white sore of eating energy was dulled, but around it rock crumbled. As he blinked against the tears in his eyes, he saw a piece of the wall disappear outward. He turned, loosed the cart, and, with all his strength, rammed it against the broken wall.

There was a moment of resistance before the corrosion of the chewer prevailed and the cart pierced into the open. Joktar jerked it back to use it again and again as a battering ram until he had a hole which was more doorway than window. The roar of surf came from below and a wind carrying the damp of sea spray beat in, dispelling the fumes of the chewer, cooling the rock of the broken wall.

Once more he set the battered cart to act as a door lock before climbing through the hole. Outside, above and slightly to the right was the illuminated line of the bridge link to the next island. The point where he now crouched was well below the ground surface of the clinic island, and Joktar could hear the slap and lick of the waves not too far away. Returning to the cart he unrolled one of the dust sucker hoses. Quickly he fed the line through the hole and then climbed out to use the coil in support.

The rock of the island had not been, as he had feared, smoothed when the buildings were erected. Having hooked himself to the hose with the belt of his tunic, the Terran used his hands to explore. And well within reaching distance he discovered in a promising shadow what he needed—climbing holds. Working his way sidewise he began to climb. He had gained some six feet and the bridge was still several yards above him yet when he was forced to loosen the hose. When it was free, the Terran gave the supple length a quick jerk, activating the coiling mechanism to have it withdrawn into the room.

There were no ledges on which he could pause and his muscles ached with strain and tension when he at length swung up on one of the underbraces of the bridge. For a moment, he sat astride of a beam, studying the path ahead. To venture up on the surface of that span under the lights was to court instant discovery. His charred, torn clothing and his sudden appearance would be enough to rivet the attention of any guard.

So, if one could not cross on the surface of the bridge, one had to take an under way. And from his present perch that operation did not promise to be easy. Once up on the next island, he must somehow get a scout tunic and then . . . Joktar shook his head. One move at a time, concentrate on what was immediately before him now. His luck had held amazingly and somehow he knew that he *was* riding a gambler's winning streak tonight and that he must push it to the limit.

Water washed high below, beat in white edged lashes on the rocks. And he could not swim. To crawl along the half-seen supports before him was going to be an ordeal which would require all his energy and will-power. And waiting was not going to make him any more sure-footed. He was past the first fatigue of his climb, it was time to move.

Joktar crept, he edged, twice he swung from one shadowy hold to another. The training he had taken in what now seemed a very distant past came to his aid as his body responded to the demands he made upon it.

There was some traffic on the bridge about him and the vibration carried to him, just as the constant sound of the sea was a warning of menace below. Now and then when he came upon a resting place he paused to wipe his sweating hands on his breeches before making the swing ahead. His world had narrowed to those supports, most of which lay in dangerous pools of shadow.

Time stretched endlessly until his hands fastened in the last hold, and before him again was a rock wall of island. Once up that he would stand again at ground level. He leaned against the wall, forced his breath into a slow and even pattern. Now—

Once more his nails gritted on stone as he groped for fingerholds. Then, long minutes later, he lay belly-down on a ledge, backed by a man-made parapet which guarded the approach to the bridge. As Joktar raised to look over that, he saw that the medic had been right in his warning of the extra security Lennox had planted to seal off the clinic. There was the uniform of the local police; also, Joktar's hands caught hard on the parapet, one of the gray-clad scouts, plain under the floodlights.

He watched the conference between the two, hardly daring to hope that the scout was not on regular guard duty. But his luck held. Gray tunic was walking away, heading into the island. Joktar scuttled along his ledge to the end of the parapet. Here were some small ornamental shrubs set out in a fan of soil, a pocket-sized park.

The lights were not the powerful glares of the floods and there were patches of helpful dusk here and there. Once more, the Terran followed a well-known pattern. Such a stalking game as this was native to the streets. He skulked from one bit of cover to the next, to sprint on into the dark well of a doorway.

So normal was the hum of city noise that he could blot it from his consciousness, to concentrate on that other sound, the click of the gravity plates on the scout's space boots. So announced, his prey drew opposite the doorway.

With a larger man, or a suspicious one, Joktar might not have had such unqualified success. But the blow delivered in just the right spot, the sweep of arm to bring the limp body in against him, flowed, one into the other, with the timing of an instructor's exhibition. He lowered the unconscious scout to the ground and set about stripping off his uniform. As he sealed the tunic and buckled on the other's blaster belt, he marveled at his own success. This was certainly one of those nights when luck was pouring his way across the table and he couldn't lose even if he wanted to.

The Terran settled the tight gray cap on his head and rolled the unconscious scout into the back of the doorway. Unless the fellow was superhuman, he would be out for at least an hour, and groggy for a while afterwards. Wearing Joktar's singed tunic he would have a lot of questions to answer if he were found before he was able to stagger out on his own wobbly feet seeking help.

There were a few other pedestrians on the street, but none near enough to matter. Joktar stepped out of the doorway and began to walk toward the other side of the island and that second bridge which should take him to the Seven Stars, stopping only once by a brightly illuminated shop window to study the identification folder he had taken from his victim.

So, he was Rog Kilinger, detached for special duty with Commander Lennox, perfect! He smiled at the center display in the window, a collection of Styrian pearl flowers, their colors flushing faintly under the pull of the light. The flowers were beautiful. This was a fine night, and Scout Kilinger after arduous service, doubtless on the barbaric rim, was entitled to plush relaxation at the Seven Stars. The best was none too good for brave Rog Kilinger, Commander Lennox's doughty right, or maybe left-hand man.

There were police on the second bridge but Joktar's momentary hesitation as he sighted that guard did not even break his steady gait. Nor did any of the guards pay him attention until he reached the other end of the span where the vast pile of the Seven Stars loomed in a display of lighting and fantastic, scrambled architecture from the edge of the sea well into Loki's sky.

"Ident, Gentlehomo?"

With a gesture he hoped careless enough, Joktar drew out the folder, flipped it open.

"Your business here, scout?"

Joktar grinned. "Just in from the rim, officer, what do you think?"

The police sentry laughed. "From what I've heard, scout, you'd better keep off the joy juice. That commander of yours isn't too easy in judging a morning-after alibi."

"You got it," Joktar agreed. "But then, what commander ever is?"

"Lift one for me." The sentry handed back the case. "It's going to be a long night."

"Something special up?" Joktar made that question as casual as he could.

The sentry shrugged. "Alert B, not that that means much. We get that thrown in our teeth every time a vip has one over five and something leers at him from the vapor shower the next morning. Keep your ident handy, though, they may ask you your name pretty often under a B."

"Thanks for the tip." Joktar sketched a salute and walked on passing from the bridge into the rim of garden beyond. So there was an alert on. But he could not believe that it had been triggered by the discovery of his escape from the clinic. Certainly there would have been a tighter control at the bridge if that were true.

Joktar stepped into the shadow of a fantastically twisted tree and stopped short, watching his back trail. But if anyone had shadowed him from the second island that simplest of checks did not smoke him out. The sounds of music, laughter, and a kind of muted roar issued from the Seven Stars, with the wash of waves making a dull undertone. He could detect no such footfalls as announced the scout.

A party of four gaily dressed couples came out of a flowery clump and ran laughing toward the building. Joktar cut across their path, reached a terrace set with tables, all occupied, and threaded a way between them to the door. Another dining room, and the clothing styles of a dozen planets or systems, a babble of tongues which branched from basic Terran speech to mutate into almost incomprehensible idioms used on the planets of far flung stars.

He looked for a gray tunic to match his own; saw only one at a far table so he turned in the opposite direction. The smell of good food tickled his nostrils, offered a temptation which was hard to resist. But he kept on toward the next door. And he had almost reached that point when he checked, his startled gaze centering on two men who had just arisen from a small side booth intended for privacy and were now on their way to the same exit he had marked. One of them turned his head a fraction and Joktar knew he was right: Samms!

The Terran rounded a last table, took the two steps up to the door in a quick scramble, and came out, not into a hall or lounge as he had expected, but into a vast bubble which was a city in itself, rising in levels, each crowded with shops, ribboned with move-belts carrying full quotas of passengers, a kaleidoscope of ever-moving color in which it would be very easy to lose any quarry.

But Samms' rather drab jacket was the exception in this fashionable world. A glimpse of his wide shoulders drew Joktar into one of the belts and he began moving along it to draw closer to the man from Fenris. Luckily there were other impatient passengers and he did not make himself conspicuous by his stalking. And Samms and his diner companion appeared content to allow the belt to transport them at its slower rate. Joktar was close enough to follow them when they did move, leaving the wider belt with a skip for a narrower one winding into a side corridor. There were fewer riders here and Joktar was forced to allow several passengers to get between him and the pair he trailed.

He knew that the party from Fenris had been housed together and he was certain that sooner or later Samms would guide him to their quarters, for he dared not make any enquiry for Hogan. Now Samms' companion stepped courteously aside for a woman and Joktar saw that he was Sa—Sa of Harband! Yet from their attitude one would believe those two ahead to be good friends, rather than enemies who less than three weeks ago had been exchanging blaster shots . . . if not exactly at each other, then by proxy. The old suspicion of Samms' possible double game flowered. And the Terran began to wonder about the wisdom of trailing this ill-assorted pair.

They were leaving the belt; he must make up his mind in a hurry. Joktar, his hand resting near the butt of his blaster, allowed the belt to carry him parallel with the door to the grav-plate shaft where the others now stood, then he jumped off, to come up behind Sa.

Samms glanced around and Joktar expected recognition, but that did not come. For what broke Samms' stolid expression was sharp surprise, a surprise with a touch of wariness in it. And for the first time there was a spark of some emotion in his pale gray eyes.

"What are you doing here?" he demanded. "I told the commander not to move in before nineteen hours."

"The commander likes to take out insurance," Joktar ad-libbed. "I'm the insurance."

Sa looked over his shoulder. On his thin, well-chiseled features there was a distant shadow of annoyance.

"Such last-minute additions to well-conceived plans," he commented, "always lead to difficulties. If you go up with us now, it will jeopardize our chances of coming to an agreement."

He had fallen into something, Joktar knew that, though he still could not understand why Samms did not know him. Or did he? Was the outlaw from Fenris doubling on an already-muddled trail? But how did the scouts and Lennox come into this?

"I have my orders," he returned shortly.

A grav-plate came to a halt before them and the two from Fenris moved on it reluctantly. The Terran guessed that Samms, at least, longed to order him to remain where he was. They arose in a stomach-rocking sweep, Samms' inner agitation betrayed by that snap of full power. Joktar braced himself at the hand rail. If they stopped short now. . .

But Samms slowed the plate and the jar of the halt did not shake them from their footing. In the hall facing them, he saw both the green tunic of the planet police and the blue of a patrolman. He waited tensely for Samms to protest to both or either concerning his own presence, but no protest came.

The Fenrian outlaw moved on to the door, placed his palm on its lock, and stepped aside to usher Sa past him. His shoulder half-blocked Joktar, but the Terran nudged him on.

They came into a luxurious apartment which now held an odd scene. Hogan and Rysdyke were both stretched out in the soft embrace of eazee-rests. But neither of them was resting easily. A small disc in the hand of a second patrol officer insured that. They were effectively webbed in the bonds of a tangle.

"It would seem," Joktar spoke, "that there's a little trouble here."

The patrolman turned his head to face the muzzle of the scout blaster.

"Pin up!" the Terran snapped.

When he saw the other's finger rise from the disc and Rysdyke and Hogan move, Joktar held out one hand.

"Toss!" he gave his second order, "And make it center!"

The patrolman tossed and the Terran's fingers closed about the tangle control.

"Now, all of you, over there!" His gesture included Samms, Sa, and the patrol officer, sending them to the other side of the room. Holstering his blaster he pushed in the tangle pin.

"You know," he informed them, "there is a way of jamming these so they can't be turned off . . . they have to be burned out. Now I wonder how good my memory is . . . Sorry." His three captives twisted under a tightening of the coils which held them. And Samms spat a quite exotic suggestion concerning Joktar's past. "There, that ought to do it!" The pin was well-wedged to one side and he dropped the tangle to the floor. "Now you'll all stay put until that's burnt out."

Samms made a biting comment concerning Commander Lennox.

"What's Lennox got to do with it?" demanded Rysdyke.

"Yes, that I would like to know . . . Oh," Hogan laughed, "my good friends have really given themselves away this time, haven't they? They accept the false as readily as the real because they were expecting some such move." His hand dropped on Joktar's shoulder. "How did you manage to arrive like the space marines, all ready for battle in good time?"

Samms' eyes narrowed and he stared at the Terran, for the first time seeing more than the uniform. Again that spark glowed in his eyes. And Joktar knew that Samms would never either forgive or forget this particular meeting.

"The scouts tried to pry me loose from the clinic. I preferred to make the trip under my own power. What I want to know is why?"

"Samms," Hogan reseated himself. "I sadly fear I made a grave error in your case, the error of underestimating you. Lennox got to you, didn't he? I would very much like to know how the commander is so well-informed concerning our movements. There has been a bad slip somewhere."

Sa wriggled as if he were trying to find a more easy fit within the invisible ties which held him prisoner.

"Hogan, I am a reasonable individual. You have impressed me that you possess a certain sense of logic; you are able to rise above such dramatics as these. I also believe that Harband is not the primary objective of your present moves. I believe that we may, as you say, be able to make a deal."

Hogan listened with an expression of placid interest. "I am, of course, flattered by your estimate of my character, Gentlehomo. Yes, I am attracted to logic, sense, and reason as much as any man. Now, what do you have to offer?"

"Profit . . . and perhaps your life."

Hogan settled closer into the embrace of his chair. "Both those points are able to hold my full interest, Gentlehomo. Will you please turn up your first card?"

* ✳ **12** ✳ *

Behind Sa's slender elegance Samms backed the wall. Of the three prisoners, Joktar paid him the closest attention. Those shallow eyes were fastened on Hogan and there was an odd deliberation in that gaze. Was his the study of a knife fighter picking out his mark? Samms' control was back, he was assured . . . or waiting. Joktar spoke: "They're playing for time."

Hogan smiled, answered lazily. "But of course. However, we must preserve the aura of courtesy if not the quality itself. Gentlehomo, Sa has not come here to represent anyone but his own company."

Sa nodded his head, his body still held rigid by the grip of the tangle.

"Do you wish me to swear to that on the Truth of the Ancestors?" he inquired with a half-sneer.

"Not at all, Gentlehomo. I made a statement, I did not ask for reassurance. Now, what do you have to offer?"

"Suppose the companies relax the import regulations on Fenris, allow free traders to planet?"

"And in return for such a concession?"

"You do not push your case before Cullan."

"Ah, that's the nip, is it? But I am a little surprised at you, Gentlehomo. You immediately offer us what men have died vainly

116

to obtain. And yet you have the reputation of being an astute, sly man. So I shall make some guesses, you need not even signify as to whether I am right or am failing to judge correctly what must be in progress behind several different curtains at this moment.

"First, the companies have been warned their monopolies are in danger. A manifest piece of mismanagement or public scandal now will wreck them and Councilor Cullan is the avowed enemy of their present way of conducting business. In answer to that, Gentlehomo, may I say that the end of the companies in their present form is already upon us. You cannot build a dam when a river is in flood. But by granting graciously such concessions as you have already outlined, you might be in a position six months or a year from now, to have the backing of new friends when you need them most. Because the companies are needed on the frontier worlds, but with their policies modified."

Sa smiled. "We understand each other perfectly," there was almost a note of humor in that. "May I also point out, Gentlehomo, that you are now engaged in a war covering more than one sector. To turn one of your opponents, a minor one that is true, but nevertheless an enemy of sorts, into a neutral or even a friend at this juncture might also divert the tide in your favor."

"In other words you have information of value." Hogan picked up a com-mike with attached mirror from the table. "You have been dealing with Samms, now you offer me certain advantages. Why change? Surely the temporary turning of tables in this room has not had so great an influence . . ."

"You have an argument which counts over this." Sa pointed with his chin to the tangle on the floor.

"And that?"

"We do not have time to spare, Gentlehomo. An hour ago, Lennox thought he had what he wanted. Without that particular advantage on his side, the whole government policy, even our way of life, may crack wide open. No, Lennox is not top, you are!"

Hogan held the mirror steady, his face still wore an urban half-smile, but Joktar knew he was on guard.

"Your information sources appear extremely efficient."

"I assure you that they are, Hogan. And this, too, I will concede: we of the companies must change course or cease to cruise space. You dare not continue to hammer down a cap upon the forces the vips have tried to control. So I tell you, Lennox will move to take back what he wants. He's preparing to move against you tonight."

There was an odd strangled sound out of Samms. Hogan's finger tapped the code key of the mike. A face flashed on the mirror, its eyes regarded Hogan briefly before it disappeared. Now a code pattern of interwoven light followed. Hogan spoke twice, unknown words, into the mike and the pattern swirled in answer.

"Hogan here, Councilor, we have information that Lennox—"

He did not add another word. He could not. Out of the walls, the floor under them, the very air of the room, the enemy struck.

"Vibrator!" Joktar got that word out, his body twisting involuntarily as he fought against the agonizing pull of the energy beam which must be near, judging by the intensity of its torturing volume.

Rysdyke was already on the floor, writhing, small choking moans being wrung from him as he rolled. Hogan fought, beads of moisture gathering on his forehead, trickling down his flat cheeks. He clutched the mike close to his lips, tried to force out words as his limbs jerked and twitched.

Joktar staggered halfway toward the door panel. The action was like trying to run through thick mud, a mud which in addition sent fiery whips up his body in great stinging cuts. But somehow he kept his feet, was able to take his blaster from the holster and bring its barrel up in line with the door.

An inarticulate cry from Hogan made him look around. The other was signaling with his eyes, demanding. In his hands the mike oscillated back and forth but somehow he made the gesture of holding it out. Joktar stumbled back, to half-collapse beside Hogan. His right arm lay across the other's thighs, the blaster held still to face the door.

Then, using all his will power and what remained of his control over his own muscles, Joktar pulled the mike to his mouth. Whether the vibrator had already muted him he did not know, but this was their one chance for help. He worked his lips, trying to conquer their spasmodic fluttering.

"Vi-vibrator here," that was ragged about the edges but the words made sense. If they only did the same for the unseen listener!

There was a ripple of light on the mirror. For one long moment, Joktar looked at a face, as the other must sight him. Then the mirror went blank, the hum of an open com died. And the device flew across the room as an involuntary convulsion of Hogan's muscles hurled it.

They must have stepped up the vibrator to the outer limit. Hogan rolled, Rysdyke was drooling blood, and Sa had gone entirely limp, supported by the tangle. While the patrolman was moaning and only half-conscious. Of them all Samms clung to some measure of awareness.

And yet, though he was in agony, Joktar could still move. He knew a dim and fleeting wonder at that. The only thing was to use this partial immunity to the utmost. He began to crawl, avoiding Rysdyke, heading for a table he could use as a crutch to regain his feet. He clawed his way up. Before he could again face the door squarely, the panel moved.

Hogan lay on the eazee-rest. He was inert, only his eyes still had a small spark of consciousness. Now he made a convulsive struggle to rise as a figure in a protective non-vi suit strode into the room.

Joktar, seeing that suit, knew how pitiful his own hopes of defiance were. A blaster beam, unless snapped up to a concentration which made it dangerous to its user, could make no impression on that kind of armor. Nevertheless, the Terran was on his feet and able after a fashion to use a weapon and the stranger in the suit would be expecting no opposition.

The newcomer stooped over Rysdyke, examined him briefly, and kicked him aside, to advance on Hogan. His hand was half-raised and flat against the palm Joktar caught the glisten of metal. There were several very small, very deadly arms which could be carried that way. Suddenly he knew that this was not a matter of taking prisoners, but of murder!

There was no way of crossing the space between them in time, not with most of his muscles knotted by the vibrator. But—

Using both hands, he swung the blaster around, aimed it, not at the man advancing on Hogan, but at one vital spot on the floor. That crack of bolt was followed by a spurt of white fire leaping from the carpet. Joktar had already lunged forward as men, suddenly released from the destroyed tangle, slumped to the floor, bearing with them the startled stranger.

Joktar lay half-across Hogan and his blaster, brought down as a club, had dazed the man in the non-vi suit. But the blow had not landed clean and the other was not stunned as the Terran had gambled. His own reflexes were so slowed by the vibrator that he could not raise his hand in time to ward off a return blow, the force of which sent him rolling to the floor and rendered him so weak he could not struggle up again.

He saw that hand sweep up with the bright spark cupped in the palm, swing over him. Then the other paused. Through the transparent face mask his face wore an expression of complete astonishment. With his other hand he jerked Joktar into a sitting position, slammed him back against the eazee-rest and tore open the front of his tunic. But whatever he sought, he did not find. Instead he stared at the burn scar on the Terran's shoulder and his gaze was bleak as his lips moved, he was speaking into the throat mike of his suit.

His answer came in the halting of the vibrator waves. Only none of the men freed from that torture were able to move and most of them were unconscious. The man in the suit spun Joktar around, whipped the Terran's limp hands behind him, and made fast his wrists, before shoving him roughly back to floor level. So Joktar's attack had been a forlorn hope after all.

Others were entering the room. Hands on his shoulders, pulling him up to face the gray-clad man he had last seen in the clinic. The commander surveyed him coldly, nodded. Joktar looked around. They were all prisoners, it would seem. Sa, Rysdyke, the patrolman were still out. Of Samms and Hogan, he was not so sure.

Lennox went to the latter. He reached down, caught a fistful of the trader's hair and pulled his head around. Hogan's eyes were still open, now his lips moved in a wry grimace. The commander smiled thinly.

"This is the end, snooper."

Again Hogan's lips moved without sound. But Lennox appeared to read some protest.

"We'll take you to headquarters where we know how to keep mouths shut. I'd like to know how your employer will keep on with his plans after we finish mopping up. Nobody, *nobody*, you understand," his mouth tightened, the hand entangled in Hogan's hair moved so that the head on which that hair grew, thumped hard against the chair, "nobody makes fools of the scouts! Nor dirties their records, present or past." He looked past Hogan to Joktar with the same deadly coldness he had displayed at the clinic. "We'll run our tests, and if you have found your monster . . . well, he won't survive long! Kelse!" At his call another gray-clad man stepped forward. "The 'copter on the west terrace, see these are loaded in that and get them to headquarters at once."

"You sound in a hurry, Commander."

Bluecoats were pushing aside the gray at the door. Lennox whirled, half-crouching, a fighting man ready for an attack. But the man who had spoken wore no weapons, his official cloak, thrown back over one shoulder, had the star within star of the Council, and his face was the one Joktar had last seen on the com-mirror.

"This is a service matter, no civil rights, Councilor."

"No civil rights? Yet to my certain knowledge none of these prisoners of yours are enlisted in the scouts. Let me see . . . that is Gentlehomo Sa Kim, one of the directors of the Harband Company, and that one is a patrolman. Correct me, of course, if I am not right, Commander, but the patrol is *not* answerable to the scouts, though you are answerable to their admiral. And these here," he glanced at Samms, Hogan and Rysdyke, "are all petitioners in council from Fenris. I was to interview them tomorrow, or rather today, since it is now past midnight. No, you cannot in truth claim any of these gentlehomos as members of the scouts, subject to your discipline."

Lennox's hand shot out, fastened on the collar of Joktar's tunic, dragging him to his wavering feet. "This one I can and do!"

"So?" Cullan advanced deliberately across the room, gave Joktar a measuring stare, beginning at his tousled head and descending to his scuffed boots. "Dober!" One of the patrolmen at the door came to him. "Correct me if I am wrong, do the scouts not wear special ident-discs at all times!"

"Yes, Gentlehomo."

"Will you please search this man for his disc." The patrolman hesitated. Lennox had pulled Joktar half-behind him and seemed ready to resist such action.

"Come now, Commander, do not be difficult. If this man is one of yours, he will wear such a disc; if he is not and is masquerading as a member of the service, then he has committed an offense which it is my duty as Councilor to investigate."

Lennox's heavy space tan was darkened by a greenish undercast. He moved with a vast reluctance, and the patrolmen pulled Joktar's tunic half-off his shoulders, the undershirt following.

"No disc, Gentlehomo," he reported woodenly.

"Ah, then, I must be right. This man is an impostor and so will be dealt with along proper channels. I think we must get to the bottom of this whole strange business as soon as possible. Patrolmen, escort all these civilians, and Commander Lennox, to my quarters. You need have no fear concerning escapes, Commander, I have been granted a maximum security apartment. Also, medical attention must be provided for those in need of it. We shall assemble later for an informal inquiry."

At that inquiry, an hour or so later, Joktar occupied a seat he had chosen for himself, the ledge of a window. Behind him, the wide sweep of unbreakable op-glass framed the pink-orange of dawn. He raised the cup he balanced between his two hands to his lips and drank. The liquid was cool, but inside him warm, mellow; it was relaxing and renewing. Over the rim of that cup he watched the other occupants of the room with wary intentness.

Rysdyke half-reclined in an eazee-rest. The dribble of blood was gone from his chin, but his face was that of a spent runner from whose body the last precious spark of energy had been drawn. And next to him was Samms, far more alert, his flat, silver, platelike eyes moving slowly from one face to the next. Sa was sipping at a cup, a little shrunken in his finely cut, lusterless silks, but ready. Then a small space and Lennox—Lennox who sat as if he had been forced into that seat by external pressure, held there by a tangle. Beyond Lennox, next to his own perch, Hogan. Only the patrolman was missing from their first company and his place was taken by the strange man wearing the plum tunic of a bureau chief, the man who had tapped Hogan lightly on the shoulder with the familiarity of old camaraderie when he had entered the room minutes earlier, to take his place at Cullan's right, facing the others, and to be introduced as Director Kronfeld.

The Councilor turned his head to the view from the second window behind his chair. "Dawn," he remarked, "symbolically fitting in a way that we should have a dawn hour for this particular discussion." He picked up a sheet of petition parchment. "I have here a petition in order from a body calling themselves 'Free Men of Fenris,' represented here by Gentlehomos Samms, Rysdyke and Hogan. Do you, Gentlehomo Sa, offer any reasons why the complaint set forth here should not be investigated?"

Sa smiled wearily. "Councilor, one does not win a race by flogging a dead horse. I have already agreed with Gentlehomo Hogan to negotiate terms with those he represents. I can speak only for Harband, but—"

"But with their united front broken, the other companies will be moved to follow your example? Very well, negotiations will be ordered, to be carried out by a representative of the Council within the legal term of time. May I congratulate you, Gentlehomo Sa, upon your reasonable and sensible handling of a difficult situation."

Again Sa smiled. "Which is more than any of my conferees shall do," he remarked.

"Now we come to the next point," Cullan's manner changed abruptly. "Your liberty was threatened, your persons put into danger, through the misguided efforts of a service officer. Do you wish to register an official complaint?"

Sa's smile grew broader. He put down his cup. "Councilor, it is my impression that this particular matter is none of my affair, not does it concern matters on Fenris in any way. I beg your leave to withdraw. The overzealous officer I leave to your discretion." He stood up, put out one hand to Samms.

"Gentlehomo, since our business here is complete, shall we go?"

Samms evaded that touch. He leaned forward, to stare past Sa . . . at Hogan? Or Lennox? It was Cullan who broke the momentary silence.

"Gentlehomo, if you believe that you have a private understanding with this officer, its provisions are now cancelled. You do not control anything or anyone that he desires. Furthermore, he is no longer in a position where he can hope to bargain. Correct me if I am wrong, Commander."

Lennox continued to look straight ahead, past Cullan, out at the advance of the dawn. As Sa had appeared a few moments earlier, now he in turn was a little shrunken, diminished. Samms got to his feet.

"What about you?" the Fenrian's voice was ragged as he asked that of Hogan.

The ex-trader rested one hand as if to wave farewell. "Samms," he replied with all his old lazy lightness of tone, "I am about to make you a gift, a large, enticing gift, which no growing boy could possibly resist—Fenris. You will make a good deal now for those who backed us, of that I am reasonably sure . . . for two reasons. First, because Gentlehomo Sa has admitted he sees the writing on the wall of outer space and is ready to lead a vanguard of pioneers into a bright new era . . ."

Sa bowed urbanely, with a gentle chuckle.

"And second, since Fenris is now your undisputed preserve, you will do all you can to make yourself vip there. Which entails a certain continuing regard for the rights of your future co-workers and liege men. You leave with my blessing and a free field. Don't bother to inform me in return that you hate my insides, and now all the more for this withdrawal on my part. We are both well aware of that."

A flicker of light in Samms' eyes. He ignored Hogan, bowed to Cullan. With a dignity Joktar could not deny him, he then took Sa's arm and they left together, already linked more than physically by a future both could visualize, even if those visions did not exactly coincide.

As the door panel closed behind them, Hogan added more briskly: "End of chapter, perhaps of book."

"That one," amended Kronfeld."

"Now," Cullan once more regarded the spreading blanket of color in the sky. He watched that display a long moment before he spun his chair around to face Lennox. "We know," he said quietly, but with an emphasis which bit, "everything, including much that you do not, Commander. But by what right under all the stars of this galaxy, or the next, dare you move against the Ffallian?"

✳ ✳ **13** ✳ ✳

Lennox lost his detachment. His face screwed into a mask of hate.

"If you know everything, then you also know why."

"Yes, I know why. Because twenty years ago a man who was bringing with him an offer of the greatest gift our species could have, appealed to you for help in the name of friendship, and you betrayed him to his death."

"Oh, no," Lennox shook his head, "you can't fasten what *you* claim to be a crime on me, Councilor. I did what I had to do, what my loyalty, not only to the service, but all our kind, demanded of me. Nor will I deny that I agreed with every word of the orders I obeyed when I turned Marson in. He wasn't even human anymore! What I did, I did for the good of every human being, in or out of space.

"That traitor," his mouth twisted, "was a monster. What he came to offer was vile. You should thank whatever gods you believe in, on your knees, that he did not carry out his mission."

"One way of looking at it," Kronfeld's judicial evenness of speech was the more impressive in contrast to the other's hot vehemence. "That fanaticism has had official approval for quite a while. Only there's another side to the same story. Marson had, in the pursuit of his scout duty, made contact with the Others who we have long-known shared our galactic space. The period of Marson's contact began involuntarily on his part because he answered a strange distress signal and became involved in a rescue. He could not be as inhuman as his orders demanded he be; therefore, he discovered that this other species was entirely different from the official descriptions circulated by his superiors. He then joined them, lived among them, and only because he learned something which would benefit both races equally, did he volunteer to return to human-held territory, knowing that such an act might well mean his death. He hoped that some man of good will would listen and examine his proof.

"He came as an ambassador. But before he had a chance to reach those who might have understood, he was caught and killed, the whole affair covered up. This ended the matter—for all time your service believed. Then, fifteen or so years ago, there came a second attempt at communication. Because the situation on the other side was growing critical, though our short Terran life span does not limit those Others. This time the volunteer ambassadors numbered two, with a third individual brought to prove their point."

Lennox's fingers plucked at the empty blaster's holster on his belt.

"A scout named Ksanga had followed Marson's earlier orbit and been attracted into the same pattern of cooperation. He came back as pilot of a ship which landed on the planet Kris, two passengers on board, a woman and her child. He dared to return even though he knew that he was outlawed as no other wolf-head since the beginning of time. Unfortunately, he was recognized on Kris, picked up by your police. He contrived to die before he was forced to betray those he had brought with him. How they escaped we shall never know. But eventually they reached Terra.

"The woman, although fully armed against the dangers her people could anticipate, was not immune to terrestrial disease. She died in N'Yok, in JetTown, where she had found a temporary hideout. The child remained."

Joktar put down his empty cup. Now he was as fascinated as the commander by Kronfeld's story.

"By Terran standards, that child appeared to be about six years old, he was closer to twelve. And he had been provided with a mental block for his own protection. In JetTown, he found a place for himself, eventually fitted into the pattern of the streets. Neither he, nor those about him, knew how important he was."

Kronfeld picked up a paper, but he recited rather than read. "What was the driving motive behind Marson's return, Ksanga's sacrifice, and the woman's? Oh, I've heard all the wild tales the services have fostered through the years since our first contact with the aliens—"

"Wild tales?" Lennox spat between his teeth. "Just because you don't believe the truth?"

"What is the truth? That the aliens are immortal? That fact could be difficult for us to accept. But it isn't true. Not only can they die by accident, but also, though their life span is immeasurably longer than ours, they are mortal in the ordinary fashion. That they are our superiors mentally and physically? Yes, that gives us a feeling of inferiority which many little men find impossible to face. But they have also one overwhelming disadvantage on their side of the scales."

Now Lennox actually did spit. The droplet of moisture beaded on the dark surface.

"They want us!" his face flushed darkly. "They have to have us to breed."

Kronfeld regarded him somberly. "Fifty years ago," he said in a remote tone, "a hysterical and perverted man put his own interpretation on a secret report. Perhaps he made an understandable human error, under the influence of his warped background; perhaps he had another reason for what he did. He slammed a door for his whole species. But it is an axiom that truth cannot be hidden forever. Other men have been searching for those hidden files, for the true meaning of that report ever since. Three years ago, the real story came to those who dared to believe. All the garbled nonsense which Morre fed his followers was sifted. Then the facts underneath and the monstrous crimes he fathered on the aliens were discovered to be something quite different. Yes, these galactic neighbors must have another species allied with them for breeding, but that act does not follow the unspeakable pattern Morre pictured out of the vileness of his own evil imagination.

"The aliens are humanoid, but not human. They have voyaged the star lanes for a length of time we cannot measure. They were comrades-in-arms and good friends to other races who preceded us into space, those who built the ruins we now find on dead worlds, for we are new to come into an old, old region. But long ago, their species suffered a mutation which has almost doomed them to extinction. If they mate among themselves, the resulting children are female only. If they mate with a kindred humanoid race, the children are the Ffallian, and all male.

"In turn, the Ffallian may mate fruitfully with either human or alien and produce children of both sexes. And the children of that second generation, as the Ffallian themselves, will have an increased life span, certain distinct physical and mental advantages over our kind. A long time has ensued since the aliens have found a race with whom they could have common offspring, and the Ffallian grow fewer every year. So they were overjoyed when they discovered that we were a species they could—"

"Use to produce their half-breed monsters!" Lennox exploded.

"Half-breeds, yes; monsters, no! Very far from monsters. Luckily all minds have not been corrupted by Morre's poison. A woman of the aliens chose to mate with Marson. Their son is true Ffallian. She brought him to Terra after her husband's death to prove that point, beg help for her people. Now, years too late, we may succeed in making her mission worthwhile. We do not have the gifts of the aliens, but our sons and daughters will. As human time is reckoned it may take many years, but the Ffallian will increase in number, linking us with the aliens in a pattern of sharing which will give us both something close to immortality."

"You're mad!" There was horrified conviction in Lennox's answer. "Try urging people to mate with monsters and see how quickly you'll have a war on your hands!"

"I said it would have to come slowly. We've already made a start. I head a colonization project in which we are educating a picked group. And we have pulled the whole subject out of hiding. The right kind of publicity is as good as the wrong kind, and we shall use the right."

"You can't do it! They've fed you a pretty story and you've swallowed it. The real story is anything but pretty. Morre knew, he saw the results. You talk of supermen, he saw the devils that really issue from such cross-breeding."

"Devils? You have seen one of these 'devils,' too. In what way is he a monster? Does he resemble the ogres Morre dreamed up to support his edited records?"

Lennox's head turned, his hot eyes fastened on Joktar. And then, when none of them expected such a move, he launched himself straight at the younger man, his hands reaching for the Terran's throat. Reflexes trained on the streets moved in Joktar's defense. But he was borne back across the ledge until his head cracked against the unbreakable substance of the window. In a matter of seconds, the Terran knew that he was battling for his life against a man in a frenzy, a man who scratched, tore, snapped teeth in a hideous attempt to maim and kill. A little dazed by the madness of the other's fury, Joktar fought back.

Then Lennox's dusky color deepened, he snarled and whined, as his head was forced back by an arm clamped under his chin, levering him away from Joktar. He clawed at the air, fought against that merciless bar of flesh and bone closing off his breath. Joktar raised a hand to dripping scratches on his cheek and watched Hogan choke the commander into submission.

There was a scuffle as Cullan summoned patrolmen, had the half-conscious Lennox removed. But Joktar had turned his back on the room. He was trying to blot out what he had just heard. That old chill thrust of loneliness struck into him . . . spreading . . . walling him off from the men in the room behind him, and in a measure from the room itself.

Monster . . . half-breed! Lennox had fastened those tags on him. And there would be hundreds . . . millions of other all around the galaxy to raise the same cry. He had been well-tutored on the streets. Since the beginning of the human species, there had been in them that dark and evil urge to turn upon and rend the one who was different, to hunt him down with a mob. And to be the hunted awoke in Joktar a wave of sheer terror which washed through his brain.

✳ ✳ ✳

Loki's sun was up now. A blaze above the golden brown of the sea . . . warmer than the sun which touched snow drifts on Fenris. The life of the streets had existed at night, there were few times when he had really looked at the sun.

A golden planet, a world where the sun was warm and kind . . .

Joktar heard movements in the room, closed his ears to them. They were all men there and he was something else. In those few moments of speech, Lennox had raised a barrier between him and every living being he had ever known.

Sun on the waves . . . a golden world . . . well, he would have to face those others, and his future some time. Joktar turned his back to the sun, his face to the room.

Only Hogan stood there. He was studying the younger man with the same searching measurement he had once used on Fenris. He spoke softly.

"But it isn't that way at all, you know. Don't let that poison Lennox spouted mean anything. You aren't alone."

"Half-breed," Joktar said the ugly word.

"Ffallian," Hogan corrected. "It is very different. I know believe me, I know."

"How?" challenged Joktar.

"Do you think that your father and Ksanga were the only humans to join the aliens? Four years ago . . . I came back."

"But you were on Fenris . . . a trader!"

"Hiding out . . . just as much of a wolf-head as if I were Ffallian. I was waiting for Kronfeld to move. He had to find you. That you existed, we knew. *Where*—that we had to discover. Yes, Lennox was wrong, pitifully horribly wrong. Do you believe me?"

And Joktar, seeing what lay in the other's eyes, was moved to a conviction which banished all the wariness he had learned from his father's unpredictable breed.

STAR
HUNTER

* ✳ **1** ✳ *

Nahuatl's larger moon pursued the smaller, greenish globe of its companion across a cloudless sky in which the stars made a speckled pattern like the scales of a huge serpent coiled around a black bowl. Ras Hume paused at the border of scented spike-flowers on the top terrace of the Pleasure House to wonder why he thought of serpents. He understood. Mankind's age-old hatred, brought from his native planet to the distant stars, was evil symbolized by a coil in a twisted, belly-path across the ground. And on Nahuatl, as well as a dozen other worlds, Wass was the serpent.

A night wind was rising, stirring the exotic, half-dozen other worlds' foliage planted cunningly on the terrace to simulate the mystery of an off-world jungle.

"Hume?" The inquiry seemed to come out of thin air over his head.

"Hume," he repeated his own name calmly.

A shaft of light brilliant enough to dazzle the eyes struck through the massed vegetation, revealing a path. Hume lingered for a moment, offering a counterstroke of indifference in what he had always known would be a test of wits. Wass was Veep of a shadowy empire, but that was apart from the world in which Ras Hume moved.

He strode deliberately down the corridor illuminated between leaf and blossom walls. A grotesque lump of crystal leered at him from the heart of a tharsala lily bed. The intricate carving of a devilish nonhuman set of features was a work of alien art. Tendrils of smoke curled from the thing's flat nostrils, and Hume sniffed the scent of a narcotic he recognized. He smiled. Such measures might soften up the usual civ Wass interviewed here. But a star pilot turned outhunter was immunized against such mind clouding.

There was a door, the lintel and posts of which had more carving, but this time Terran, Hume thought—old, very old. Perhaps rumor was right, Milfors Wass might be truly native Terran and not second-, third-, nor fourth-generation star stock as most of those who reached Nahuatl were.

The room beyond that elaborately carved entrance was, in contrast, severe. Rust walls were bare of any pattern save an oval disk of cloudy golden shimmer behind the chair at the long table of solid ruby rock from Nahuatl's poisonous sister planet of Xipe. Without a pause he walked to the chair and seated himself without invitation to wait in the empty room.

That clouded oval might be a com device. Hume refused to look at it after his first glance. This interview was to be person to person. If Wass did not appear within a reasonable length of time he would leave.

And Hume hoped, that to any unseen watcher, he presented the appearance of a man not impressed by stage settings. After all he was now in the seller's space boots, and it was a seller's market.

Ras Hume rested his right hand on the table. Against the polished glow of the stone, the substance of it was flesh-tanned brown—a perfect match for his left. And the subtle difference between true flesh and false was no hindrance in the use of those fingers or their strength. Save that it had pushed him out of command of a cargo-cum-liner and hurled him down from the pinnacle of a star pilot. There were bitter brackets about his mouth, set there by that hand as deeply as if carved with a knife.

It had been four years—planet time—since he had lifted the Rigal Rover from the launch pad on Sargon Two. He had suspected it might be a tricky voyage with young Tors Wazalitz, who was a third owner of the Kogan-Bors-Wazalitz line, and a Gratz chewer. But one did not argue with the owners, except when the safety of the ship was concerned. The Rigal Rover had made a crash landing at Alexbut, and a badly injured pilot had brought her in by will, hope and a faith he speedily lost.

He received a plasta-hand, the best the medical center could supply and a pension for life, forced by the public acclaim for a man who had saved ships and lives. Then—the sack because a crazed Tors Wazalitz was dead. They dared not try to stick Hume with a murder charge; the voyage record tapes had been shot straight through to the Patrol Council, and the evidence on those could be neither faked nor tampered with. They could not give him a quick punishment, but they could try to arrange a slow death. The word had gone out that Hume was off pilot boards. They had tried to keep him out of space.

And they might have done it, too, had he been the usual type of pilot, knowing only his trade. But some odd streak of restlessness had always led him to apply for the rim runs, the very first flights to newly opened worlds. Outside of the survey men, there were few qualified pilots of his seniority who possessed such a wide and varied knowledge of the galactic frontiers.

So when he learned that the ships' boards were irrevocably closed to him, Hume had signed up with the Out-Hunters Guild. There was a vast difference between lifting a liner from a launching pad and guiding civ hunters to worlds surveyed and staked out for their trips into the wild. Hume relished the exploration part—he disliked the leading-by-the-hand of nine-tenths of the Guild's clients.

But if he had not been in the Guild service he would never have made that find on Jumala. That lucky, lucky find! Hume's plasta-flesh fingers curved, their nails drew across the red surface of the table. And where was Wass? He was about to rise and go when the golden oval on the wall smoked, its substance thinning to a mist as a man stepped through to the floor.

The newcomer was small compared to the former pilot, but he had breadth of shoulder which made the upper part of his torso overbalance his thin hips and legs. He was dressed most conservatively except for a jeweled plaque resting on the tightly stretched gray silk of his upper tunic at heart level. Unlike Hume he wore no visible arms belt, but the other did not doubt that there were a number of devices concealed in that room to counter the efforts of any assassin.

The man from the mirror spoke with a flat, toneless voice. His black hair had been shaven well above his ears, the locks left on top of his skull trained into a kind of bird's crest. As Hume, his visible areas of flesh were deeply browned, but by nature rather than exposure to space, the pilot guessed. His features were harsh, with a prominent nose, a back-slanting forehead, eyes dark, long and large, with heavy lids.

"Now—" He spread both his hands, palm down and flat on the table, a gesture Hume found himself for some unknown reason copying, "you have a proposition?"

But the pilot was not to be hurried, any more than he was to be influenced by Wass' stage settings.

"I have an idea," he corrected.

"There are many ideas." Wass leaned back in his chair, but he did not remove his hands from the table. "Perhaps one in a thousand is the kernel of something useful. For the rest, there is no need to trouble a man."

"Agreed," Hume returned evenly. "But that one idea in a thousand can also pay off in odds of a million to one, when and if a man has it."

"And you have such a one?"

"I have such a one." It was Hume's role now to impress the other by his unshakable confidence. He had studied all the possibilities. Wass was the right man, perhaps the only partner he could find. But Wass must not know that.

"On Jumala?" Wass returned.

If that stare and statement were intended to rattle Hume, it was a wasted shot. To discover that he had just returned from that frontier planet required no ingenuity on the Veep's part.

"Perhaps."

"Come, Out-Hunter Hume. We are both busy men, this is no time to play tricks with words and hints. Either you have made a find worth the attention of my organization or you have not. Let me be the judge."

This was it—the corner of no return. But Wass had his own code. The Veep had established his tight control of his lawless organization by set rules; and one of them was, don't be greedy. Wass was never greedy, which is why the patrol had never been able to pull him down, and those who dealt with him did not talk. If you had a good thing, and Wass accepted temporary partnership, he kept his side of the bargain rigidly. You did the same—or regretted your stupidity.

"A claimant to the Kogan estate—that good enough for you?"

Wass showed no surprise. "And how would such a claimant be profitable to us?"

Hume appreciated the "us"; he had an in now.

"If you supply the claimant, surely you can claim a reward, in more ways than one."

"True. But one does not produce a claimant out of a Krusha dream. The investigation for any such claim now would be made by a verity lab and no imposture will pass those tests. While a real claimant would not need your help or mine."

"Depends upon the claimant."

"One you discovered on Jumala?"

"No." Hume shook his head slowly. "I found something else on Jumala—an L-B from Largo Drift, intact and in good shape. From the evidence now in existence it could have landed there with survivors aboard."

"And the evidence of such survivors living on—that exists also?"

Hume shrugged, his plasta-flesh fingers flexed slightly. "It has been six planet years, there is a forest where the L-B rests. No, no evidence at present."

"The Largo Drift," Wass repeated slowly, "carrying, among others, Gentlefem Tharlee Kogan Brodie."

"And her son, Rynch Brodie, who was at the time of the Largo Drift's disappearance a boy of fourteen."

"You have indeed made a find." Wass gave that simple statement enough emphasis to assure Hume he had won. His one-in-a-thousand idea had been absorbed, was now being examined, amplified, broken down into details he could never have hoped to manage for himself, by the most cunning criminal brain in at least five solar systems.

"Is there any hope of survivors?" Wass attacked the problem straight on.

"No evidence even of there being any passengers when the L-B planeted. Those are automatic and released a certain number of seconds after an accident alarm. For what it's worth the hatch of this one was open. It could have brought in survivors. But I was on Jumala for three months with a full Guild crew and we found no sign of any castaways."

"So you propose—?"

"On the basis of my report, Jumala has been put up for a safari choice. The L-B could well be innocently discovered by a client. Everyone knows the story with the case dragging through the Ten Sector-Terran Courts now. Gentlefem Brodie and her son might not have been news ten years ago. Now, with a third of the Kogan-Bors-Wazalitz control going to them, any find linked with the Largo Drift would gain full galactic coverage."

"You have a choice of survivor? The Gentlefem?"

Hume shook his head. "The boy. He was bright, according to the stories since, and he would have the survival manual from the ship to study. He could have grown up in the wilds of an unopened planet. To use a woman is too tricky."

"You are entirely right. But we shall require an extremely clever imposter."

"I think not." Hume's cool glance met Wass'. "We only need a youth of the proper general physical description and the use of a conditioner."

Wass' expression did not change; there was no sign that Hume's hint had struck home. But when he replied there was a slight change in the monotone of his voice.

"You seem to know a great deal."

"I am a man who listens," Hume replied, "and I do not always discount rumor as mere fantasy."

"That is true. As one of the Guild, you would be interested in the root of fact beneath the plant of fiction," Wass acknowledged. "You appear to have done some planning on your own."

"I have waited and watched for just such an opportunity as this," Hume answered.

"Ah, yes. The Kogan-Bors-Wazalitz combine incurred your displeasure. I see you are also a man who does not forget easily. And that, too, I understand. It is a foible of my own, Out-Hunter. I neither forget nor forgive my enemies, though I may seem to do so and time separates them from their past deeds for a space."

Hume accepted that warning—both must keep any bargain. Wass was silent for a moment, as if to leave time for the thought to root itself, then he spoke again.

"A youth with the proper physical qualifications. Have you any such in mind?"

"I think so." Hume was short.

"He will need certain memories; those take time to tape."

"Those dealing with Jumala I can supply."

"Yes. You will have to provide a tape beginning with his arrival on that world. For such family material as is necessary I shall have ready. An interesting project, even apart from its value to us. This is one to intrigue experts."

Expert psycho-techs—Wass had them. Men who had slipped over the border of the law, had entered Wass' organization and prospered there. There were some techs crooked enough to enjoy such a project for its own sake, indulging in forbidden experimentation. For a moment, but only for a moment, something in Hume jibbed at the intent of carrying through his plan. Then he shrugged that tinge aside.

"How soon do you wish to move?"

"How long will preparation take?" Hume asked in return, for the second time battling a taste of concern.

"Three months, maybe four. There's research to be done and tapes to be made."

"It will be six months probably before the Guild sets up a safari for Jumala."

Wass smiled. "That need not worry us. When the time comes for a safari, there shall also be clients, impeccable clients, asking for it to be planned."

There would be, too, Hume knew. Wass' influence reached into places where the Veep himself was totally unknown. Yes, he could count on an excellent, well-above-suspicion set of clients to discover Rynch Brodie when the time came.

"I can deliver the boy tonight, or early tomorrow morning. Where?"

"You are sure of your selection?"

"He fulfills the requirements, the right age, general appearance. A boy who will not be missed, who has no kin, no ties, and who will drop out of sight without any questions to be asked."

"Very well. Get him at once. Deliver him here."

Wass swept one hand across the table surface. On the red of the stone there glowed for seconds an address. Hume noted it, nodded. It was one in the center of the port town, one which could be visited at an odd hour without exciting any curiosity. He rose.

"He will be there."

"Tomorrow, at your convenience," Wass added, "you will come to tin's place." Again the palm moved and a second address showed on the table.

"There you will begin your tape for our use. It may take several sessions."

"I'm ready. I still have the long report to make to the Guild, so the material is still available on my note tapes."

"Excellent. Out-Hunter Hume, I salute a new colleague." At last Wass' right hand came up from the table. "May we both have luck equal to our industry."

"Luck to equal our desires," Hume corrected him.

"A very telling phrase, Out-Hunter. Luck to equal our desires. Yes, let us both deserve that."

✳ ✳ **2** ✳ ✳

The Starfall was a long way down scale from the pleasure houses of the upper town. Here strange vices were also merchandise, but not such exotics as Wass provided. This was strictly for crewmen of the star freighters who could be speedily and expertly separated from a voyage's pay in an evening. The tantalizing scents of Wass' terraces were reduced here to simply smells, the majority of which were not fragrant.

There had already been two fatal duels that evening. A tubeman from a rim ship had challenged a space miner to settle a difference with those vicious whips made from the tail casings of Flangoid flying lizards, an encounter which left both men in ribbons, one dead, one dying. And a scarred, ex-space marine had blaster-flamed one of the Star-and-Comet dealers into charred human ash.

The young man who had been ordered to help clear away the second loser retired to the stinking alley outside to lose the meal which was part of his meager day's pay. Now he crawled back inside, his face greenish, one hand pressed to his middle section.

He was thin, the fine bones of his face tight under the pallid skin, his ribs showing even through the sleazy fabric of the threadbare tunic with its house seal. When he leaned his head back against the grime-encrusted wall, raising his face to the light, his hair had the glint of bright chestnut, a gold which was also red. And for his swamper's labor he was almost fastidiously clean. "You—Lansor!"

143

He shivered as if an icy wind had found him and opened his eyes. They seemed disproportionately large in his skin-and-bone face and were of an odd shade, neither green nor blue, but somewhere between.

"Get going, you! Ain't paying out good credits for you to sit there like you was buying on your own!" The Salarkian who loomed above him spoke accentless, idiomatic Basic Space which came strangely from between his yellow lips. A furred hand thrust the handle of a mop-up stick at the young man, a taloned thumb jerked the direction in which to use that evil-smelling object. Vye Lansor levered himself up the wall, took the mop, setting his teeth grimly.

Someone had spilled a mug of Kardo and the deep purple liquid was already patterning the con-stone floor past any hope of cleaning. But he set to work slapping the fringe of the noisome mop back and forth to sop up what he could. The smell of the Kardo uniting with the general effluvia of the room and its inhabitants heightened his queasiness. Working blindly in a half-stupor, he was not aware of the man sitting alone in the booth until his mop spattered the ankle of one of the drinking girls. She struck him sharply across the face with a sputtering curse in the tongue of Altar-Ishtar.

The blow sent him back against the open lattice of the booth. As he tried to steady himself another hand reached up, fingers tightened about his wrist. He flinched, tried to jerk away from that hold, only to discover that he was the other's prisoner.

And looking down at his captor in apprehension, he was aware even then of the different quality of this man. The patron wore the tunic of a crewman, lighter patches where the ship's badges should have been to show that he was not engaged. But, though his tunic was shabby, dirty, his magnetic boots scuffed and badly worn, he was not like the others now enjoying the pleasures of the Starfall.

"This one—he makes trouble?" The vast bulk of the Vorm-man who was the Starfall's private law moved through the crowd with serene confidence in his own strength, which no one there, unless blind, deaf, and out-of-the-senses drunk, could dispute. His scaled, six-fingered claw hand reached out for Lansor and the boy cringed.

"No trouble!" There was the click of authority in the voice of the man in the booth. His face, moments earlier taut and sharp with intelligence, was suddenly slack, his tone slurred as he answered: "Looks like an old shipmate. No trouble, just want a drink with an old shipmate."

But the grip which had pulled Vye forward swung him around and down on the other bench in the booth, was anything but slack. The Vorm-man glanced from the patron of the Starfall to its least important employee and then grinned, thrusting his fanged jaws close to Lansor's.

"If the master wants to drink, you dirt-rat, you drink!"

Vye nodded vigorously, and then put his hand to his mouth, afraid his stomach was about to betray him again. Apprehensive, he watched the Vorm-man turn away. Only when that broad, green-gray back was lost in the smoky far reaches of the room did he expel his breath again.

"Here—" The grip was gone from his wrist, but fingers now put a mug into his hand. "Drink!"

He tried to protest, knew it was hopeless, and used both hands to get the mug to his lips, mouthing the stinging liquid in dull despair. Only, instead of bringing nausea with it, the stuff settled his stomach, cleared his head with an afterglow with which he managed to relax from the tense state of endurance which filled his hours in the Starfall.

Half of the mug's contents inside him and he dared to raise his eyes to the man opposite him. Yes, this was no common crewman, nor was he drunk as he had pretended for the Vorm-man. Now he watched the milling crowd with a kind of detachment, though Vye was sure he was aware of every move he himself made.

Vye finished the liquid. For the first time since he had come into this place two months earlier, he felt like a real person again. And he had wits enough to guess that the potion he had just swallowed contained some drug. Only now he did not care at all. Anything which could wipe out in moments all the shame, fear, and sick despair the Starfall had planted in him was worth swallowing. Why the other had drugged him was a mystery, but he was content to wait for enlightenment.

Lansor's companion once more applied that compelling pressure to the younger man's bony forearm. Linked by that hold, they left the Starfall, came into the cooler, far more pleasant atmosphere of the street. They were a block away before Vye's guide halted, though he did not release his prisoner.

"Forty names of Dugor!" he spat.

Lansor waited, breathing in the air of early morning. The confidence of the drug still held. At the moment he was certain nothing could be as bad as the life behind him; he was willing to face what this strange patron of the Starfall had in mind.

The other slapped his hand down on an air-car call button, stood waiting until one of the city flitters landed on beam before them.

From the seat of the air-car Vye noted they were heading into the respectability of the upper city, away from the stews ringing the launch port. He tried to guess their destination or purpose, not that either mattered much. Then the car descended on a landing stage.

The stranger waved Lansor through a doorway, down a short corridor into a room of private quarters. Vye sat down gingerly on the foam seat extending from the wall as he neared. He stared about. Dimly he could just remember rooms which had this degree of comfort, but so dimly now he could not be sure they did not exist only in his vivid imagination. For Vye's imagination had buoyed him first through the drab existence in a State Child's Créche, then through a state-found job which he had lost because he could not adapt to the mechanical life of a computer tender, and had been an anchor and an escape when he had sunk through the depths of the port to the last refuge in the Starfall.

Now he pressed both his hands into the soft stuff of the seat and gaped at a small tri-dee on the wall facing him, a miniature scene of life on some other planet wherein a creature enveloped in short black-and-white striped fur crept belly flat, to stalk long-legged, short-winged birds making blood-red splotches against yellow reed banks under a pale violet sky. He feasted on its color, on the sense of freedom and off-world wonders which it raised in him.

"Who are you?"

The stranger's abrupt question brought him back, not only to the room but to his own precarious position. He moistened his lips, no longer quite so aglow with confidence.

"Vye—Vye Lansor." Then he added his other identification, "S. C. C. 425061."

"State child, eh?" The other had pushed a button for a refresher cup, then was sipping its contents slowly. He did not ring for a second to offer Vye. "Parents?"

Lansor shook his head. "I was brought in after the Five-Hour Fever epidemic. They didn't try to keep records, there were too many of us."

The man was watching him levelly over the rim of that cup. There was something cold in that study, something which curbed Vye's pleasant feeling of only moments earlier. Now the other set down his drink, crossed the room. Cupping his hand under Lansor's chin, he brought up his head in a way which stirred a sullen resentment in the younger man, yet something told him resistance would only bring trouble.

"I'd say Terran stock—not more than second generation." He was talking to himself more than to Vye. He loosed his hold on the boy's chin, but he still stood there surveying him from head to foot. Lansor wanted to squirm, but he fought that impulse, and managed to meet the other's gaze when it reached his face again.

"No—not the usual port-drift. I was right all the way."

Now he looked at Vye again as if the younger man did have a brain, emotions, some call on his interest as a personality. "Want a job?"

Lansor pressed his hand deeper into the foam seat. "What—*what* kind?" He was angry and ashamed at that small betraying break in his voice.

"You have scruples?" The stranger appeared to think that amusing. Vye reddened, but he was also more than a little surprised that the man in the worn space uniform had read hesitancy right. Someone out of the Starfall should not be too particular about employment, and he could not tell why he was.

"Nothing illegal, I assure you." The man crossed to set his refresher cup in the empty slot. "I am an Out-Hunter."

Lansor blinked. This had all taken on some of the fantastic aura of a dream. The other was eyeing him impatiently, as if he had expected some reaction.

"You may inspect my credentials if you wish."

"I believe you," Vye found his voice.

"I happen to need a gearman."

But this wasn't happening! Of course, it couldn't happen to him, Vye Lansor, state child, swamper in the Starfall. Things such as this did not happen, except in a thaline dream, and he wasn't a smoke eater! It was the kind of dream a man didn't want to wake from, not if he was port-drift.

"Would you be willing to sign on?"

Vye tried to clutch reality to himself, to remain level-headed. A gearman for an Out-Hunter! Why five men out of six would pay a large premium for a chance at such rating. The chill of doubt cut through the first hazy rosiness. A swamper from a portside dive simply did not become a gearman for a Guild Hunter.

Again it was as if the stranger read his thoughts. "Look here," he spoke abruptly. "I had a bad time myself, years ago. You resemble someone to whom I owe a debt. I can't repay him, but I can make the scales a little more even this way."

"Make the scales even." Vye's fading hope brightened. Then the Out-Hunter was a follower of the Fata Rite. That would explain everything. If you could not repay a good deed to the one you owed, you must balance the Eternal Scales in another fashion. He relaxed again, a great many of his unasked questions so answered.

"You will accept?"

Vye nodded eagerly. "Yes, Out-Hunter." He still could not believe that this was happening.

The other pressed the refresher button, and this time he handed Lansor the brimming cup. "Drink on the bargain." His words had the ring of command.

Lansor drank, gulping down the contents of the cup, and suddenly was aware of being tired. He leaned back against the wall, his eyes closed.

Ras Hume took the cup from the lax fingers of the young man.

So far, very good. Chance appeared to be playing on his side of the board. It had been chance which had steered him into the Starfall just three nights ago when he had been in quest of his imposter. And Vye Lansor was better than he dared hope to find. The boy had the right coloring, he had been batted around enough to fall for the initial story, he was malleable now. And after Wass' techs worked on him he would be Rynch Brodie—heir to one-third of Kogan-Bors-Wazalitz!

"Come!" He touched Vye on the shoulder. The boy opened his eyes, but his gaze did not focus as he got slowly to his feet. Hume glanced at his planet-time watch. It was still very early; the chance he must run in getting Lansor out of this building was small if they went at once. Guiding the younger man with a light hold above the elbow, he walked him out back to the flitter landing stage. The air-car was waiting. Hume's sense of being a gambler facing a run of good luck grew as he shepherded the boy into the flitter, punched a cover destination and took off.

On another street he transferred himself and his charge into a second air-car, set the destination to within a block of the address Wass had given him. Not much later he walked Vye into a small lobby with a discreet list of names posted in its rack. No occupations attached to those colored streamers Hume noted. This meant either that their owners represented luxury trades, where a name signified the profession or service, or that they were covers—perhaps both. Wass' world fringed many different circles, intermingled with some quite surprising professions dedicated to the comfort, pleasure or health of the idle rich, off-world nobility, and the criminal elite.

Hume fingered the right call button, knowing that the thumb pattern he had left on Wass' conference table would have already been relayed as his symbol of admission here. A flicker of light winked below the name, the wall to the right shimmered, and produced a doorway. Steering Vye to it, Hume nodded to the man waiting there. He was a flat-faced Eucorian of the servant caste, and now he reached out to draw Lansor over the threshold.

"I have him, Gentlehomo." His voice was as expressionless as his face. There was another shimmer and the door disappeared.

Hume brushed his hand down the outer side of his thigh, wiping flesh against the coarse stuff of the crew uniform. He left the lobby frowning at his own thoughts.

Stupid! A swamper from one of the worst rat holes in the port. Like as not that youngster would have had his brains kicked out in a brawl, or been fried to a crisp when some drunk got wild with a blaster, before the year was out. He'd done him a real kindness, given him a chance at a future less than one man in a billion ever had the power to even dream about. Why, if Vye Lansor had known what was going to happen to him, he would have been so willing to volunteer, that he would have dragged Hume here. There was no reason to have any regrets over the boy, he had never had it so good— never! There was only one small period of risk for Vye to face. Those days he would have to spend alone on Jumala between the time Wass' organization would plant him there and the coming of Hume's party to "discover" him. Hume himself would tape every possible aid to cover that period. All the knowledge of a Guild Out-Hunter, added to the information gathered by the survey, would be used to provide Rynch Brodie with the training necessary for wilderness survival. Hume was already listing the items to be included as he strode down the street, his bread once more assured.

* ✳ **3** ✳ *

His head ached dully, of that he was conscious first. As he turned, without opening his eyes, he felt the brush of softness against his cheek, and a pungent odor fill his nostrils.

He opened his eyes, stared up past a rim of broken rock toward the cloudless, blue-green sky. A relay clicked into proper place deep in his mind.

Of course! He had been trying to lure a strong-jaws out of its traphole with hooked bait, then his foot had slipped. Rynch Brodie sat up, flexed his bare thin arms, and moved his long legs experimentally. No broken bones, anyway. But still he frowned. Odd—that dream which jarred with the here and now.

Crawling to the side of the creek, he dipped head and shoulders into the water, letting the chill of the stream flush away some of his waking bewilderment. He shook himself, making the drops fly from his uncovered torso and arms, and then discovered his hunting tackle.

He stood for a moment fingering each piece of his scanty clothing, recalling every piece of labor or battle which had added pouch, belt, strip of fabric to his equipment. Yet—there was still that odd sense of strangeness, as if none of this was really his.

Rynch shook his head, wiped his wet face with his arm. It was all his, that was sure, every bit of it. He'd been lucky, the survival manual on the L-B had furnished him with general directions and this was a world which was not unfriendly—not if one was prepared for trouble.

He climbed up and loosened the net, coiling its folds into one hand, taking the good spear in his other. A bush stirred ahead, against the pull of the light breeze. Rynch froze, then the haft of his spear slid into a new hand grip, the coils of his net spun out. A snarl cut over the purr of water.

The scarlet blot which sprang for his throat was met with the flail of the net. Rynch stabbed twice at the creature he had so swept off balance. A water-cat, this year's cub. Dying, its claws, overlong in proportion to its paws, drew inch-deep furrows in the earth and gravel. Its eyes, almost the same shade as its long, burr-entangled body fur, glared up at him in deathly enmity.

As Rynch watched, that feeling that he was studying something strange, utterly alien, came to him once again. Yet he had hunted water-cats for many seasons. Fortunately, they were solitary, evil-tempered beasts that marked out a roaming territory to defend it from others of their kind, and not too many were to be encountered in cross-country travel.

He stooped to pull his net from the now still paws. Some definite place he must reach. The compulsion to move on in that sudden flash shook him, raised the dull ache still troubling his temples into a punishing throb. Going down on his knees, Rynch once more turned to the stream water; this time after splashing it onto his face, he drank from his cupped hands.

Rynch swayed, his wet hands over his eyes, digging fingertips into the skin of his forehead to ease that pain bursting in his skull. Sitting in a room, drinking from a cup—it was as if a shadow picture fitted over the reality of the stream, rocks and brush about him. He had sat in a room, had drank from a cup—that action had been important!

A sharp, hot pain made him lose contact with that shadow. He looked down. From the gravel, from under rocks, gathered an army of blue-black, hard-shelled things, their clawed fore-limbs extended, blue sense organs raised on fleshy stalks well above their heads, all turned towards the dead feline.

Rynch slapped out vigorously, stumbled into the water loosening the hold of two vicious scavengers on the torn skin of his ankle when he waded out knee-deep. Already that black tongue of small bodies licked across the red-haired side of the hunter. Within minutes the corpse would be only well-cleaned bones.

Retrieving his spear and net, Rynch immersed both in the water to clean off attackers, and hurried on, splashing through the creek until he was well away from the vicinity of the kill. A little later he flushed a four-footed creature from between two rocks and killed it with one blow from his spear haft. He skinned his kill, feeling the substance of the skin. Was it exceedingly rough hide, or rudimentary scales? And knew a return of that puzzlement.

He felt, he thought painfully as he toasted the dry-looking, grayish meat on a sharpened stick, as if a part of him knew very well what manner of animal he had killed. And yet, far inside him, another person he could not understand stood aloof watching in amazement.

He was Rynch Brodie, and he had been traveling on the Largo Drift with his mother.

Memory presented him automatically with a picture of a thin woman with a narrow, rather unhappy face, a twist of elaborately dressed hair in which jeweled lights sparkled. There had been something bad—memory was no longer exact but chaotic. And his head ached as he tried to recall that time with greater clarity. Afterwards the L-B and a man with him in it—

"Simmons Tait!"

An officer, badly hurt. He had died when the L-B landed here. Rynch had a clear memory of himself piling rocks over Tait's twisted body. He had been alone then with only the survival manual and some of the L-B supplies. The important thing was that he must never forget he was Rynch Brodie.

He licked grease from his fingers. The ache in his head made him drowsy. He curled up on a patch of sun-warmed sand and slept.

Or did he? His eyes were open again. Now the sky above him was no longer a bowl of light, but rather a muted halo of evening. Rynch sat up, his heart pounding as if he had been racing to outdistance the rising wind now pushing against his half-naked body.

What was he doing here? Where *was* here?

Panic, carried through from that awakening, dried his mouth, roughened his skin, made wet the palms of the hands he dug into the sand on either side of him. Vaguely, a picture projected into his mind—he had sat in a room, and watched a man come to him with a cup. Before that, he had been in a place of garish light and evil smells.

But he was Rynch Brodie, he had come here on an L-B when he was a boy, he had buried the ship's officer under a pile of rocks, managed to survive by himself because he had applied the aids in the boat to learn how. This morning he had been hunting a strong-jaw, tempting it out of its hiding by a hook and line and a bait of fresh-killed skipper.

Rynch's hands went to his face, he crouched forward on his knees. That all was true, he could prove it—he would prove it! There was the strong-jaw's den back there, somewhere on the rise where he had left the snapped haft of the spear he had broken in his fall. If he could find the den, then he would be sure of the reality of everything else.

He had only had a very real dream—that was it! Only, why did he continue to dream of that room, that man, and the cup? Of the place of lights and smells, which he hated so much that the hate was a sour taste in his fright-dried mouth? None of it had ever been a part of Rynch Brodie's world.

Through the dusk he started back up the stream bed, towards the narrow little valley where he had wakened after that fall. Finally, finding shelter within the heart of a bush, he crouched low, listening to the noises of another world which awoke at night to take over the stage from the day dwellers.

As he plodded back, he fought off panic, realizing that some of those noises he could identify with confidence, while others remained mysteries. He bit down hard on the knuckles of his clenched fist, attempting to bend that discovery into evidence. Why did he know at once that that thin, eerie wailing was the flock call of a leather-winged, feathered tree dweller, and that a coughing grunt from downstream was just a noise?

"Rynch Brodie—Largo Drift—Tait." He tasted the blood that his teeth drew from his own skin as he recited that formula. Then he scrambled up. His feet tangled in the net, and he went down again, his head cracking on a protruding root.

Nothing tangible reached him in that brush shelter. What did venture out of hiding to investigate was a substance none of his species could have named. It was neither body, nor mind—perhaps it was closest to alien emotion.

Making contact stealthily, but with confidence, it explored after its own fashion. Then, puzzled, it withdrew to report. And since that to which it reported was governed by a set pattern which had not been altered for eons, its only answer was a basic command reaffirmed. Again it made contact, strove to carry out that order fruitlessly. Where it should have found easy passage, a clear channel to carry influence to the sleeper's brain, it found a jumble of impressions, interwoven until they made a protective barrier.

The invader strove to find some pattern, or meaning—withdrew baffled. But its invasion, as ghostly as that had been, loosened a knot here, cleared a passage there.

Rynch awoke at dawn, slowly, dazedly, sorting out sounds, smells, thoughts. There was a room, a man, trouble and fear, then there was he, Rynch Brodie, who had lived in this wilderness on an unmapped frontier world for the passage of many seasons. That world was about him now; he could feel its winds, hear its sounds, taste, smell. It was not a dream—the other was the dream. It had to be!

Prove it. Find the L-B, retrace the trail of yesterday past the point of the fall which had started all this. Right there was the slope down which he must have tumbled. Above, he would find the den he had been exploring when the accident had occurred.

Only—he did not find it. His mind had produced a detailed picture of that rounded depression, at the bottom of which the strong-jaw lurked. But when he reached the crown of the bluff, nowhere did he sight the mounded earth of the pit's rim. He searched carefully for a good length, both north and south. No den—no trace of one. Yet his memory told him that there had been one here yesterday.

Had he fallen elsewhere and stumbled on, dazed, to fall a second time?

Some disputant inside him said no to that. This was where he had regained consciousness yesterday and there was no den!

He faced away from the river, breathing fast. No den—was there also no L-B? If he had passed this way dazed from a former fall, surely he would have left some trace.

There was a crushed, browned plant flattened by weight. He stooped to finger the wilted leaves. Something had come in this direction. He would back-track. Rynch gave a hunter's attention to the ground.

A half-hour later he found nothing but some odd, almost obliterated marks on grass too resilient to hold traces very long. And from them he could make nothing.

He knew where he was, even if he did not know how he got here. The L-B—if it did exist—was to the west. He had a vivid mental picture of the rocket shape, its once silvery sides dulled by exposure, canted crookedly amid trees. And he was going to find it!

Beyond the edge of any conscious sense there was a new stir. He was contacted again, tested. A forest called delicately in its alien way. Rynch had a fleeting thought of trees, was not aware of more than a mild desire to see what lay in their shade.

For the present his own problem held him. That which beckoned was defeated, repulsed by his indifference. While Rynch started at a steady distance to trot towards the east, far away a process akin to a relay clicked into a second set of impulse orders.

Well above the planet, Hume spun a dial to bring in the image of the wide stretches of continents, the small patches of seas. They would set down on the western land mass. Its climate, geographical features and surface provided the best site. And he had the very important coordinates for their camp already taped in the directo.

"That's Jumala."

He did not glance around to see what effect that screen view had on the other four men in the control cabin of the safari ship. Just now he was striving to master his impatience. The slightest hint could give birth to a suspicion which would blast their whole scheme. Wass might have had a hand in the selection of the three clients, but they would certainly be far from briefed on the truth of any discovery made on Jumala—they had to be for the safety of the whole enterprise.

The fourth man, serving as his gearman for this trip, was Wass' own insurance against any wrong move on Hume's part. And the Out-Hunter respected him as being man enough to be wary of giving any suspicion of going counter to the agreed plan.

Dawn was touching up the main points of the western continent, and he must set this spacer down within a day's journey of the abandoned L-B. Exploration in that direction would be the first logical move for his party. They could not be openly steered to the find, but there were ways of directing a hunt which would do as well.

Two days ago, according to schedule, their castaway had been deposited here with a subconscious command to remain in the general area. There had been a slight element of risk in leaving him alone, aimed only with the crude weapons he could manipulate, but that was part of the gamble.

They were down—right on the mark. Hume saw to the unpacking and activating of those machines and appliances which would protect and serve his civ clients. He slapped the last inflate valve on a bubble tent, watched it critically as it billowed from a small roll of fabric into a weather-resistant, one-room, air-conditioned and heated shelter.

"Ready and waiting for you to move in, Gentlehomo," he reported to the small man who stood gazing about him with a child's wondering interest in the new and strange.

"Very ingenious, Hunter. Ah—now just what might that be?" His voice was also eager as he pointed a finger to the east.

⁎ ⁎ **4** ⁎ ⁎

Hume glanced up alertly. There was a bare chance that "Brodie" might have witnessed their arrival and might be coming in now to save them all a great amount of time and trouble by acting the overjoyed, rescued castaway.

But he could sight nothing at all in that direction to excite any attention. The distant mountains provided a stark, dark blue background. Up their foothills and lower slopes was a thick furring of trees with foliage of so deep a green as to register black from this distance. And on the level country was the lighter blue-green of the other variety of wood edging the open country about the river. In there rested the L-B.

"I don't see anything!" he snapped, so sharply the little man stared at him in open surprise. Hume forced a quick smile.

"Just what did you sight, Gentlehomo Starns? There is no large game in the woodlands."

"This was not an animal, Hunter. Rather a flash of light, just about there." Again he pointed.

Sun, Hume thought, could have been reflected from some portion of the L-B. He had believed that small spacer so covered with vines and ringed in by trees that it could not have been so sighted. But a storm might have disposed of some of nature's cloaking. If so Starns' interest must be fed, he would make an ideal discoverer.

"Odd." Hume produced his distance glasses. "Just where, Gentlehomo?"

"There." Starns obligingly pointed a third time. If there had been anything to see it was gone now. But it did lie in the right direction. For a second or two, Hume was uneasy. Things seemed to be working too well; his cynical distrust was triggered by fitting so smoothly.

"Might be the sun," he observed.

"Reflected from some object you mean, Hunter? But the flash was very bright. And there could be no mirror surface in there, surely there could not be?"

Yes, things were moving too fast. Hume might be overly cautious but he was determined that no hint of any pre-knowledge of the L-B must ever come to these civs. When they would find the Largo Drift's life boat and locate Brodie, there would be a legal snarl. The castaway's identity would be challenged by a half-dozen distant and unloving relatives, and there would be an intense inquiry. These civs must be the impartial witnesses.

"No, I hardly believe in a mirror in an uninhabited forest, Gentlehomo," he chuckled. "But we are on a hunting planet and not all its life forms have yet been classified."

"You are thinking of an intelligent native race, Hunter?" Chambriss, the most demanding of the civ party, strode up to join them.

Hume shook his head. "No native intelligence on a hunting world, Gentlehomo. That is assured before the planet is listed for a safari. However, a bird or flying thing, perhaps with metallic plumage or scales to catch the sunlight, might under the right circumstances seem a flash of light. That has happened before."

"It was *very* bright," Starns said doubtfully. "We might look over there later."

"Nonsense!" Chambriss spoke briskly as one used to overriding the conflicting wishes in any company. "I came here for a water-cat, and a water-cat I'm going to have. You don't find those in wooded areas."

"There will be a schedule," Hume announced. "Each of you has signed up, according to contract, for a different trophy. You for a water-cat, Gentlehomo. And you, Gentlehomo Starns, want to make tri-dees of the pit-dragons. While Gentlehomo Yactisi wishes to try electo-fishing in the deep holes. To alternate days is the fair way. And, who knows, each of you may discover your own choice near the other man's stake out."

"You are quite right, Hunter," Starns nodded. "And since my two colleagues have chosen to try for a water creature, perhaps we should start along the river."

It was two days, then, before they could work their way into the woods. One part of Hume protested, the more cautious section of his mind was appeased. He saw, beyond the three clients now turning over and sorting space bags, Wass' man glanced at the woods and then back to Starns. And, being acutely aware of all undercurrents here, Hume wondered what the small civ had actually seen.

The camp was complete, a cluster of seven bubble tents not too far from the ship. At least this crowd did not appear to consider that the Hunter was there to do all the serious moving and storing of supplies. All three of the clients pitched in to help, and Wass' man went down to the river to return with half a dozen silver-fins cleaned and threaded on a reed, ready to broil over the cook unit.

A fire in the night was not needed except to afford the proper stage setting. But it was enjoyed. Hume leaned forward to feed the flames, and Starns pushed some lengths of driftwood closer.

"You have said, Hunter, that hunting worlds never contain intelligent native life. Unless the planet is minutely explored, how can your survey teams be sure of that fact?" His voice bordered on the pedantic, but his interest was plain.

"By using the verifier." Hume sat cross-legged, his plasta-hand resting on one knee. "Fifty years ago, we would have had to keep rather a lengthy watch to be sure of a free world. Now, we plant verifiers at suitable test points. Intelligence means mental activity of some sort—any of which would be recorded on the verifier."

"Amazing!" Starns extended his plump hands to the flames in the immemorial gesture of a human attracted not only to the warmth of the burning wood, but to its promise of security against the forces of the dark. "No matter how few or how scattered your native thinkers may be, you record them without missing any?"

Hume shrugged. "Maybe one or two," he grinned, "might get through such a screening. But we have yet to discover a planet with such a sparse native life as that at the level of intelligence."

Yactisi juggled a cup in and out of the firelight. "I agree, this is most interesting." He was a thin man, with scanty drab gray hair and dark skin, perhaps the result of the mingling of several human races. His eyes were slightly sunken, so that it was difficult in this light to read their expression. He was, Hume had already decided, a class-one brain and observant to a degree, which could either be a help or a menace. "There have been no cases of failure?"

"None reported," Hume returned. All his life he had relied on machines operating, of course, under the competent domination of men trained to use them properly. He understood the process of the verifier, had seen it at work. At the Guild Headquarters, there were no records of its failure; he was willing to believe it was infallible.

"A race residing in the sea now—could you be sure your machine would discover its presence?" Starns continued to question.

Hume laughed. "Not to be found on Jumala, you may be sure of that—the seas here are small and shallow. Such, not to be picked up by the verifier, would have to exist at great depths and never venture on land. So we need not fear any surprises here. The Guild takes no chances."

"As it always continues to assure one," Yactisi replied. "The hour grows late. I wish you rewarding dreams." He arose to go to his own bubble tent.

"Yes, indeed!" Starns blinked at the foe and then scrambled up in turn. "We hunt along the river, then, tomorrow?"

"For water-cat," Hume agreed. Of the three, he believed Chambriss the most impatient. Might as well let him pot his trophy as soon as possible. The ex-pilot deduced there would be little cooperation in exploration from that client until he was satisfied in his own quest.

Rovald, Wass' man, lingered by the fire until the three civs were safe in their bubbles.

"River range tomorrow?" he asked.

"Yes. We can't rush the deal."

"Agreed." Rovald spoke with a curtness he did not use when the civs were present. "Only don't delay too long. Remember, our boy's roaming around out there. He might just get picked off by something before these stumble-footed civs catch up with him."

"That's the chance we knew we'd have to take. We don't dare raise any suspicion. Yactisi, for one, is no fool, neither is Starns. Chambriss just wants to get his water-cat, but he could become nasty if anyone tried to steer him."

"Too long a wait might run us into trouble. Wass doesn't like trouble."

Hume spun around. In the half-light of the fire his features were set, his mouth grim. "Neither do I, Rovald, neither do I!" he said softly, but with an icy promise beneath the words.

Rovald was not to be intimidated. He grinned. "Set your fins down, fly-boy. You need Wass—and I'm here to hold his stakes for him. This is a big deal, we won't want any misses!"

"There won't be any—not from my side." Hume stepped away from the fire, approached a post which gleamed with a dull, red line of fire down either side. He pressed a control button. That red line flared into a streak of brilliance. Now encircling the bubble tents and the spaceship was a force field: routine protection of a safari camp on a strange world and one Hume had set as a matter of course.

He stood for a long moment staring through that invisible barrier toward the direction of the wood. It was a dark night, there were scudding clouds to hide the stars, which meant rain probably before morning. This was no time to be plagued by uncertain weather.

Somewhere out there Brodie was holed up. He hoped the boy had long ago reached the "camp" so carefully erected and left for his occupancy. The L-B, that stone-covered "grave" showing signs of several years' occupancy, was all assembled and constructed to the last small detail. Far less might have deceived the civs in this safari. But as soon as the story of their find leaked, there would be others on the scene, men trained to assess the signs of a castaway's fight for survival. His own Guild training and the ability of Wass' renegade techs should bring them through that test.

What had Starns seen? The glint of sun on the tail of the L-B, tilted now to the sky? Hume walked slowly back to the fire, when he saw Rovald going up the ramp into the spacer. He smiled. Did Wass think he was stupid enough not to guess that the Veep's man would be in com-touch with his employer? Rovald was about to report along some channel of the shadow world that they had landed and that the play was about to begin. Hume wondered idly how far and through how many relays that message would pass before it reached its destination.

He stretched and yawned, moving to his sleeping pad. Tomorrow they must find Chambriss a water-cat. Hume shoved Brodie into the back of his mind to center his thoughts on the various ways of delivering, to the waiting sportsman, a fair-sized alien feline.

The lights in the bubbles went out one by one. Within the circle barrier of the force field men slept. And by midnight the rain began to fall, streaming down the sides of the bubbles, soaking the ashes of the fire.

Out of the dark crept that which was not thought, not substance, but alien to the off-world men. But the barrier, meant to deter multi-footed creatures, with wings or no visible limbs at all, proved to be a better protection than its creators had hoped. There was no penetration—only a baffled butting of one force against another. And then the probe withdrew as undetected as it had come.

Only, the thing which had no intelligence, as humankind rated intelligence, did possess the ability to fathom the nature of that artificial barrier. The force field was examined, its nature digested. First approach had failed. The second was now ready—ready as it had not been months before when the first coming of these creatures had alerted the very ancient watchdog on Jumala.

Deep in the darker woods on the mountain sides there was a stirring. Things whimpered in their sleep, protested subconsciously commands they could never understand, only obey. With the coming of dawn there would be a marshaling of hosts, a new assault—not on the camp, but on any leaving its protection. And also on the boy now sleeping in a shallow cave formed by the swept roots of a tree—a tree which had crashed when the L-B landed.

Again, fortune favored Hume. With the dawn, the rain was over. There was a cloudy sky overhead, but he believed the day would clear. The roily, rushing water of the river would aid Chambriss' quest. Water-cats holed up in the banks, but rising water often forced them out of such dens. A coarse parallel to the stream bed could well show them the tracks of one of the felines.

They started off in a group, Hume leading, with Chambriss treading briskly behind him, Rovald bringing up the rear in the approved trail technique. Chambriss carried a needler. Starns was unarmed except for a small protection stunner, his tri-dee box slung on his chest by well-worn carrying straps. Yactisi shouldered an electric pole, wore its control belt buckled about his middle, though Hume had warned him that the storm would prevent any deep-hole fishing.

Only a short distance from the campsite they came upon the unmistakable marks of a water-cat's broad paws, pressed in so heavy and distinct a pattern that Hume knew the animal could not be far ahead. The indentations were deep, and he measured the distance between them with the length of his hand.

"Big one!" Chambriss exclaimed in satisfaction. "Going away from the river, too."

That point puzzled Hume slightly. The red-coated felines might be washed out of their burrows, but they did not willingly head so sharply away from the water. He squatted on his heels and surveyed the stretch of countryside between them and the distant wood with care.

The grass was this season's, still growing, not tall enough to afford cover for an animal with paws as large as these prints. There were two clumps of brush. It could have holed up in either, waiting to attack any trailer—but why? It had not been wounded, nor frightened by their party; there was no reason for it to set an ambush on its back trail.

Starns and Yactisi dropped back, though Starns was fussing with his tri-dee. Rovald caught up. He had drawn his ray-tube in answer to Hume's hand wave. Any action foreign to the regular habits of an animal was to be mistrusted.

Getting to his feet, Hume paced along the line of marks. They were fresh—hot fresh. And they still led in a straight line for the woods. With another wave of his hand, he stopped Chambriss. The civ was trained in spite of his eagerness and obeyed. Hume left the tracks, made a detour which brought him to a point from which he could study those clumps of brush. No sign except that line of prints pointed to the woods. And if the party kept on, they might well come upon the L-B!

He decided to risk it. But when they were less than a couple of yards from the tree fringe, his hand shot up to direct Chambriss to fire towards the quivering bush.

Only, that formless half-seen thing, hardly to be distinguished in color from the vegetation, was no water-cat. There was a thin, ragged cry. Then the creature plunged backward, was gone.

"What in the name of nine gods was that?" Chambriss demanded.

"I don't know." Hume went forward, jerked the needler dart from a tree trunk. "But don't shoot again—not unless you are sure of what you are aiming at!"

∗ ∗ **5** ∗ ∗

Moisture from the night's rain hung on the tree leaves, clung in globules to Rynch's sweating body. He lay on a wide branch trying to control the heavy panting which supplied his laboring lungs. And he could still hear the echoes of the startled cries which had come from the men who had threaded through the woods to the up-pointed tail fins of the L-B.

Now he tried to reason why he had run. They were his own kind, they would take him out of the loneliness of a world heretofore empty of his species. But that tall man—the one who had led the party into the irregular clearing about the life boat—

Rynch shivered, dug his nails into the wood on which he lay. At the sight of that man, dream and reality had crashed together, sending him into panic-stricken flight. That was the man from the room—the man with the cup!

As his heart quieted, he began to think more coherently. First, he had not been able to find the strong-jaws' den. Then the marks on the ground at the point from which he had fallen and the L-B were here, just as he remembered. But not far from the small ship he had discovered something more—a campsite with a shelter fashioned out of spalls and vines, containing possessions a castaway might have accumulated.

That man would come, Rynch was sure of that, but he was too spent to struggle on.

166

No, the answer to every part of the puzzle lay with that man. To go back to the ship clearing was to risk capture—but he had to know. Rynch looked with more attention at his present surroundings. Deep mold under the trees here would hold tracks. There might just be another way to move. He eyed the spread of limbs on a neighbor tree.

His journey through those heights was awkward and he sweated and cringed when he disturbed vocal treetop dwellers. He was also to discover that close to the site of the L-B crash others waited.

He huddled against the bole of a tree when he made out the curve of a round bulk holding tight to the tree trunk aloft. Though it was balled in upon itself he was sure the creature was fully as large as he, and the menacing claws suggested it was a formidable opponent.

When it made no move to follow him, Rynch began to hope it had only been defending its own hiding place, for its present attitude suggested concealment.

Still facing that featureless blob in the tree, the man retreated, alert for the first sign of advance on the part of the creature above. None came, and he dared to slip around the bole of the tree under which he stood, listening intently for any corresponding movement overhead. Now he was facing that survivor's camp.

Another object crouched in the dark of the lean-to shelter, just as its fellow was on sentry duty in the tree! Only this one did not have the self-color of the foliage to disguise it. Four-limbed, its long forearms curved about its bent knees, its general outline almost that of a human—if a human went clothed in a thick fuzz. The head hunched right against the shoulders as if the neck were very short, or totally lacking, was pear-shaped, with the longer end to the back, and the sense organs of eyes and nose squeezed together on the lower quarter of the rounded portion, with a line of wide mouth to split the blunt round of the muzzle. Dark pits for eyes showed no pupil, iris, or cornea. The nose was a black, perfectly rounded tube jutting an inch or so beyond the cheek surface. Grotesque, alien and terrifying, it made no hostile move. And, since it had not turned its head, he could not be sure it had even sighted him. But it knew he was there, he was certain of that. And was waiting—for what? As the long seconds crawled by, Rynch began to believe that it was not waiting for him. Heartened, he pulled at the vine loop, climbed back into the tree.

Minutes later, he discovered that there were more than two of the beasts waiting quietly about the camp, and that their sentry line ran between him and the clearing of the L-B. He withdrew farther into the wood, intent upon finding a detour which would bring him out into the open lands. Now he wanted to join forces with his own kind, whether those men were potential enemies or not.

As time passed, the beasts closed about the clearing of the camp. Afternoon was fading into evening when he reached a point several miles downstream near the river. Since he had come into the open he had not sighted any of the watchers. He hoped they did not willingly venture out of the trees where the leaves were their protection.

Rynch went flat on the stream bank, made a worm's progress up the slope to crouch behind a bush and survey the land immediately ahead. There stood an off-world spacer, fins down, nose skyward, and grouped not too far from its landing ramp, a collection of bubble tents. A fire burned in their midst and men were moving about it.

Now that he was free from the wood and its watchers and had come so near to his goal, Rynch was curiously reluctant to do the sensible thing: to rise out of concealment and walk up to that fire, to claim rescue by his own kind.

The man he sought stood by the fire, shrugging his arms into a webbing harness which brought a box against his chest. Having made that fast he picked up a needler by its sling. By their gestures the others were arguing with him, but he shook his head, came on, to be a shadow stalking among other shadows. One of the men hailed him, but as they reached a post planted a little beyond the bubble tents he stopped, allowed the explorer to advance alone into the dark.

Rynch went to cover under a bush. The man was heading to the stream bed. Had they somehow learned of his own presence nearby? Were they out to find him? But the preparations the tall man had made seemed more suited to going on patrol. The watchers! Was the other out to spy on them? That idea made sense. And in the meantime he would let the other past him, follow along behind until he was far enough from the camp so that his friends could not interfere—*then,* they would have a meeting!

Rynch's fingers balled into fists. He would find out what was real, what was a dream in this crazy, mixed up mind of his! That other would know, and would tell him the truth!

Alert as he was, he lost sight of the stranger who melted into the dusky cover of the shadows. Then came a quiet ripple of water close to his own hiding place. The man from the spacer camp was using the stream as his road.

In spite of his caution, Rynch was close to betrayal as he edged around a clump of vegetation growing half-in, half-out of the stream. Only a timely rustle told him that the other had sat down on a drift log.

Waiting for him? Rynch froze, so startled that he could not think clearly for a second. Then he noted that the outline of the other's body was visible, growing brighter by the moment.

Minute particles of pale-greenish radiance were gathering about the other. The dark shadow of an arm flapped, the radiance swirled, broke again into pinpoint sparks.

Rynch glanced down at his own body—the same sparks were drifting in about him, edging his arms, thighs, chest. He pushed back into the bushes while the sparks still flitted, but they no longer gathered in strength enough to light his presence. Now he could see they drifted about the vegetation, about the log where the man sat, about rocks and reeds. Only they were thicker about the stranger as if his body were a magnet. He continued to keep them whirling by means of waving hand and arm, but there was enough light to show Rynch the fingers of his other hand, busy on the front panel of the box he wore.

That fingering stopped, then Rynch's head came up as he heard a very faint sound. Not a beast's cry—or was it?

Again those fingers moved on the panel. Was the other sending a message by that means? Rynch watched him check the webbing, count the equipment at his belt, settle the needler in the crook of his arm. Then the stranger left the stream, headed towards the woods.

Rynch jumped to his feet, a cry of warning shaping, but not to be uttered. He padded after the other. There was plenty of time to stop the man before he reached the danger which might lurk under the trees.

However the other was as wary of that dark as if he suspected what might lie in wait there. He angled along northward, avoiding clumps of scattered brush, keeping in the open where Rynch dared not tail him too closely.

Their course, parallel to the woods, brought them at last to a second stream, the size of a river, into which the first creek emptied. Here the other settled down between two rocks with every indication of remaining there for a period.

Thankfully, Rynch found his own lurking place from which he could keep the other in sight. The light points gathered, hung in a small luminous cloud over the rocks. But Rynch had prudently withdrawn under a bush, and the scent of its aromatic leaves must have discouraged the sparks, for no such crown came to his sentry post.

Drugged with fatigue, the younger man slept, awaking to full day, a fog of bewilderment and disorientation. To open his eyes to this blue-green pocket instead of to four dirty walls, was wrong.

Remembering, he started up and slunk down the slope, angry at his failure. He found the other's track, not turning back as he had half-feared, cleanly printed on level spots of wet earth—eastward now. What was the purpose of the other's expedition? Was he going to use the open cut through which the river ran as a way of penetrating the wooded country?

Now Rynch considered the problem from his own angle. The man from the spacer had made no effort to conceal his trail; in fact it would almost seem that he had deliberately gone out of his way to leave boot prints on favorable stretches of ground. Did he guess that Rynch lurked behind, was now leading him on for some purpose of his own? Or were those traces left to guide another party from the camp?

To advance openly up the stream bed was to invite discovery. Rynch surveyed the nearer bank. Clumps of small trees and high growing bushes dotted that expanse, an ideal cover.

He was hardly out of sight of the bush which had sheltered him when he heard the coughing roar of a water-cat. And the feline was attacking an enemy, enraged to the pitch of vocal frenzy. Rynch ran a zig-zag course from one clump of bush to the next. That sound of snarling, spitting hate ended in mid-cry as Rynch crawled to the river bank.

The man from the spacer camp had been the focus of a three-prong attack from a female and her cubs. Three red bodies were flat and still on the gravel as the off-worlder leaned back against a rock breathing heavily. As Rynch sighted him, he stooped to recover the needler he had dropped, lurched away from the rock towards the water, and so blundered straight into another Jumalan trap.

His unsteady foot advancing for another step came down on a slippery surface, and he fell forward as his legs were engulfed in the trap burrow of a strong-jaws. With a startled cry, the man dropped the needler again, clawed at the ground about him. Already he was buried to his knees, then his mid-thighs, in the artificial quicksand. But he had not lost his head and was jerking from side to side in an effort to pull free.

Rynch got to his feet, walked with slow deliberation down to the river's brink. The trapped prisoner had shied halfway around, stretching out his arms to find a firmer grip on some rock large and heavy enough to anchor him. After his first startled cry he had made no sound, but now, as he sighted Rynch, his eyes widened and his lip parted.

The box on his chest caught on a stone he had dragged to him in a desperate try for support. There was a spitting of sparks and the stranger worked frantically at the buckle of the webbing harness to loosen it and toss the whole thing from him. The box struck one of the dead water-cats, flashed as fur and flesh were singed.

Rynch watched dispassionately before he caught the needler, jerking it away from the prisoner. The man eyed him steadily, and his expression did not alter even when Rynch swung the off-world weapon to center its sights on the late owner.

"Suppose," Rynch's voice was rusty sounding in his own ears, "we talk now."

The man nodded. "As you wish, Brodie."

✳ ✳ **6** ✳ ✳

"Brodie?" Rynch squatted on his heels.

Those gray eyes, *so* light in the other's deeply tanned face, narrowed the smallest fraction, Rynch noted with an inner surge of triumph.

"Were you looking for me?" he added.

"Yes."

"Why?"

"We found an L-B—we wondered if there were survivors."

Slowly Rynch shook his head. "No—you knew I was here. Because you brought me!" He fashioned his suspicions into one quick thrust.

This time there was not the slightest hint of self-betrayal from the other.

"You see," Rynch leaned forward, but still well out of reach from the captive, "I remember!"

Now there was a faint flicker of answer in the man's eyes. He asked quietly: "What do you remember, Brodie?"

"Enough to know that I am not Brodie. That I did not get here on the L-B, did not build that camp."

He ran one hand over the stock of the needler. Whatever motive lay behind this weird game into which he had been unwillingly introduced, he was now sure that it was serious enough to be dangerous.

172

"You have no cup this time."

"So you do remember." The other accepted that calmly. "All right. That need not necessarily spoil our plans. You have nothing to return to on Nahuatl—unless you *liked* the Starfall." His voice was icy with contempt. "To play our roles will be for your advantage, too." He paused, his gaze centering on Rynch with the intensity of one willing the desired answer out of his inferior.

Nahuatl. Rynch caught at that. He had been on or in Nahuatl— a planet? a city? If he could make this man believe he remembered everything clearly, more than just the scattered patches that he did . . .

"You had me planted here, then came back to hunt me. Why? What makes Rynch Brodie so important?"

"Close to a billion credits!" The man from the spacer leaned well back in the hole, his arms spread flat out on either side to keep his body from sinking deeper. "A billion credits," he repeated softly.

Rynch laughed. "You'll have to think of a better one than that, fly-boy."

"The stakes would have to be high, wouldn't they, for us to go to all this staging? You've been conditioned, Brodie, illegally brain-channeled!"

To Rynch the words meant nothing. If they ever had, that was gone, lost in the maze of other things which had been blotted out of his mind by the Brodie past. But he would not give the other the advantage of knowing his uncertainty.

"You need a Brodie for a billion credits. But you don't have a Brodie now!"

To his surprise the prisoner in the earth trap laughed. "I'll have a Brodie when he's needed. Think about a good share of a billion credits, boy, keep thinking of that hard."

"I will."

"Thoughts alone won't work it, you know." For the first time there was a hint of some emotion in the man's voice.

"You mean I need you? I don't think so. I've stopped being a plaque for someone to play across the board." That expression brought another momentary flash of hazy memory—a smoky, crowded room where men slid counters back and forth across tables—not one of Brodie's edited recalls, but his own.

Rynch stood up, started for the rise of the slope, but before he topped that he glanced back. The damaged com-box still smoked where its wearer had flung it. Now the man was already straining forward with both arms, trying to reach a rock just a finger space beyond. Lucky for him the burrow was an old one, uninhabited. In time he should be able to work his way out. Meanwhile there was the whole of a wide countryside in which Rynch could discover a hideout—no one would find him now against his will.

He tried, as he strode along, to piece together more of his memories and the scanty information he had had from the Nahuatl man. So he had been "brain-channeled," given a set of false memories to fit a Rynch Brodie whose presence on this world meant a billion credits for someone. He could not believe that this was the spaceman's game alone, for hadn't he spoken of "we"?

A billion credits! The sum was fantastic, the whole story unbelievable.

There was a hot stab of pain on his instep. Rynch cried out, stamped hard. One of the clawed scavengers was crushed. The man leaped back in time to avoid another step into a swarming mass of them at work on some unidentifiable carrion. Staring down at the welter of scaled, segmented bodies and busy claws, he gasped.

Three dead water-cats were near the man trapped in the pit. Bait to draw these voracious eaters straight to the prisoner. Rynch's empty stomach heaved. He swung around, ran across the grassy verge of the upper bank, hoping he was not too late.

As he half-fell, half-slid down to the water, he saw that the man had managed to hook the webbing of the smoldering box to him, was casting it out and dragging it back patiently, aiming at the nearest rock of size, fruitlessly attempting to hitch its straps over the round of stone.

Rynch dashed on, caught at that loop of webbing, and dug his heels into the loose gravel as he began a steady pull. With his aid the other crawled out, lay panting. Rynch grabbed the man's shoulder, jerked him away from the body of the female water-cat.

He was sure he had seen a telltale scurrying around the smaller of the dead cubs.

The man straightened, glanced toward Rynch who was backing off, the needler up and ready between them.

"My turn to ask why?"

Then his gaze followed Rynch's. The smallest cub twitched from side to side. Not with any faint trace of life, but under the attack of the scavengers. More scuttled towards the second cub.

"Thanks!" The stranger was on his feet. "My name is Ras Hume. I don't think I told you that when we last met."

"This doesn't make any difference. I'm not your man, not Brodie!"

Hume shrugged. "You think about it, Brodie, think about it with care. Come back to camp with me and—"

"No!" Rynch interrupted. "You go your way, I go mine from here on."

Again the other laughed. "Not so simple as all that, boy. We've started something which can't just be turned off as easily as you snap down a switch." He took a step or two in Rynch's direction.

The younger man brought up the needler. "Stay right where you are! Your game, Hume? All right, you play it—but not with me."

"And what are you going to do, take to the woods?"

"What I do is my business, Hume."

"No, my business, too, very much so. I'm giving you a warning, boy, in return for your help here." He nodded at the pit. "There's something in that woods—something which didn't show up when the Guild had their survey exploration here."

"The watchers." Rynch retreated step by step, keeping the needler ready. "I saw them."

"You've seen them!" Hume was eager. "What do they look like?"

In spite of his desire to be rid of Hume, Rynch found himself answering that in detail, discovering that on demand he could recall minutely the description of the animal hiding in the tree, the one who had waited in the shelter, and those he had glimpsed drawing in about the L-B clearing.

"No intelligence." Hume turned his head to survey the distant wood. "The verifier reported no intelligence."

"These watchers—you don't know them?"

"No. Nor do I like what you've seen of them, Brodie. So I'm willing to call a truce. The Guild believed Jumala an open planet, our records accredited it so. If that is not true we may be in for bad trouble. As an Out-Hunter I am responsible for the safety of three civs back there in the safari camp."

Hume made sense, much as Rynch disliked admitting it. And the Hunter must have read something of his agreement in his face for now he nodded and added briskly:

"Best place now is the safari camp. We'll head back at once."

Only time had run out. A noise sounded with a metallic ring. Rynch whirled, needler cocked. A glittering ball about the size of his fist rolled away from contact with a boulder, came to rest in the deep depression of one of Hume's boot tracks. Then another flash through the air, a clatter as a second ball spun across a patch of gravel.

The balls seemed to appear out of the air. Displaying rainbow glints they rolled in a semicircle about the two men. Rynch stooped, then Hume's fingers latched about his wrist, dragging his hand away from the globe. It was only then that he realized that sharp action had detached his attention from that ball he had wanted to take up.

"Don't touch!" Hume barked. "And don't look at that too closely! Come along!" He pulled Rynch forward through the yet-unclosed arc of the globe circle.

Hume detoured around the feasting scavengers and brought Rynch with him at a trot. They could hear behind them the plop and tinkle of more globes. Glancing back Rynch saw one fall close to the bodies of the water-cats.

"Wait a minute!" He pulled back against Hume's hold. Here was a chance to see what effect that crystal had on the clawed carrion eater.

There was a change in the crystal: yellow now, then red—red as the few scraps of fur remaining on the rapidly disappearing body.

"Look!"

The pulsating carpet which had covered the dead feline ceased to move. But towards that spot rolled two more of the globes, approaching the scavengers. Now the clawed things were stirring, dropping away from their prey. They spread out in a patch, moved purposefully forward. Behind them, as guardians might head a flock, rolled three globes, flushing scarlet, then more.

Hume's hand came up. From the cone tip of the ray-tube spat a lance of fire, to strike the middle crystal. The beam was reflected into the block of scavengers. Scaled bodies, twisted, crisped, were ash. But the crystal continued to roll at the same pace.

"Move!" Hume's other hand hit Rynch's shoulder, knocked him forward in an impetuous shove which nearly took him off his feet. Both men began to run.

"What—what are those things?" Rynch appealed between panting breaths.

"I don't know—and I don't like their looks. They're between us and the safari camp if we keep to the river—"

"Between us and the river now." Rynch saw that glittering swoop through the air, marked the landing of a ball near the water's edge.

"Might be trying to box us in. But that's not going to work. See— ahead there where that log's caught between two rocks? Run out on that when we reach there and take to the water. I don't think those things can float and if they sink to the bottom that ought to fix them as far as we are concerned."

Rynch ran, still holding the needler. He balanced along the drift log Hume had pointed out and a jump sent him floundering in the brown stream thigh deep. Hume joined him, his face grim.

"Downstream—"

Rynch looked. One shape—two—three—clearly detailed where matching vegetation gave them no covering camouflage, the watchers had come out of the woods at last. A line of them were walking quietly and upright towards the humans, their blue-green fuzz covering like a mist under the direct rays of the sun. Quiet as they seemed at present, the things out of the Jumalan forest were a picture of sheer brute strength as they moved.

"Let's get out of here—fast!"

The men kept moving, and always after them padded that silent line of green-blue, pushing them farther and farther away from the safari camp, on towards the rising mountain peaks. Just as the globes had shaken the scavengers loose from their meal and sent them marching on, so were the humans being herded for some unknown purpose.

At least, once the march of the beasts began, they saw and heard no more of the globes. And as they reached a curve in the river, Hume stopped, swung around, stood studying the line of decorously pacing animals.

"We can pick them off with the needler or the ray."

The Hunter shook his head. "You don't kill," he recited the credo of his Guild, "not until you are sure. There is a method behind this, and method means intelligence."

Handling of X-tee creatures and peoples was a part of Guild training. In spite of his devious game here on Jumala, Hume was Guild-educated and Rynch was willing to leave such decisions to him.

The other held out the ray-tube. "Take this, cover me, but don't use it until I say so. Understand?"

He waited only for Rynch's nod before he started at a deliberate pace which matched that of the beasts, back through the river shallows to meet them. But that advancing line halted, stood waiting in silence. Hume's hands went up, palm out, he spoke slowly in Basic-X-Tee clicks:

"Friend." This was all Rynch could make out of that sing-song of syllables Rynch knew to be a contact pattern.

The dark eye pits continued to stare. A light breeze ruffled the fuzz covering of wide shoulders, long muscular arms. Not a head moved, not one of those heavy, rounded jaws opened to emit any answering sound. Hume halted. The silence was threatening, a portending atmosphere spread from the alien things as might a tangible wave.

For perhaps two breaths they stood so, man facing alien. Then Hume turned, walked back, his face set. Rynch offered him the ray-tube.

"Fight our way out?"

"Too late. Look!"

Moving lines of blue-green coming down to the river. Not five or six now—a dozen—twenty. There was a small trickle of moisture down the side of the Hunter's brown face.

"We're penned—except straight ahead."

"But we're going to fight!" Rynch protested.

"No. Move on!"

✳ ✳ **7** ✳ ✳

It was some time before Hume found what he wanted, an islet in midstream lacking any growth and rising to a rough pinnacle. The sides were seamed with crevices and caves which promised protection for one's back in any desperate struggle. And they had discovered it none too soon, for the late afternoon shadows were lengthening.

There had been no attack, just the trailing to herd the men to the northeast. And Rynch had lost the first tight pinch of panic, though he knew the folly of underestimating the unknown.

They climbed with unspoken consent, going clear to the top, where they huddled together on a four-foot tableland. Hume unhooked his distance lenses, but it was toward the rises of the mountains that he aimed them, not along the back trail.

Rynch wriggled about, studied the river and its banks. The beasts there were quiet, blue-green lumps, standing down on the river bank or squatting in the grass.

"Nothing." Hume lowered the lenses, held them before his broad chest as he still watched the peaks.

"What did you expect?" Rynch snapped. He was hungry, but not hungry enough to abandon the islet.

Hume laughed shortly. "I don't know. Only I'm sure they are heading us in that direction."

"Look here," Rynch rounded on him. "You know this planet, you've been here before."

"I was one of the survey team that approved it for the Guild."

"Then you must have combed it pretty thoroughly. How is it that you didn't know about them?" He gestured to their pursuers.

"That is what I would like to ask a few assorted experts right about now," Hume returned. "The verifiers registered no intelligent native life here."

"No native life." Rynch chewed that over, came up with the obvious explanation. "All right—so then maybe our blue-backed friends are imported. Suppose someone's running a private business of his own here and wants to get rid of visitors?"

Hume looked thoughtful. "No." He did not enlarge upon his negative. Sitting down he pulled a cylinder container from a belt loop and shook out four tablets, handing two to Rynch, mouthing the others.

"Vita-blocks—good for twenty-four hour's sustenance."

The iron rations depended upon by all exploring services did not have the satisfying taste of real food. However Rynch swallowed them dutifully before he descended with Hume to river level. The Hunter splashed water from the stream into a depression in the rock and dropped a pinch of clarifying powder into it.

"With the dark," he announced, "we might be able to get through their lines."

"You believe that?"

Hume laughed. "No—but one doesn't overlook the factor of sheer luck. Also, I don't care to finish up at the place they may have chosen for us." He tilted his chin to study the sky. "We'll take watches and rest in turn. No use trying anything until it is dark—unless they start to move in. You take the first one?"

As Rynch nodded, Hume edged back into a crevice as a shelled creature withdrawing to natural protection, going to sleep as easily as if he could control that state by will.

Rynch, watching him curiously for a second or two before climbing up to a position from which he judged he could see all sides of their refuge, determined not to be surprised.

The watchers were crouched down, waiting with that patience which had impressed him from his first sight of the camp sentries back in the forest. There was no movement, no sound. They were simply there—on guard. And Rynch did not believe that the darkness of night would bring any relaxation of that vigilance.

He leaned back, feeling the grit of the rocky surface against his bare back and shoulders. Under his hand was the most efficient and formidable weapon known to the frontier worlds, from this post he could keep the enemy trader surveillance and think.

Hume had had him planted here, in the first place, provided with the memory of Rynch Brodie—the reward for him was to be a billion credits. Too much staff work had gone into his conditioning for just a small stake.

So Rynch Brodie was on Jumala, and Hume had come with witnesses to find him. Another part of his mind stood aloof now, applauding the clearness of his reasoning. Rynch Brodie was to be discovered a castaway on Jumala. Only, matters had not worked out according to Hume's plan. In the first place he was certain he had not been intended to know that he was *not* Rynch Brodie. For a fleeting second he wondered why that conditioning had not completely worked, then went back to the problem of his relationship with Hume.

No, the Out-Hunter had expected a castaway who would be just what he ordered. Then this affair of the watcher creatures the Guild men had not found here a few months ago—Rynch felt a small cold dull along his spine. Hume's game was one thing, something he could understand, but the silent beasts were another and somehow far more disturbing threat.

Rynch edged forward, watching the mist on the water, his brain striving to solve this other puzzle as neatly as he thought he had discovered the reason for his scrambled memories and his being on Jumala.

The mist was an added danger. Thick enough and those watchers could move in under its curtain. A needler was efficient, yes, but it could wipe out only an enemy at which it was aimed. Blind cross sweeping with its darts would only exhaust the clip without results, save by lucky chance.

On the other hand, suppose they could turn that same gray haze to their own advantage—use it to blanket their withdrawal? He was about to go to Hume with that suggestion when he sighted the new move in their odd battle with the aliens.

A wink of light—two more—blinking, following the erratic course by the pull of the stream. All bobbing along toward the rugged coastline of the islet. Those had appeared out of nothingness as suddenly as the globes when this chase had begun.

The globes and the winking lights on the water connected in his mind, argued new danger. Rynch took careful aim, fired a dart at one which had grounded on the pointed tip of the rocks where the river current came together after its division about the island. For the first time, Rynch realized those things below were moving *against* the current—they had come upstream as if propelled.

He had fired and the light was still there, two more coming in behind it, so that now there was an irregular cluster of them. And there was activity on the water-washed rocks before them. Just as the scavengers had moved ahead of the globes on land, so now aquatic creatures had come out of the river, were flopping higher on the islet. And those lights were changing color—from white to reddish-yellow.

Rynch scrabbled with one hand in a rock crevice, found a stone he had noted earlier. He hurled that at the cluster of lights. There was a puff of brilliant red, one was gone. Something flopping on the rocks gave a mewling cry and somersaulted back into the water. Then a finger of mist drew between Rynch and the lights which were now only faint, glowing patches. He swung down from his perch, shook Hume awake.

The Out-Hunter made that instant return to full consciousness which was another defense for the men who live long on the rim of wild worlds.

"What—?"

Rynch pulled him forward. The mist had thickened, but there were more of those ominous lights at water level, spreading down both sides of the point, forming a wall. Dark forms moved out of the water ahead of them, flopping on the rocks, pressing higher, towards the ledge where the men stood.

"Those globes—I think they're moving in the river now." Rynch found another stone, took careful aim, and smashed a second one. "The needler has no effect on them," he reported. "Stones do—but I don't know why."

They searched about them in the crevices for more ammunition, laying up a line of fist-sized rocks, while the lights gathered in, spreading farther and farther down the shores of the islet. Hume cried out suddenly, and aimed his ray-tube below. The lance of its blast cut the dark as might a bolt of lightning.

With a shrill squeal, a blot shadow detached from the slope immediately below them. A vile, musky scent, now mingled with the stench of burning flesh, set them coughing.

"Water spider!" Hume identified. "If they are driving those out and up at . . ."

He fumbled at his equipment belt and then tossed an object downward to disintegrate in a shower of fiery sparks. Wherever those sparks touched rock or ground they flared up in tall thin columns of fire, lighting up the nightmare on the rocks and up the ledges.

Rynch fired the needler, Hume's ray-tube flashed and flashed again. Things squealed, or grunted, or died silently, while clawing to reach the upper ledges. He could not be sure of the nature of some of those things. One, armed and clawed as the scavengers, was nearly as large as a water-cat. And a furry, man-legged creature, with a double-jawed head, bore also a ring of phosphorescent eyes set in a complete circle about its skull. They were alien life routed out of the water.

"The lights—smash the lights!" Hume ordered.

Rynch understood. The lights had driven these attackers out of the river. Put out the lights and the boiling broth of water dwellers might conceivably return to their homes. He dropped the needler, took up stones and set about the business of finishing off as many of the lights as he could.

Hume fired into the crawling mass, pausing only once to send another of those flame bombs crashing to illuminate the scene. The water creatures bewildered, clumsy out of their element, were so far at his mercy. But their numbers, in spite of the piling dead, were still a dangerous threat.

Rynch tore gaping holes in that line of lights. But he could see, through the mist, more floating sparks, gathering to take their places, perhaps herding before them more water things to attack. Except for those few gaps he had wrought, the islet was now completely enveloped.

"Ahhhh—" Hume's voice arose in a roar of anger and defiance. He stabbed his ray down at a spot just below their ledge. A huge segmented, taloned leg kicked, caught on the edge of the stone at the level of their feet, twisted aloft again and was gone.

"Up!" Hume ordered. "To the top!"

Rynch caught up two handfuls of stones, holding them to his chest with his left arm as he made a last cast to see one light puff out in answer. Then they both scrambled on to that small platform at the top of the islet. By the aid of the burning flame-torches the Hunter had set, they could see that most of the rocky slopes below them now squirmed with a horrible mass of water life.

Where Hume had fired his ray there was fierce activity, as the living feasted on the slain and quarreled over the bounty. But from other quarters the crawling advance pressed on.

"I have only one more flame flare," Hume stated.

One more flare—then they would be in the dark with the mist hiding the forward-moving enemy.

"I wonder if they are watching out there?" Rynch scowled into the dark.

"They—or what sent them. They know what they are doing."

"You mean they must have done this before?"

"I think so. That L-B back there—it made a good landing, and there are supplies missing from its lockers."

"Which you removed—" Rynch countered.

"No. There might have been real castaways landed here. Not that we found any trace of them. Now I can guess why—"

"But you Guild men were here, and you didn't run into this!"

"I know." Hume sounded baffled. "Not a sign then."

Rynch threw the last of his stones, heard it clink harmlessly against a rock. Hume balanced an object on the palm of his hand.

"Last flare!"

"What's that? Over there?" Rynch had sighted the flashing out of the dark from the river bank, making a pattern of flickers which bore no relation to the infernal lights at the water's edge.

Hume's ray-tube pointed skyward as he answered with a series of short bursts.

"Take cover!" The call came weirdly out over the water, the tone dehumanized. Hume cupped his mouth with one hand, shouted back: "We're on top—no cover."

"Then flatten down—we're blasting!"

They flattened, lay almost in each other's arms, curled on that narrow space. Even through his closed eyelids Rynch caught the flash of vivid, man-made lightning crashing first on one side of the islet and then on the other, and sweeping every crawling horror out of life, into odorous ash. The backlash of that blast must have caught the majority of the lights also. For when Rynch and Hume cautiously sat up, they saw only a handful of widely scattered and dulling globes below.

They choked, coughed, rubbed watering eyes as the fumes from the scorched rocks wreathed up about their perch.

"Flitter with life line—above you!"

That voice had come out of what should have been empty air over their heads. A gangling line trailed across their bodies, a line with a safety belt locked to it, and a second was uncoiling in a slow loop as they watched.

In unison they grabbed for those means of escape, buckled the belts about them.

"Haul away!" Hume called. The lines tightened, their bodies swung up clear of the blasted river island, as their unseen transport headed for the eastern shore.

✳ ✳ **8** ✳ ✳

A subdued but steady light all around him issued from stark gray walls. He lay on his back in an empty cell room. And he'd better be on the move before Darfu comes to enforce a rising order with a powerful kick or one of these back-handed blows which the Salarkian used to reduce most humans to helpless obedience.

Vye blinked again. But this wasn't his cubby-hole at the Starfall, his nose as well as his eyes told him that. There was no hint of uncleanliness or corruption here. He sat up stiffly, looked down at his own body in dull wonder. The only covering on his bare, brown self was a wide, scaled belt and a loin cloth. Clumsy sandals shod his feet, and his legs, up to thigh level, were striped with healing scratches and blotched with bruises.

Painfully, with mental processes as stiff as his arms and his legs, he tried to think back. Sluggishly, memory associated one picture with another.

Last night—or yesterday—Rynch Brodie had been locked in here. And "here" was one of the storage compartments of a spacer belonging to a man named Wass. It had been Wass' pilot in the flitter which snaked them from the river islet where the monsters had besieged them.

This was a concealed, fortified camp—Wass' hide-out. And he was a prisoner with a very uncertain future, depending upon the will of the Veep and a man named Hume.

Hume, the Out-Hunter, had shown no surprise when Wass stood up in the lamplight to greet the rescued. "I see you have been hunting." His eyes had moved from Hume to Rynch and back again.

"Yes—but that does not matter!" the Hunter had returned impatiently.

"No? Then what does?"

"This is not a free world, I have to report that. Get my civs off-planet before something happens to them!"

"I thought all safari worlds were certified as free," Wass countered.

"This one isn't. I don't know how or why. But that fact has to be reported and the civs lifted—"

"Not so fast." Wass' voice had been quiet, almost gentle. "Such a report would interest the Patrol, would it not?"

"Of course—" Hume began and then stopped abruptly.

Wass smiled. "You see—complications already. I do not wish to explain anything to the Patrol. Nor do you either, my young friend, not when you stop to think about what might result from such explanations."

"There wouldn't have been any trouble if you'd kept away from Jumala." Hume's control had returned; both voice and manner were under tight rein. "Weren't Rovald's reports explicit enough to satisfy you?"

"I have risked a great deal on this project," Wass replied. "Also, it is well from time to time for a Veep to check upon his field operatives. Men do not grow careless when personal supervision is ever in mind. And it is well that I did arrive here, is it not, Hunter? Or would you have preferred remaining on that island? Whether any of our project may be salvaged is a point we must consider. But for the moment we make no moves. No, Hume, your civs will have to take their chances for a time."

"And if there is trouble?" Hume challenged him. "A report of an alien attack will bring in the Patrol quickly enough."

"You forget Rovald," Wass corrected. "The chance that one of your civs can activate and transmit from the spacer is remote, and Rovald will see that it is impossible. You have picked up Brodie, I see."

"Yes."

"No!" What had possessed him at that moment to contradict? He had realized the folly of his outburst the moment Wass had looked at him.

"This becomes more interesting," the Veep had remarked with that deceptive gentleness. "You are Rynch Brodie, castaway from the Largo Drift, are you not? I trust that Out-Hunter Hume has made plain to you our concern with your welfare, Gentlehomo Brodie."

"I'm not Brodie." Having taken the leap into the dangerous truth he was stubborn enough to continue swimming.

"I find this enlightening indeed. If you are not Brodie—then who are you?"

That had been it. At that moment he couldn't have told Wass who he was, explain that his patchwork of memories had gaping holes.

"And you, Out-Hunter," Wass' reptilian regard had moved again to Hume, "perhaps you have an adequate explanation for this discovery."

"None of his doing," he burst out. "I remembered—"

Some inexplicable emotion made Rynch defend Hume then.

Hume laughed, and there was a reckless edge to that sound. "Yes, Wass, your techs are not as good as they pretend to be. He didn't follow the pattern of action they set for him."

"A pity. But there are always errors when one deals with the human factor. Peake!" One of the other three men moved towards them. "You will escort this young man to the spacer, see him safely stowed for the present. Yes, a pity. Now we must see just how much can be salvaged."

Then Vye had been brought into the shop, supplied with a ration container, and left to himself within this bare-walled cabin to meditate upon the folly of talking too freely. Why had he been so utterly stupid? Veeps of Wass' caliber did not swim through the murky channels of the Starfall, but their general breed had smaller but just as vicious representatives there, and he knew the man for what he was, ruthless, powerful and thorough.

A sound, slight, but easily heard in the silent vacuum of the storage cabin, alerted him. The crack of the sliding panel door opened and Vye crouched, his hand cupping the only possible weapon, the ration container. Hume edged through, shut the door behind him. He stood there, his head turned so his ear rested against the wall; obviously he was listening.

"You brain-smoothed idiot!" The Hunter's voice was a thread of whisper. "Why couldn't you have kept that swinging jaw of your closed last night? Now listen and listen good. This is a slim try, but it's one we have to take."

"We?" Vye was startled into asking.

"Yes, we! By rights I ought to leave you right here to do the rest of your big, brave speechmaking for Wass' benefit. If I didn't need you, that's just what I would do! If it weren't for those civs—" His head snapped back, cheek to panel, he was listening again. After a long moment his whisper came once more. "I don't have time to repeat this. In about five minutes, Peake'll be here with rations. I'll leave this door unlatched. There's another storage cabin across the corridor—see if you can hide there, then trick him into getting in here and lock him in. Got it?"

Vye nodded.

"Then—make for the exit port. Here." He snapped a packet loose from his belt. "This is a flare pak, you saw how they worked on the island. When you get on the ramp beyond the atom lamp, throw this. It should hit the camp force barrier. And the result ought to hold their attention. Then you head for the flitter. Understand?"

"Yes." The flitter, yes, that was the perfect escape. With a camp force barrier on, any fugitive could only break out by going straight up.

Hume gazed at him soberly, listened once more, and then went. Vye counted a slow five before he followed. The cabin across the corridor was open, just as Hume had promised. He slipped inside, waited.

Peake was coming now, the metallic plates on his spaceboots clicking in regular pattern of sound. He carried another ration container and crooked it in his arm as he snapped up the lock bar on the other cabin.

There was an exclamation of surprise. Vye went into action. His hand, backed by all the strength of his thrusting arm, thumped between Peake's shoulders, sending him staggering into the prison compartment. Before the other could recover either his balance or his wits, Vye had the panel shut, the bar locked into place.

He ran down the corridor to the well ladder, swung down its rungs with an agility born of necessity. Then he was in the air lock, getting his bearings. The flitter stood to his left, the flashing atom lamp, where the men were gathered, to his right.

Vye stepped out on the ramp. He wiped his sweating hand across his thigh. There had to be no failures in the tossing of the flare pak.

Choosing a spot, not directly in line with the lamp but near enough to dazzle the men, he hurled it with all the force he could muster. Then he was running down the ramp, forward to the area of the ship.

There was a flash—shouting—Vye curbed the impulse to look back, darted for the flitter. He jerked open the cabin compartment, scrambled into the cramped space behind the pilot's seat, leaving that free for Hume's quick entrance. More shouting—now he saw the lines of fire wavering from earth to sky along the barrier.

A black shape put on a burst of speed, was silhouetted against that flaming wall, then passed the spacer, grabbed at the open cockpit, and slid in behind the controls. Hume pulled the levers with flying fingers. They arose vertically at a pace which practically slapped Vye's stomach up into the lower regions of his throat.

The searing line of at least one blaster reached after them—too slowly, too low. He heard Hume grunt, and they again leaped higher. Then the Hunter spoke: "Half an hour at the most—"

"The safari camp?

"Yes."

They no longer climbed. The flitter was boring forwards on a projectile flight, into the dark of the night.

"What're those?" Vye suddenly leaned forward.

Had some of the stars across the space void broken free from their fixed orbits? Flecks of light, moving in an arc, headed towards the speeding flitter.

Hume hit a button. Again they arose in a violent leap above those wandering lights. But ahead on this new level more such dots flocked, moving fast to close in on the flyer.

"A straight ram course," Hume muttered, more to himself than Vye.

Again the flyer drove forward in a rising thrust of speed. Then the smooth purr of the propulsion unit faltered, broke into protesting coughs. Hume worked over the controls, beads of sweat showing on his forehead and cheek in the gleam of the cabin light.

"Deading—deading out!"

He brought the flitter around in a wide circle, the purr smoothed out once more in a steady reassuring beat.

"Outrun them!"

But Vye feared they were back again on the losing side of a struggle with the unknown alien power. As they had been herded along the river, so now they were being pushed across the sky, towards the mountains. The enemy had followed them aloft!

Some core of stubborn will in Hume would not yet allow him to admit that. Time and time again he climbed higher—always to meet climbing, twisting, spurting lines of lights which reacted on the engine of the flitter and threatened it with complete failure.

Where they were now in relation to Wass' camp or that of the safari, Vye had no idea, and he guessed that Hume could not be too certain.

Hume switched on the flitter's com-unit, tried a channel search until he picked up a click of signal—the automatic reply of the safari camp. His fingertip beat out in return the danger warning, then the series of code sounds to give an edited version of what must be guarded against.

"Wass has a man in your camp. His skin is in just as much danger as the rest. He may not relay it to the Patrol, but he'll keep the force barrier up and the civs inside—anything else would be malicious neglect and a murder charge when the Guild check tape goes in. This call is on the spacer tape now and will be a part of that— he can't possibly alter such a report and he knows it. This is the best we can do now—"

"We're close to the mountains, aren't we?"

"Do you know much about this part of the country?" Vye persisted. Hume's knowledge might be their only hope.

"Flew over the range twice. Nothing to see."

"But there has to be something there."

"If there is, it didn't show up during our survey." Hume's voice was dull with fatigue.

"You're a Guild man, you've dealt with alien life forms before—"

"The Guild doesn't deal with intelligent aliens. That's X-Tee Patrol business. We don't land on any planet with unknown intelligent life forms. Why should we court trouble—couldn't run a safari in under those conditions. X-Tee certified Jumala as a wild world, our survey confirmed that."

"Someone or something landed here after you left?"

"I don't believe so. This is too well-organized an action. And since we have a satellite guard in space, any ship landing would be taped and recorded. No such record appeared on the Guild screens. One small spacer—such as Wass'—could slip through by knowing procedure—just as he did. But to land all those beasts and equipment they'd need a regular transport. No—this must be native." Hume leaned forward again, flipped a switch.

A small red light answered on the central board.

"Radar warn-off," he explained.

So they wouldn't end up smeared against some cliff face anyway. Which was only small comfort amid terrifying possibilities.

Hume had taken the precaution just in time. The light blinked faster, and the speed of the flyer was checked as the automatic control triggered by the warn-off came into command. Hume's hands were still on the board, but a system of relays put safety devices into action with a speed past that which a human pilot could initiate.

They were descending and had to accept that, since the warn-off, operating for the sake of the passengers, had ruled that move best. The directive would glide the flitter to the best available landing. It was only moments before the shock gear did touch surface. Then the engine was silent.

"This is it," Hume observed.

"What do we do now?" Vye wanted to know.

"Wait."

"Wait! For what?"

Hume consulted his planet-time watch in the light of the cabin.

"We have about an hour until dawn—if dawn arrives here at the same time it does in the plains. I don't propose to go out blindly in the dark."

Which made sense. Except that to sit here, quietly, in their cramped quarters, not knowing what might be waiting outside, was an ordeal Vye found increasingly harder to bear. Maybe Hume guessed his discomfort, maybe he was following routine procedure, but he turned, thumbed open one of the side panels in Vye's compartment, and dug out the emergency supplies.

$*$ $*$ **9** $*$ $*$

They sorted the crash rations into small packs. A blanket of the water-resistant, feather-heavy Ozakian spider silk was cut into a protective covering for Vye. That piece of tailoring occupied them until the graying sky permitted them a full picture of the pocket in which the flitter had landed. The dark foliage of the mountain growth was broken here by a ledge of dark-blue stone on which the flyer rested.

To the right was a sheer drop, and a land slip had cut away the ledge itself a few feet behind the flitter. There was only a steadily narrowing path ahead, slanting upward.

"Can we take off again?" Vye hoped to be reassured that such a feat was possible.

"Look up!"

Vye backed against the cliff wall, stared up at the sky. Well above them those globes still swam in unwearied circles, commanding the air lanes.

Hume had cautiously approached the outer rim of the ledge, was using his distance glasses to scan what might lie below.

"No sign yet."

Vye knew what he meant. The globes were overhead, but the blue beasts, or any other fauna those balls might summon, had not yet appeared.

Shouldering their packs they started along the ledge. Hume had his ray-tube, but Vye was weaponless, unless somewhere along their route he could pick up some defensive and offensive arm. Stones had burst the lights of the islet, they might prove as effective against the blue beasts. He kept watch for any of the proper size and weight.

The ledge narrowed, one shoulder scraped the cliff now as they rounded a pinnacle to lose sight of the flitter. But the globes continued to hover over them.

"We are still traveling in the direction they want," Vye speculated.

Hume had gone to hands and knees to negotiate an ascent so steep he had to search for hand and toe holds. When they were safely past that point they took a breather, and Vye glanced aloft again. Now the sky was empty.

"We may have arrived, or are about to do so," said Hume.

"Where?"

Hume shrugged. "Your guess is as good as mine. And both of us can be wrong."

The steep ascent did not quite reach the top of the cliff around the face of which the ledge curled. Instead their path now leveled off and began to widen out so that they could walk with more confidence. Then it threaded into a crevice between two towering rock walls and sloped downward.

A path unnaturally smooth, Vye thought, as if shaped to funnel wayfarers on. And they came out on the rim of a valley, a valley centered with a wood-encircled lake. They stepped from the rock of the passage onto a springy turf which gave elastically to their tread.

Vye's sandal struck a round stone. It started from its bed in the black-green vegetation, turned over so that round pits stared eyelessly up at him. He was faced by the fleshless grin of a human skull.

Hume went down on one knee, examined the ground growth, gingerly lifted the lace of vertebrae forming a spine. That ended in a crushed break which he studied briefly before he laid the bones gently back into the concealing cover of the mossy stuff.

"That was done by teeth!"

The cup of green valley had not changed, it was the same as it had been when they had emerged from the crevice. But now every clump of trees, every wind-rippled mound of brush promised cover.

Vye moistened his lips, diverted his eyes from the skull.

"Weathered," Hume said slowly, "must have been here for seasons, maybe planet years."

"A survivor from the L-B?" Yet this spot lay days of travel from that clearing back in the plains.

"How did he get here?"

"Probably the same way we would have, had we not holed up on that river island."

Driven! Perhaps the lone human on Jumala herded up into this dead-end valley by the globes or the blue beasts. "This process must have been in action for some time."

"Why?"

"I can give you two reasons." Hume studied the nearest trees narrowly. "First—for some purpose, whatever we are up against wants all interlopers moved out of the lowlands into this section, either to imprison them, or to keep them under surveillance. Second—" He hesitated.

Vye's own imagination supplied a second reason, a revolting one he tried to deny to himself even as he put it into words:

"That broken spine—food . . ." Vye wanted Hume to contradict him, but the Hunter only glanced around, his expression already sufficient answer.

"Let's get out of here!" Vye was fighting down panic with every ounce of control he could summon, trying not to bolt for the crevice. But he knew he could not force himself any farther into that sinister valley.

"If we can!" Hume's words lingered direly in his ears.

Stones had smashed the globes by the river. If they still waited out there Vye was willing to try and break them with his bare hands, should escape demand such action. Hume must have agreed with those thoughts; he was already taking long strides back to the cliff entrance.

But that door was closed. Hume's foot, raised for the last step toward the crevice corridor, struck an invisible obstruction. He reeled back, clutching at Vye's shoulder.

"Something's there!"

The younger man put out his hand questioningly. What his fingers flattened against was not a tight, solid surface, but rather an unseen elastic curtain which gave a little under his prodding and then drew taut again.

Together they explored by touch what they could not see. The crevice through which they had entered was now closed with a curtain they could not pierce or break. Hume tried his ray-tube. They watched thin flame run up and down that invisible barrier, but not destroy it.

Hume relooped the tube. "Their trap is sprung."

"There may be another way out!" But Vye was already despondently sure there was not. Those who had rigged this trap would leave no bolt holes. But because they were human and refused to accept the inevitable without a fight, the captives set off, not down into the curve of the cup, but along its slope.

Tongues of brush and tree clumps brought about detours which forced them slowly downward. They were well away from the crevice when Hume halted, flung up a hand in silent warning. Vye listened, trying to pick up the sound which had alarmed his companion.

It was as Vye strained to catch a betraying noise that he was first conscious of what he did not hear. In the plains there had been squeaking, humming, chitterings, the vocalizing of myriad grass dwellers. Here, except for the sighing of the wind and a few insect sounds—nothing. All inhabitants bigger than a Jumalan fly might have long ago been routed out of the land.

"To the left." Hume faced about.

There was a heavy thicket there, too stoutly grown for anything to lie within its shadow. Whatever moved must be behind it.

Vye looked about him frantically for anything he could use as a weapon. Then he grabbed at the long bush knife in Hume's belt sheath. Eighteen inches of tri-fold steel gleamed wickedly, its hilt fitting neatly into his fist as he held it point up, ready.

Hume advanced on the bush in small steps, and Vye circled to his left a few paces behind. The Hunter was an expert with ray-tube; that, too, was part of the necessary skill of a safari leader. But Vye could offer other help.

He shrugged out of the blanket pack he had been carrying on his back, tossed that burden ahead.

Out of cover charged a streak of red, to land on the bait. Hume blasted, was answered by a water-cat's high-pitched scream. The feline writhed out of its life in a stench of scorched fur and flesh. As Vye retrieved his clawed pack, Hume stood over the dead animal.

"Odd." He reached down to grasp a still-twitching foreleg, stretched the body out with a sudden jerk.

It was a giant of its species, a male, larger than any he had seen. But a second look showed him those ribs starting through mangy fur in visible hoops, the skin tight over the skull, far too tight. The water-cat had been close to death by starvation; its attack on the men probably had been sparked by sheer desperation. A starving carnivore in a land lacking the normal sounds of small birds and animal life, in a valley used as a trap.

"No way out and no food." Vye fitted one thought to another out loud.

"Yes. Pin the enemy up, let them finish off one another."

"But why?" Vye demanded.

"Least trouble that way."

"There are plenty of water-cats down on the plains. All of them couldn't be herded up here to finish each other off; it would take years—centuries."

"This one's capture may have been only incidental, or done for the purpose of keeping some type of machinery in working order," Hume replied. "I don't believe this was arranged just to dispose of water-cats."

"Suppose this was started a long time ago, and those who did it are gone, so now it goes on working without any real intelligence behind it. That could be the answer, couldn't it?

"Some process triggers into action when a ship sets down on this portion of Jumala, maybe when one planet's under certain conditions only? Yes, that makes sense. Only why wasn't the first Patrol explorer flaming in here caught? And the survey team—we were here for months, cataloguing, mapping, not a whisper of any such trouble."

"That dead man—he's been here a long time. And when did the Largo Drift disappear?"

"Five—six years ago. But I can't give you any answers. I have none."

It began as a low hum, hardly to be distinguished from the distant howling of the wind. Then it slid up-scale until the thin wail became an ululating scream torturing the ears, dragging out of hiding those fears of a man confronting the unknown in the dark.

Hume tugged at Vye, drew the other by force back into the brush. Scratched, laced raw by the whip of branches, they stood in a small hollow with the drift of leaves high about their ankles. And the Hunter pulled into place the portions of growth they had dislodged in their passage into the thicket's heart. Through gaps they could see the opening where lay the body of the water-cat.

The wail was cut off short, that cessation in itself a warning. Vye's body, touching earth with knee and hand as he crouched, picked up a vibration. Whatever came towards them walked heavily.

Did the smell of death draw it now? Or had it trailed them from the closed gate? Hume's breath hissed lightly between his teeth. He was sighting the ray-tube through a leaf gap.

A snuffling, heavier than a man's panting. A vast blot, which was neither clearly paw nor hand, swept aside leaves and branches on the other side of the small clearing, tearing them casually from the shrubs.

What shuffled into the open might be a cousin of the blue beasts. But where they had given only an impression of brutal menace, this was savagery incarnate. Taller than Hume, but hunched forward in its neckless outline, the thing was a monster. And over the round of the lower jaw, tusks protruded in ugly promise.

Being carnivorous and hungry, it scooped up the body of the water-cat and fed without any prolonged ceremony. Vye, remembering the crushed spine of the human skeleton, was sickened.

Done, it reared on hind feet once again, the pear-shaped head swung in their direction. Vye was half-certain he had seen that tube-nose expand to test the air and scent them.

Hume pressed the button of the ray-tube. That soundless spear of death struck in midsection of that barrel body. The thing howled, threw itself in a mad forward rush at their bush. Hume snapped a second blast at the head, and the fuzz covering it blackened.

Missing them by a precious foot, the creature crashed straight on through the thicket, coming to its knees, writhing in a rising chorus of howls. The men broke out of cover, raced into the open where they took refuge behind a chimney of rock half-detached from the parent cliff. Down the slope the bushes were still wildly agitated.

"What was that?" Vye got out between sobbing breaths.

"Maybe a guardian, or a patrol stationed to dispose of any catch. Probably not alone, either." Hume fingered his ray-tube. "And I am down to one full charge—just one."

Vye turned the knife he held around in his fingers, tried to imagine how one could face up to one of those tusked monsters with only this for a weapon. But if that thing had companions, none were coming in answer to its dying wails. After it had been quiet for a while, Hume motioned them out of hiding.

"From now on, we'll keep to the open, better see trouble like that before it arrives. And I want to find a place to hole up for the night."

They trailed along the steep upper slope and in time found a place where a now dried stream had once formed a falls. The empty watercourse provided an overhang, not quite a cave, but shelter. Gathering brush and stones, they made a barricade and settled behind it to eat sparingly of their rations.

"Water—a whole lake of it down there. The worst of it is that a water supply in a dry country is just where hunters congregate. That lake's entirely walled in by woodland and provides cover for a thousand ambushes."

"We might find a way out before our water bulbs fail," Vye offered.

Hume did not answer directly. "A man can live for quite a while on very thin rations, and we have tablets from the flitter emergency supplies. But he can't live long without water. We have two bulbs. With stretching that is enough for two days—maybe three."

"We ought to get completely around the cliffs in another day."

"And if we do find a way out, which I doubt, we're still going to need water for the trek out. It's right down there waiting until our need is greater than either our fear or our cunning."

Vye moved impatiently, his blanket-clad shoulders scraping the rock at their backs. "You don't think we have a chance!"

"We aren't dead. And as long as a man is breathing, and on his feet, with all his wits in his skull, he always has a chance. I've blasted off-world with odds stacked high on the other side of the board." He flexed that plasta-flesh hand which was so nearly human and yet not by the fraction which had changed the course of his life. "I've lived on the edge of the big blackout for a long time now—after a while you can get used to anything."

"One thing I would like—to get at the one who set this trap," commented Vye.

Hume laughed with dry humor. "After me, boy, after me. But I think we might have to wait a long time for that meeting."

✶ ✳ **10** ✳ ✶

Vye crawled weakly from the area of a rock outcrop. The sun, reflected from the cliffside, was a lash of fire across his emaciated body. His swollen tongue moved a pebble back and forth in his dry mouth. He stared dimly down the slope to that beckoning platter of water open under the sun, rimmed with the deadly woodland.

What had happened? They had gone to sleep that first night under the ledge of the dried waterfall. And all of the next day was only a haze to him now. They must have moved on, though he could remember nothing, save Hume's odd behavior—dull-eyed silence while stumbling on as a brainless servio-robot, incoherent speech wherein all the words came fast, running together unintelligibly. And for himself—patches of blackout.

At some time, they had come to the cave and Hume had collapsed, not rousing in answer to any of Vye's struggles to awaken him. How long they had been there Vye could not tell now. He had the fear of being left alone in this place. With water perhaps Hume could be returned to consciousness, but that was all gone.

Vye believed he could scent the lake, that every breeze up-slope brought its compelling enticement. Just in case Hume might awake to a state of semi-consciousness and wander off, Vye tethered him with blanket bonds.

Vye fingered Hume's knife, which had been painstakingly lashed to a trimmed shaft of wood. Since he had emerged from that clouding of mind which still gripped the Hunter, he had done what he could to prepare for another attack from any roving beast. And he also had Hume's ray-tube—its single charge to be used only in dire need.

Water! His cracked lips moved, ejected the pebble. Their four empty water bulbs were in the front of his blanket tunic, pressing against his ribs. It was now—or die, because soon he would be too weak to make the attempt at all. He darted for the first stand of bush downhill.

As the brooding silence of the valley continued, he reached the edge of the wood unhindered, intent on his mission with a concentration which shut out everything save his need and the manner of satisfying it.

He squatted in the bush, eyeing the length of woodland ahead. Then he tried the only action he had been able to think out. That beast Hume had killed had been too heavy to swing up in trees. But Vye's own weight now did not prohibit that form of travel.

With spear and ray-tube firmly attached to him, Vye climbed into the first tree. A slim chance—but his only defense against a possible ambush. A wild outward swing brought him, heart-thudding, to the next set of limbs. Then he had a piece of luck, a looped vine tied together a whole group of branches from one treetop to the next.

Hand grips, balance, sometimes a walk along a branch—he threaded towards the lake. Then he came to a gap. With hands laced into tendrils, Vye hunched to look down on a beaten ribbon of gray earth—a trail well-used by the evidence of its pounded surface.

That area had to be crossed on foot, but his passage through the brush below would leave traces. Only—there was no other way. Vye checked the lashings of his weapons again before leaping. Almost in the same instant, his sandals hit the packed earth he was running. His palms skinned raw on rough bark as he somehow scrambled aloft once more.

No more vines, but broad limbs shooting well out. He dropped from one to another—stopped for breath—listened.

The dark gloom of the wood was broken by sunlight. He was at the final ring of trees. To get to the water he must descend again. A dead trunk extended over the water. If he could run out on that and lower the bulb, it could work.

Eerie silence. No flying things, no tree dwelling reptiles or animals, no disturbance of any water creature on the unruffled surface of the lake. Yet the sensation of life, inimical life, lurking in the depths of the wood, under the water, bore in upon him.

Vye made the light leap to the bole of the dead tree, balanced out on it over the water, moving slowly as the trunk settled a little under his weight. He hunkered down, brought out the first bulb tied fast to a blanket string.

The water of the river had been brown, opaque. But here the liquid was not so cloudy. He could see snags of dead branches below its surface.

And something else!

Down in those turgid depths he made out a straight ridge running with a trueness of line which could not be nature's unassisted product. That ridge joined another in a squared corner. He leaned over, strained his eyes to follow through the murk the farther extent of those two ridges., and looked along both pointed protuberances aimed at the surfaces of the lake, like fangs in an open jaw. Down there was something—something artificially fashioned which might be the answer to all their questions. But to venture into the lake himself—he could not do it! If he could bring the Out-Hunter to his senses the other might find the solution to this puzzle.

Vye filled his bulbs, working speedily, but still studying what he could see of the strange erection under the lake. He thought it was curiously free of silt, and its color, as far as he could distinguish, allowing for the dark hue of the water, was light gray—perhaps even white. He lowered his last bulb.

Down in the bleached forest of dead branches, well to one side of the mysterious walls, there was movement, a slow rolling of a shadow so hidden by a stirring of bottom mud that Vye could not make out its true form. But it was rising to the bulb.

Vye hated to lose a single precious drop. Once he might have the luck to make this journey unmolested, a second time the odds could be too high.

A flash—the slowly rising shadow was transformed into a whizzing spear of attack. Vye snapped the bulb out of the water just as a nightmarish, armored head arose on a whiplash of coiled, scaled neck, and a blunt nose thudded against the tree trunk with a hollow boom. Vye clung to his perch as the thing flopped back into deeper water from a froth of beaten foam, leaving a patch of odorous scum and slime to bracelet the water-logged wood.

He ran for the shelter of the trees to get away. This time there was no rear, no thump of feet in warning. Out of the ground itself, or so it seemed to Vye's startled terror, reared one of the tusked beasts. To reach his tree and its dubious safety he had to wind past that chimera. And the creature waited with a semblance of ease for him to come to it.

Vye brought around his spear. The length of the haft might afford him a fighting chance if he could send the point home in some vulnerable spot. Yet he knew that the beasts were hard to kill.

The mouth opened in a wide grin of menace. Vye noted a telltale tightening of shoulder muscles. It was going to rush for him now with those clawed forepaws out to rip.

To wait was to court disaster. Vye shouted, his battle cry piercing the silence of the lake and wood. He sprang, aiming the spear point at the beast's protuberant belly, and then swerved to the side as the knife bit home, raking his weapon to open a gaping wound.

The spear was jerked from Vye's hold as both those taloned paws closed on it. Then the creature pulled it free, snapped the haft in two. Vye fired a short blast from the ray-tube before it could turn on him, saw fur-fuzz afire, as he ran for the tree.

Beneath its branches he looked back. The beast was pawing at the burning fur on its head, and he had perhaps a second or two. He jumped and his fingers caught on the low-hanging branch, then he made a superhuman effort, was up out of the path of the thing which rushed blindly for the tree, shrieking in frenzied complaint.

The huge body crashed against the trunk with force which nearly shook Vye from his hold. As the giant forepaws belabored the wood, strove to lift the body from the ground, Vye worked his way out on another branch. In the end it was the shaking of that limb under him which aided his swing to the next tree. And from there he traveled recklessly, intent only on getting out of the woods as fast as he could.

By the noise the beast was still assaulting the tree, and Vye marveled at its vitality, for the belly wound would long ago have killed any creature he knew. Whether it could trace his flight aloft, or whether its howls would bring more of its kind, he could not guess, but every second he could gain was all important now.

At the gap over the trail he hesitated. That path ran in the direction of the open, and to go on foot meant the possibility of greater speed. Vye slipped from the bough, hit the ground, and ran. His ragged lungsful of air came in great gasps and he doubted it he could take the exertion of more tree travel now. He raced down the path.

Those mewling cries were louder, he was sure of it. Now he heard the thump of the beast's blundering pursuit behind him. But its bulk and hurts slowed it. In the open he could find cover behind a rock, use the ray again.

The trees began to thin. Vye summoned power for a last burst of speed, came out of the shadow of the wood as might a dart expelled from a needler. Before him, up slope, was the closed door of the valley. And moving in from the left was another of the blue beasts.

He could not retreat to the trees. But the newcomer was moving with the same ponderous self-confidence its fellow had shown earlier. Vye dodged right, headed for the rocks by the gap. As he pulled himself into that temporary fortification, the wounded beast dragged out of the woods below. He thought it was blind, yet some instinct drove it after him.

Shaking from fatigue, Vye steadied his forearm on the top of the rock, brought up the ray-tube. Less than two yards away now was the deceptively open mouth of the gap. If he threw himself at that, would the elasticity of the unseen curtain hurl him back into the claws of the enemy? He fired his blast at the head of the unwounded beast. It screeched, threw out its arms, and one of those paws struck against its wounded fellow. With a cry, that one flung itself at its companion in the hunt, and they tangled in a body-to-body battle terrible in its utter ferocity. Vye edged along the cliff, determined to reach the cave and Hume. And the two blue things seemed intent on finishing each other off.

The one from the wood was done, the fangs of the other ripping out its throat. Tearing viciously the victor made sure of its kill, then its seared head came up, swung about to face Vye. He guessed it was aware of his movements whether it could see or not.

But he was not prepared for the speed of its attacking lunge. Heretofore the creatures had given the impression of brute strength rather than agility. And he had been almost fatally deceived. He jumped backwards, knowing he must elude that attack, for he could not survive hand-to-hand combat with the alien thing.

There was a moment of dazed disorientation, a weird sensation of falling through unstable space in which there had never been and never would be firm footing again. He was rolling across rock— outside the curtain of the gap.

He sat up, the feeling of being adrift in immeasurable nothingness making him sick, to watch mistily as the blue-beast came to a halt. Whimpering it turned, but before it reached the level of the woods, it sagged to its knees, fell face forward and was still, a destructive machine no longer controlled by life.

Vye tried to understand what had happened. He had somehow broken through that barrier which made the valley a prison. For a moment all that mattered was his freedom. Then he looked apprehensively behind him along the road to the open, more than half-expecting to see a gathering of the globes, or of the less impressive lowland beasts that acted as herders. But there was nothing.

Freedom! He dragged himself to his feet. Free to go! He slipped Hume's ray-tube back into his belt. Hume was still in the valley!

Vye rubbed his shaking hands across his face. Through the barrier and free—but Hume was back there, without a weapon, defenseless against any questing beast able to nose him out. Sickly, without water and protection, he was a dead man even while he still breathed.

Keeping one hand against the wall of the gap in support, Vye started to walk, not out of the gap towards the distant lowlands, but back into the valley, forcing himself to that by his will alone and screaming inside against such suicidal folly. He put out his hand tentatively when he reached the two points of rock where that curtain had hung. There was no obstruction—the barrier was down! He must get back to Hume.

Still keeping his wall hold, Vye lurched through the gate, was once more in the valley. He stood swaying, listening. But once again there was silence, not even the wind moved through trees or bushes. Placing one foot carefully before the other he went on towards Hume's cave. The haze which had clouded his thinking processes since that first morning's awakening in this bowl was gone now. Except for the physical weakness that weighted his body, he felt once more entirely alive and alert.

Wriggling in the cave's entrance was the Hunter. He had freed the bonds Vye had put on his legs, but his hands were still tied. His face, grimy, sweat-covered, was turned up to the sunlight, and his eyes were again bright with reason.

Vye found the strength to run the last few feet between them. He was fumbling with those ties about Hume's wrists as he blurted out the news. The barrier was out—they could go.

Then he was bringing one of those precious bulbs, raising it to Hume's eager mouth, squeezing a portion of its contents between the man's cracked and bleeding lips.

Somehow they made that trip back to the valley gate. When they saw their goal, Hume broke from Vye's hold, tottered forward with a cry not far removed from a sob. He rebounded to slip full length to the ground and lie there. Sobbing dryly, his gaunt face, eyes closed, turned up to the sky. The trap had snapped shut once again.

"Why—why?" Vye found he was repeating the same words over and over, his gaze blank, unfocused, yet turned to the woods of the lake.

"Tell me what happened again."

Vye's head came around. Hume had pulled himself up so that his shoulders rested against the rock wall. His plasta-hand was outflung, slipping up and down what seemed empty air, but which was the barrier against freedom. And now his eyes seemed entirely sane.

Slowly, hesitating between words, Vye went over the full account of his visit to the lake, his reheat before the beasts, his fortunate stumble through the gap.

"But you came back."

Vye flushed. He was not going to by to explain that. Instead he said: "If it went away once, it can again."

Hume did not press the subject of his return. Rather he fastened upon the end of that action with the wounded beast, made Vye go through it verbally a third time.

"There is just this," he said when the other was done. "When you fell you were not thinking of the barrier at all—and your wits were working again. You had come out of the daze we both had."

Vye tried to remember, decided that the Hunter was correct. He had been trying to elude the charge of the beast, only, fear and that desperate desire had occupied his mind at that moment. But what did that signify?

To test just what he did not know, he crawled now to Hume's side, put up his own hand to the space where the plasta-flesh palm slid back and forth on nothingness. But he almost fell on his face, forward into the gap. Where he had been expecting the resistance of the unseen curtain there had been nothing at all! He turned to Hume with the expression of a man who had been stunned by an unexpected blow.

* ✳ **11** ✳ *

"It is open for you!" Hume broke the quiet first. His eyes were very bleak in his bony face.

Vye stood up, took one step and was on the other side of the curtain where Hume's hand still found substance. He came back with the same lack of hindrance. Yes, to him there was no longer a barrier. But why—why him when Hume was still a prisoner?

The Hunter raised his head so his eyes could meet Vye's with the authority of an order. "Go, get away while you can!"

Instead Vye dropped down beside the other. "Why?" he asked baldly. And then the most obvious of all answers came.

He glanced at Hume. The Hunter's head lolled back against the rock which supported him, his eyes were closed now, and he had the look of a man who had been driven to the edge of endurance and was now willing to relinquish his grip and let go.

Deliberately, Vye brought up his right hand, balled his fingers into a fist. And just as deliberately he struck home, square on the point of that defenseless chin. Hume sagged, would have slipped down the surface of the rock had Vye's hands not caught in his armpits.

Since he had not the strength left to get to his feet with such a burden, Vye crawled, dragging the inert body of the Hunter with him. And this time, as he had hoped, there was no resistance at the gap.

211

Unconscious, Hume was able to cross the barrier. Vye stretched him as comfortably flat as he could, used a portion of their water on his face until he moaned, muttered, and raised his hand feebly to his head.

Then those gray eyes opened, focused on Vye.

"What—"

"We're both through now, both of us!" The younger man saw Hume glance around him with waking belief.

"But how—?"

"I knocked you out, that's how," Vye returned.

"Knocked me out? I crossed when I was unconscious!" Hume's voice steadied, strengthened. "Let me see!" He rolled over on his side, threw out his arm, and this time the hand found no wall. For him, too, the barrier was gone.

"Once through, you are free," he added wonderingly. "Maybe they never foresaw any escapes." He struggled up, sitting with his hands hanging loosely between his knees.

Vye turned his head, looked down the trail. The length of distance lying between them and the safari camp now faced them with a new problem. Neither of them could make that trek on foot.

"We're out, but we aren't back—yet," Hume echoed his thought.

"I was wondering, if *this* door is open—" Vye began.

"The flitter!" Again Hume's mind matched his. "Yes, if those globes aren't hanging around just waiting for us to try."

"They might act only to get us here, not to keep us once we're in." That might be wishful thinking, they wouldn't know until they tried to prove it.

"Give me a hand." Hume held out his own, let Vye pull him to his feet. Weak as he was, he was clear-eyed, plainly clear-headed once more. "Let's go!"

Together they went back through the gap, then tested the absence of the barrier once more, to make sure. Hume laughed. "At least the front door remains open, even if we find the back one closed."

Vye left him sitting by that entrance while he made a quick trip to the cave to pick up the small pack of supplies left them. When he returned they crammed tablets into their mouths, drank feverishly of the lake water, and, with the stimulation of the new energy, set off along the cliff face.

"This wall in the lake," Hume asked suddenly, "you are sure it is artificial?"

"Runs too straight to be anything else, and those projections are evenly spaced. I don't see how it could be natural."

"We'll have to be sure."

Vye thought of that attacking water creature. "No diving in there," he protested. Hume smiled, a stretch of skin far too tight over his jaw now.

"Not us, at least not us now," he agreed. "But the Guild will send another survey."

"What could be the reason for all this?" Vye helped his companion over the loose debris of a cliff slide.

"Information."

"What?"

"Someone—or something—picked our brains while we were out of our heads. Or—" Hume paused suddenly, looked directly at Vye. "I have a vague feeling that you were able to keep going a lot better than I was. That so?"

"Some of the time," Vye admitted.

"That checks. Part of me knew what was going on, but was helpless while that other thing," his smile of moments earlier was wiped away, there was a chill edge in his voice, "picked over my brains, sorted out what it wanted."

Vye shook his head. "I didn't feel that way. Just thick-headed— as if I were sleep walking and yet awake."

"So it took me over, but didn't go all the way with you. Why? Another question for our list."

"Maybe—maybe Wass' techs fixed it so I couldn't be brain-picked, as you call it," Vye offered.

Hume nodded. "Could be—could well be. Come on." He pressed the pace now.

Vye turned to look down the slope suspiciously. Had Hume another warning of menace out of the wood? He could sight no movement there. And from this distance the lake was a topaz sheet of calm which could hide anything. Hume was already several paces ahead, scrambling as if the valley monsters were again on their track.

"What's the matter?" Vye demanded, as he caught up.

"Night coming." Which was true. Then Hume added, "If we can reach the flitter before sunset, we'll have a chance to fly over the lake down there, to make a taping of it before we go."

The energy of the tablets strengthened them so that by the time they reached the crevice door they were moving with their former agility. For a single second, Hume hesitated before that slit, almost as if he feared the test he must make. Then he stepped forward and this time into freedom.

They reached the ledge where the flitter perched just as they had seen it last. How long ago that had been they could not have told, but they suspected that days of haze hung in between. Vye searched the sky. No globes winking there—just the flyer alone.

He took his old seat behind the pilot, watched Hume test the relays and responses in the quick run-down of a man who has done this chore many times before. But the other gave a little sigh of relief when he finished.

"She's all right, we can lift."

Again they both looked aloft, half-fearing to see those malignant herders wink into being to forbid flight. But the sky was as serenely clear of even a drifting cloud as they could hope. Hume pressed a button and they arose vertically with an even progress totally unlike the leap which had taken them out of Wass' camp.

Well above the cliff wall they hovered, and were able to see below the round bowl of the valley prison. Hume touched controls, the flitter descended slowly just above the center of the lake. And from this position they were able to sight the other peculiarity of that body of water, that it was perfectly oval in shape, far too perfect to be an undeveloped product of nature. Hume took a round disk from his equipment belt, fitted it carefully into a slot on the control board and pressed the button below. Then he sent the flitter in a weaving zigzag course well above the surface of the water, so that eventually the flyer passed over every foot of its surface.

And from above, in spite of the turgid quality of the liquid, they could see what did rest on the bottom of that oval. The wall with its sharp comer which Vye had noted from shore level was only part of a water-covered erection. It made a design when seen from overhead, a six-pointed star surrounding an oval and in the midst of that oval a black blot which they could not identify.

Hume brought the flitter over in one last sweep. "That's it. We have a full taping."

"What do you think it is?"

"A device set there by an intelligent being, and set a long time ago. This valley wasn't arranged overnight, six months ago—or even a year ago. We'll have to let the experts tell us when and for what reason. Now, let's head for home!"

He brought the flitter up and over the valley wall, flying southwest so that they passed over the gap which was the main entrance to the trap. And now he tried the com unit, endeavoring to pick up a signal on which they could beam in for a safe ride.

"That's odd." Under Hume's control the direction finder passed back and forth without bringing any answering code click from the mike. "We may be too far in the mountains to pick up the beam. I wonder . . ." He swept the needle in another direction, slightly to the left.

A crackle spat from the mike. Vye could not read code but the very fury and intensity of that sound suggested panic—even terror.

"What's that?"'

Hume spoke without looking away from the control board. "Alarm."

"From the safari?"

"No. Wass." For a long second. Hume sat very still, his fingers quiet. The flitter was on the automatic course, taking them out of the mountains, and Vye thought that their air speed was such they were already well-removed from that sinister valley.

Hume made a slight adjustment to a dial, and the flitter banked, coming around on another course. Once more he spun the finder of the com. This time he was answered with a series of well-spaced clicks which lacked the urgency of that other call. Hume listened until the code rattled into silence again.

"They're all right at the safari camp."

"But Wass is in trouble. So what does that matter?" Vye wanted to know.

"It matters this much." Hume spoke slowly as if he must convince himself as well as Vye. "I'm the Guild man on Jumala, and the Guild man is responsible for all civs."

"You can't call him your client!"

Hume shook his head. "No, he's no client. But he's human."

It narrowed down to that when a man was on the frontier worlds—humans stood together. Vye wanted to deny it, but his own emotions, as well as the centuries of age-old tradition, argued him down. Wass was a Veep, one of the criminal parasites dabbling in human misery along more than one solar lane. But he was also human and, as one of their own species, had his claim on them.

Vye watched Hume take over the controls, felt the flitter answer another change of course, then heard the frantic yammer of the distress call as they leveled off to ride its beam in to the hidden camp.

"Automatic." Hume had turned down the volume of the receiver so that the clicks in the mike no longer were so strident. "Set on maximum and left that way."

"They had a force barrier around the camp and they knew about the globes and the watchers." Vye tried to imagine what had happened in that woods clearing.

"The barrier might have shorted. And without the flitter they would have been pinned."

"Could have taken off in the spacer."

"Wass doesn't have the reputation of letting any project get out of his hands."

Vye remembered. "Oh—your billion-credit deal."

To his surprise, Hume laughed. "Seems all very far and out of orbit now, doesn't it, Lansor? Yes, our billion-credit deal—but that was thought out before we knew there were more players around the table than we counted. I wonder . . ."

But what he wondered he did not put into words and a moment later he added over his shoulder, "Better try to get some rest, boy. We've some time to a set-down."

Vye did sleep, deeply, dreamlessly. And he roused after a gentle shaking to see a beam of light in the sky ahead, though around them was the solid darkness of night.

"That's a warning," Hume explained. "And I can't raise any reply from the camp except a repeat of the distress call. If there is anyone there now, he can't or won't answer.'

Against that column of light they could make out the sky-pointed taper of the spacer and the auto-pilot landed them beside that ship in the middle of an area well-lighted by the steady shaft of light from the tripod standing where the atom lamp had been on the night they had made their escape from camp.

Climbing stiffly from the small flyer they advanced with caution. A very few minutes later Hume slid his ray-tube back into its belt loop.

"Unless they've holed up in the spacer—and I can't see why they'd do that—this camp's deserted. And they haven't taken any equipment with them except maybe a few items they could backpack."

The ship proved as empty of life as the campsite. A wall seat pulled out too hastily so that it was jammed awry, the com-cabin suggested that the leave-taking, when and for what reason, had been a matter of some emergency. Hume did not touch the tape set to keep on broadcasting the call for assistance.

"What now?" Vye wanted to know as they completed the search.

"The safari camp first—and a call for the Patrol."

"Look here," Vye set down the ration container he had found, was emptying it with vast satisfaction of one who had been too long on tablets, "if you beam the Patrol you'll have to talk, won't you?"

Hume went on fitting new charges into his ray-tube. "The Patrol has to have a full report. There's no way of bypassing that. Yes, we'll have to give all the story. You needn't worry." He snapped closed the load chamber. "I can clear you all the way. You're the victim, remember."

"I wasn't thinking about that."

"Boy." Hume tossed the tube up in the air, caught it in his plasta-hand. "I went into this deal with my eyes wide open—why doesn't matter very much now. In fact," he stared beyond Vye out into the empty, lighted camp, "I've begun to wonder about a lot of things— maybe too late. No—we'll call the Patrol and we'll do it not because it is Wass and his men out there, but because we're human and they're human, and there's a nasty set-up here which has already sucked in other humans for its own purposes."

The skeleton in the valley! And how very close they had been themselves to joining that unknown in his permanent residence.

"So now we make time—back to the safari camp. Get our message off to the Patrol and then we'll try to trace Wass and see what we can do. Jumala is off a regular route. The Patrol won't be here tomorrow at sunrise, no matter how much we wish a scouter would planet then."

Vye was quiet as he stowed in the flitter again. As Hume had said, events moved fast. A little while ago he had wanted to settle with this Out-Hunter, wring out of him not only an explanation for his being here, but claim satisfaction for the humiliation of being moved about to suit some others' purposes. Now he was willing to defeat Wass, bring in the Patrol, go up against whatever hid in that lake up there, providing Hume was not the loser. He tried to think why that was so and could not, he only knew it was the truth.

They were both silent as they took off from Wass' deserted camp, sped away over the black blot of the woodland towards the safari headquarters on the plains. There were stars above again but no globes. Just as they had won their freedom from the valley, so they moved without escort on the plains.

But the lights were there—not impinging on the flitter, or patrolling along its line of flight. No, they hung in a glowing cluster ahead when in the dawn the flitter shot away from the woods, headed for the landmark of the safari camp. A crown of lights circled over the camp site, as if those below were in a state of siege.

Hume aimed straight for them and this time the bobbing circle split wide open, broke to left and right. Vye looked below. Though the grayness of the morning was still hardly more than dusk he could not miss those humps spaced at intervals on the land, just beyond the unseen line of the force barrier. The lights above, the beasts below, the safari camp was under guard.

✳ ✳ **12** ✳ ✳

"There is only one way they could be moving—toward the mountains." Hume stood in the open space among the bubble tents, facing him the four men of the camp, the three civs and Rovald. "You say it's been seven days, planet time, since I left here. They may have been five days on that trail. If possible we have to stop them before they reach that valley."

"A fantastic story." Chambriss wore the affronted expression of a man who expected no interference with his own concerns. Then catching Hume's eye he added, "Not that we doubt you, Hunter. We have the evidence in those dumb brutes waiting out there. However, by your own story, this Wass is an outside-the-law Veep, on this planet secretly for criminal purposes. Surely there is no reason for us to risk our safety in his behalf. Are you certain he is in any danger at all? You and this young man here have, by your testimony, been into enemy territory and have been able to get out again."

"Through a series of fortunate chances which might never occur again." Hume was patient, too patient, Rovald seemed to think. His hand moved, he was holding a ray-tube so that a simple movement of the wrist could send a crisping blast across all the rest of the party.

"I say, stop this yapping and get out there and pick up the Veep!"

"I intend to—after I call the Patrol."

Rovald's tube was now aimed directly at Hume. "No Patrol," he ordered.

"This wrangling has gone far enough." It was Yactisi who spoke with an authority which startled them all. And as their attention swung to him, he was already in action.

Rovald cried out, the weapon spun from his fingers, fingers which were slowly reddening. Yactisi nodded with satisfaction and he held his electo-pole ready for a second attack. Vye scooped up the tube which had whirled across the ground to strike against his borrowed boot.

"I'll set the call for the Patrol, then I'll try to locate Wass," Hume stated.

"Sensible procedure," Yactisi approved in his dry voice. "You believe that you are now immune to whatever force this alien installation controls?"

"It would seem so."

"Then, of course, you must go."

"Why?" Chambriss countered for the second time. "Suppose he isn't so immune after all? Suppose he gets out there and is captured again? He's our pilot—do you want to be planet bound *here*?"

"This man is also a pilot." Starns indicated Rovald, who was nursing his numb hand.

"Since he, too, is one of these criminals, he's not to be trusted!" Chambriss shot back. "Hunter, I demand that you take us off-planet at once! And it is only fair to inform you that I also intend to prefer charges against you and against the Guild. Empty world! Just how empty have we found this world?"

"But, Gentlehomo," Starns showed no signs of any emotion but eager curiosity, "to be here at this time is a privilege we could not hope to equal except by good fortune! The T-Casts will be avid for our stories."

What had that to do with the matter puzzled Vye. But he saw Starns' reminder produce a quick change in Chambriss.

"The T-Casts," he repeated, his expression of anger smoothing away. "Yes, of course, this is, in a manner of speaking, a truly historic occasion. We are in a unique position!"

Had Yactisi smiled? That change of lip line had been so slight Vye could not call it a smile. But Starns appeared to have found the right way to handle Chambriss. And it was the same little man who offered his services in another way when he said, diffidently to Hume:

"I have some experience with coms, Hunter. Do you wish me to send your message and take over the unit until you return? I gather," he added with a certain delicacy, "that it will not be expedient for your gearman to engage in that duty now."

So it was that Starns was installed in the com-cabin of the spacer, sending out the request for Patrol aid, while Rovald was locked in the storage compartment of the same ship, pending arrival of those same authorities. As Hume sorted out supplies and Vye loaded them into the waiting flitter, Yactisi approached the Hunter.

"You have a definite plan of search?"

"Just to cast north from their camp. If they've been gone long enough to hit the foothills we may be able to sight them climbing. Otherwise, we'll go all the way up to the valley, wait for them there."

"You don't believe that they will be released after they have been—processed?"

Hume shook his head. "I don't think we would have been free, Gentlehomo, if it hadn't been for a series of fortunate accidents."

"Yes, though you didn't give us many details about that, Hunter."

Hume put down the needler he had been charging. He studied Yactisi across that weapon.

"Who are you?" His voice was soft but carried a snap.

For the first time Vye saw the tall, lean civ really smile.

"A man of many interests, Hunter—shall we let it go at that for the present? Though I assure you that Wass is not one of them in the way you might believe."

Gray eyes met brown, held so straightly. Then Hume spoke. "I believe you. But I have told you the truth."

"I have never doubted that—only the amount of it. There must be more talking later on—you understand that?"

"I never thought otherwise." Hume set the needler inside the flitter. The civ smiled again, this time including Vye in that evidence of good will before he walked away.

Hume made no comment. "That does it," he told his companion. "Still want to go?"

"If you do—and you can't do it alone." No man could take on the valley and Wass and his men.

Hume made no comment. They had rested briefly after their return to the safari camp, and Vye had been supplied with clothing from Hume's bags, so that now he wore the uniform of the Guild. He went armed, too, with the equipment belt taken from Rovald and that other's weapons, needler and tube. At least they started on their dubious rescue mission with every aid the safari camp could muster.

It was mid-afternoon when the flitter took to the air once again, scattering the hovering globes. There was no alteration in the ranks of the blue watchers waiting—for the barrier to go down, or someone in the camp to step beyond that protection?

"They're stupid," Vye said.

"Not stupid, just geared to one set of actions," Hume returned.

"Which could mean that what sends them here can't change its orders."

"Good guess. I'd say that they were governed by something akin to our tapes. No provision made for any innovations."

"So the guiding intelligence could be long gone."

"I think it has been." Hume then changed the subject sharply.

"How did you get into service at the Starfall?"

It was hard now to think back to Nahuatl—as if the Vye Lansor who had been swamper in that den of the port town was a different person altogether. In that patch of memories into which Rynch Brodie still intruded he hunted for the proper answer.

"I couldn't hold the state jobs. And once you get the habit of eating, you don't starve willingly."

"Why not the state jobs?"

"Without premium they're all low-rung tenders' places. I tried hard enough. But to sit pressing buttons when a light flashed, hour after hour—" Vye shook his head. "They said I was too erratic and gave me the shove. One more move on and it would have been compulsive conditioning. I turned port-drift instead."

"Ever thought of trying for a loan premium?"

Vye laughed shortly. "Loan premium? That's a true fantasy if you've been job hopping. None of the companies will take a chance on a man with an in-and-out record. Oh, I tried . . ." That memory arose to the surface, clear and very chilling. Yes, he had tried to break out of the net the law and custom had put around him from the day he had been made a state child. "No—it was conditioning, or port-drift."

"And you chose port-drift?"

"I was still me—as long as I stayed away from conditioning—"

"Then you became Rynch Brodie in spite of your flight."

"No—well, maybe, for a while. But I'm still Vye Lansor here."

"Yes, here. And I don't think you'll have to worry about raising a premium to get a new start. You can claim victim compensation, you know."

Vye was silent, but Hume did not let him remain so.

"When the Patrol arrives, you put in your claim. I'll back you."

"You can't."

"That's where you're mistaken," Hume told him crisply. "I've already taped a full story back at the spacer—it's on record now."

Vye frowned. The Hunter seemed determined to ask for the worst the Patrol—or the planet police back on Nahuatl—could deal out. A case of illegal conditioning was about as serious as you could get.

They shot along the diagonal of the triangle made by three points, the mountain valley, Wass' camp, and the safari headquarters, heading to the slopes up which the men must be herded if the beasts were shepherding them to the mountain valley. Vye, surveying the forest thick below, began to doubt they would ever be able to pick them up before they reached the valley gate.

Hume took a weaving course, zig-zagging back and forth, while they both watched intently for a glint from one of the globes, any movement which would betray that trail. And it was on one of the upper slopes that the flitter passed over two of the blue beasts lumbering along. Neither of the creatures paid any attention to the flyer, they moved with purpose on some mission of their own.

"Maybe the tail-end of the hunting pack," Hume commented.

He sent the flyer hovering over a stunted line of trees and brush. Beyond that was bare rock. But though they hung for moments, nothing moved into that open.

"Wrong scent somehow." Hume brought the flitter around.

He had it on manual control now, keeping it answering to the quick changes of his will.

A longer sweep supplied the answer—a vegetation-roofed slit running back into the uplands, in a way resembling the crevice through which they had originally found their way into this country. Hume brought the flyer along that. But if the men they sought were pushing their way through below they could not be sighted from the air. At last, with evening drawing in, Hume was forced to admit failure.

"Wait by the gap?" Vye asked.

"Have to now." Hume glanced about. "I'd say maybe tomorrow—mid-morning before they make it that far—*if* they are here. We'll have plenty of time."

Time for what? To make ready for a pitched battle with Wass— or with the beasts herding him? To try in the space of hours to solve the mystery of the lake?

"Do you think we could blast that thing in the lake?" Vye asked.

"We might be able to, just might. But that must be the last resort. We want that in working order for the X-Tee men to study. No, we'd better plan to hold Wass at the gate, wait for the Patrol to come in."

Less than an hour later after a soaring approach, Hume brought the flitter down with neat skill on the top of one of the cliffs which helped to form the portal of the gap. There was no difference in the scene below, save that where the two bodies of the blue beasts had lain there were now only clean and shining bones.

Darkness spread out from the lake woods like a growing stain of evil promise as the sun fell behind the peaks. Night came earlier here than in the plains.

"Watch!" Vye had been gazing down the gap; he was the first to note that movement in the cloaking bush.

Out of the cover trotted a four-footed, antlered animal he had not seen before.

"Syken deer," Hume identified. "But why in the mountains? It's a long way from its home range."

The deer did not pause, but headed directly for the gap and, as it neared, Vye saw that its brown coat was roughed with patches of white froth, while more dripped from the pale pink tongue protruding from its open jaws, and its shrunken sides heaved.

"Driven!" Hume picked up a stone, hurled it to strike the ground ahead of the deer.

The creature did not start, nor show any sign of seeing the rock fall. It trotted on at the same wearied pace, passed the portal rocks into the valley. Then it stood still, wedge-shaped head up, black horns displayed, while the nose flaps expanded, testing the air, until it bounded toward the lake, disappearing in the woods.

Though they shared watches during the night there were no other signs of life, nor did the deer reappear from the woods. With the mid-morning there was a sudden sound to warn them—a wild cry which must have come from a human throat. Hume tossed one of the needlers to Vye, took the other, and they scrambled down to the floor of the gap passage.

Wass did not lead his men; he came behind the reeling trio as if he had joined the blasts as driver. And while his men wavered, staggered, gave the appearance of nearly complete exhaustion, he still walked with a steady tread, in command of his wits, his fears, and the company.

As the first of the men blundered on, a fresh trickle of red running down his bruised face, Hume called: "Wass!"

The Veep stopped short. He made no move to unsling the needler he carried, its barrel pointing skyward over his shoulder, but his round head with its upstanding comb of hair swung slightly from side to side.

"Stop—Wass—this is a trap!"

His three men kept on. Vye moved, for Peake leading that wavering group, stumbled, would have fallen had not the younger man advanced from the shadows to steady him.

"Vye!" Hume made his name a warning.

He had only time to glance around. Wass, his broad face

impassive except for the eyes—those burning madman's eyes—was aiming a ray-tube.

Broken free of his hold, Peake fell to the right, came up against Hume. As Vye went down he saw Wass dart forward at a speed he wouldn't have believed a driven man could summon. The Veep lunged, escaping the shot the Hunter had no time to aim, rolled, and came up with the needler Vye had dropped.

Then Hume, hampered by Peake's feeble clawing, met head on the swinging barrel of that weapon. He gave a startled grunt and smashed back against the cliff, a wave of scarlet blood streaming down the side of his head.

The momentum of Wass' charge carried him on. He collided with his men, and the last thing Vye saw, was the huddle of all four of them, flailing arms and legs, spinning on through the gate into the valley with Wass' hoarse, wordless shouting, bringing echoes from the cliffs.

✳ ✳ **13** ✳ ✳

He lay against a rock, and it was quiet again, except for a small whimpering sound which hurt, joined with the eating pain in his side. Vye turned his head, smelled burned cloth and flesh. Cautiously he tried to move, bring his hand across his body to the belt at his waist. One small part of his mind was very clear—if he could get his fingers to the packet there, and the contents of that packet to his mouth, the pain would go away, and maybe he could slip back into the darkness again.

Somehow he did it, pulled the packet out of its container pouch, worked the fingers of his one usable hand until he shredded open the end of the covering. The tablets inside spilled out. But he had three or four of them in his grasp. Laboriously he brought his hand up, mouthed them all together, chewing their bitterness, swallowing them as best he could without water.

Water—the lake! For a moment he was back in time, feeling for the water bulbs he should be carrying. Then the incautious movement of his questing fingers brought a sudden stab of raw, red agony and he moaned.

The tablets worked. But he did not slide back into unconsciousness again as the throbbing torture became something remote and untroubling. With his good arm he braced himself against the cliff, managed to sit up.

Sun flashed on the metal barrel of a needler which lay in the trampled dust between him and another figure, still very still, with a pool of blood about the head. Vye waited for a steadying breath or two, then started the infinitely long journey of several feet which separated him from Hume.

He was panting heavily when he crawled close enough to touch the Hunter. Hume's face, cheek down in the now-sodden dust, was dabbled with congealing blood. As Vye turned the hunter's head, it rolled limply. The other side was a mass of blood and dust, too thick to afford Vye any idea of how serious a hurt Hume had taken. But he was still alive.

With his good hand, Vye thrust his numb and useless left one into the front of his belt. Then, awkwardly he tried to tend Hume. After a close inspection he thought that the mass of blood had come from a ragged tear in the scalp above the temple and the bone beneath had escaped damage. From Hume's own first-aid pack he crushed tablets into the other's slack mouth, hoping they would dissolve if the Hunter could not swallow. Then he relaxed against the cliff to wait— for what he could not have said.

Wass' party had gone on into the valley. When Vye turned his head to look down the slope he could see nothing of them. They must have tried to push on to the lake. The flitter was at the top of the cliff, as far out of his reach now as if it were in planetary orbit. There was only the hope that a rescue party from the safari camp might come. Hume had set the directional beam on the flyer, when he had brought her down, to serve as a beacon for the Patrol, if and when Starns was lucky enough to contact a cruiser.

"Hmmm . . ." Hume's mouth moved, cracked the drying bloody mask on his lips and chin. His eyes blinked open and he lay staring up at the sky.

"Hume—" Vye was startled at the sound of his own voice, so thready and weak, and by the fact that he found it difficult to speak at all.

The other's head turned; now the eyes were on him and there was a spark of awareness in them.

"Wass?" The whisper was as strained as his own had been.

"In there." Vye's hand lifted from Hume's chest indicating the valley.

"Not good." Hume blinked again. "How bad?" His attention was not for his own hurt; his eyes searched Vye. And the latter glanced down at his side.

By some chance, perhaps because of his struggle with Peake, Wass' beam had not struck true, the main core of the bolt passing between his arm and his side, burning both. How deeply he could not tell, in fact he did not want to find out. It was enough that the tablets had banished the pain now.

"Seared a little," he said. "You've a bad cut on your head."

Hume frowned. "Can we make the flitter?"

Vye moved, then relaxed quickly into his former position. "Not now," he evaded, knowing that neither of them would be able to take that climb.

"Beam on?" Hume repeated Vye's thoughts of moments before. "Patrol coming?"

Yes, eventually the Patrol would come—but when? Hours? Days? Time was their enemy now. He did not have to say any of that, they both knew.

"Needler—" Hume's head had turned in the other direction; now his hand pointed waveringly to the weapon in the dust.

"They won't be back," Vye stated the obvious. Those others had been caught in the trap, the odds on their return without aid were very high.

"Needler!" Hume repeated more firmly, and tried to sit up, falling back with a sharp intake of breath.

Vye edged around, stretched out his leg and scraped the toe of his boot into the loop of the carrying sling, drawing the weapon up to where he could get his hand on it. As he steadied it across his knee Hume spoke again:

"Watch for trouble!"

"They all went in," Vye protested.

But Hume's eyes had closed again. "Trouble—maybe . . ." His voice trailed off. Vye rested his hand on the stock of the needler.

"Hoooooo!"

That beast wail—as they had heard it in the valley! Somewhere from the wood. Vye brought the needler around, so that the sights pointed in that direction. There death might be hunting, but there was nothing he could do.

A scream, filled with all the agony of a man in torment, caught up on the echoes of that other cry. Vye sighted a wild waving of bushes. A figure, very small and far away, crawled into the open on hands and knees and then crumpled into only a shadowy blot on the moss. Again the beast's cry, and a snouting!

Vye watched a second man back out of the trees, still facing whatever pursued him. He caught the glint of sun on what must be a ray-tube. Leaves crisped into a black hole, curls of smoke arose along the path of that blast.

The man kept on backing, passed the inert body of his companion, glancing now and then over his shoulder at the slope up which he was making a slow but steady way. He no longer rayed the bush, but there was the crackle of a small fire outlining the ragged hole his beam had cut.

Back two strides, three. Then he turned, made a quick dash, again facing around after he had gained some yards in the open. Vye saw now it was Wass.

Another dash and an about-face. But this time to confront the enemy. There were three of them, as monstrous as those Vye and Hume had fought in the same place. And one of them was wounded, swinging a charred forepaw before it, and giving voice to a wild frenzy of roars.

Wass leveled the ray-tube, centered sights on the beast nearest to him. The man hammered at the firing button with the flat of his other hand, and almost paid for that second of distraction with his life, for the creature made one of those lightning-swift dashes Vye had so luckily escaped. The clawed forepaw tore a strip from the shoulder of Wass' tunic, left sprouting red furrows behind. But the man had thrown the useless tube into its face, was now running for the gap.

Vye held the needler braced against his knee to fire. He saw the dart quiver in the upper arm of the beast, and it halted to pull out that sliver of dangerously poisoned metal, crumpled it into a tight twist. Vye continued to fire, never sure of his aim, but seeing those slivers go home in thick legs, in outstretched forelimbs, in wide, pendulous bellies. Then there were three blue shapes lying on the slope behind the man running straight for the gap.

Wass hit the invisible barrier full force, was hurled back, to lie gasping on the turf, but already raising himself to crawl again to the gateway he saw and could not believe was barred. Vye closed his eyes. He was very tired now—tired and sleepy—maybe the pain pills were bringing the secondary form of relief. But he could hear, just beyond, the man who beat at that unseen curtain, first in anger and fear, and then just in fear, until the fear was a lonesome crying that went on and on until even that last feeble assault on the barrier failed.

"We have here the tape report of Ras Hume, Out-Hunter of the Guild."

Vye watched the officer in the black and silver of the Patrol, a black and silver modified with the small, green, eye badge of X-Tee, with level and hostile gaze.

"Then you know the story." He was going to make no additions nor explanations. Maybe Hume had cleared him. All right, that was all he would ask to be free to go his way and forget about Jumala— and Ras Hume.

He had not seen the Hunter since they had both been loaded into the Patrol flitter in the gap. Wass had come out of the valley a witless, dazed creature, still under the mental influence of whomever, or whatever, had set that trap. As far as Vye knew the Veep had not yet recovered his full senses, he might never do so. And if Hume had not dictated that confession to damn himself before the Patrol, he might have escaped. They could suspect—but they would have had no proof.

"You continue to refuse to tape?" The officer favored him with one of the closed-jaw looks Vye had often seen on the face of authority.

"I have my rights."

"You have the right to claim victim compensation—a good compensation, Lansor."

Vye shrugged and then winced at a warning from the tender skin over ribs.

"I make no claim, and no tape," he repeated. And he intended to go on saying that as long as they asked him. This was the second visit in two days and he was getting a little tired of it all. Perhaps he should do as prudence dictated and demand to be returned to Nahuatl. Only his odd, unexplainable desire to at least see Hume kept him from making the request they would have to honor.

"You had better reconsider." Authority resumed.

"Rights of person—" Vye almost grinned as he recited that. For the first time in his pushed-around life he could use that particular phrase and make it stick. He thought there was a sour twist to the officer's mouth, but the other still retained his impersonal tone as he spoke into the intership com:

"He refused to make a tape."

Vye waited for the other's next move. This should mark the end of their interview. But instead the officer appeared to relax the restraint of his official manner. He brought a viv-root case from an inner pocket, offered a choice of contents to Vye, who gave an instant and suspicious refusal by shake of head. The officer selected one of the small tubes, snapped off the protecto-nib, and set it between his lips for a satisfying and lengthy pull. Then the panel of the cabin door pushed open, and Vye sat up with a jerk as Ras Hume, his head banded with a skin-core covering, entered.

The officer waved his hand at Vye with the air of one turning over a problem. "You were entirely right. And he's all yours, Hume."

Vye looked from one to the other. With Hume's tape in official hands why wasn't the Hunter under restraint? Unless, because they were aboard the Patrol cruiser, the officers didn't think a closer confinement was necessary. Yet the Hunter wasn't acting the role of prisoner very well. In fact he perched on a wall-flip seat with the ease of one completely at home, accepted the viv-root Vye had refused.

"So you won't make a tape," he asked cheerfully.

"You act as if you want me to!" Vye was so completely baffled by this odd turn of action that his voice came out almost plaintively.

"Seeing as how a great deal of time and effort went into placing you in the position where you *could* give us that tape, I must admit some disappointment."

"Give *us*?" Vye echoed.

The officer removed the viv-root from between his lips. "Tell him the whole sad story, Hume."

But Vye began to guess. Life in the Starfall, or as port-drift, either sharpened the wits or deadened them. Vye's had suffered the burnishing process. "A set up?"

"A set up," Hume agreed. Then he glanced at the Patrol officer a little defensively. "I might as well tell the whole truth—this didn't quite begin on the right side of the law. I had my reasons for wanting to make trouble for the Kogan estate, only not because of the credits involved." He moved his plasta-flesh hand. "When I found that L-B from the Largo Drift and saw the possibilities, did a little day dreaming—I worked out this scheme. But I'm a Guild man and as it happens, I want to stay one. So I reported to one of the Masters and told him the whole story—why I hadn't taped on the records my discovery on Jumala.

"When he passed along the news of the L-B to the Patrol, he also suggested that there might be room for fraud along the way I had thought it out. That started a chain reaction. It happened that the Patrol wanted Wass. But he was too big and slick to be caught in a case which couldn't be broken in court. They thought that here was just the bait he might snap at, and I was the one to offer it to him. He could check on me, learn that I had excellent reason to do what I said I was doing. So I went to him with my story and he liked it. We made the plan work just as I had outlined it. And he planted Rovald on me as a check. But I didn't know Yactisi was a plant, also."

The Patrol officer smiled. "Insurance," he waved the viv-root, "just insurance."

"What we didn't foresee was this complicating alien trouble. You were to be collected as the castaway, brought back to the Center and then, once Wass was firmly enmeshed, the Patrol would blow the thing wide open. Now we do have Wass, with your tape we'll have him for good, subject to complete reconditioning. But we also have an X-Tee puzzle which will keep the services busy for some time. And we would like your tape."

Vye watched Hume narrowly. "Then you're an agent?"

Hume shook his head. "No, just what I said I am, an Out-Hunter who happened to come into some knowledge that will assist in straightening out a few crooked quirks in several systems. I have no love for the Kogan clan, but to help bring down a Veep of Wass' measure does aid in reinstating one's self-esteem."

"This victim compensation—I *could* claim it, even though the deal was a set up?"

"You'll have first call on Wass' assets. He has plenty invested in legitimate enterprises, though we'll probably never locate all his hidden funds. But everything we can get open title to will be impounded. Have something to do with your share?" inquired the officer.

"Yes."

Hume was smiling subtly. He was a different man from the one Vye had known on Jumala. "Premium for the Guild is one thousand credits down, two thousand for training and say another for about the best field outfit you can buy. That'll give you maybe another two or three thousand to save for your honorable retirement."

"How did you know?" Vye began and then had to laugh in spite of himself as Hume replied:

"I didn't. Good guess, eh? Well, zoom, out your recorder, Commander. I think you are going to have some very free speech now." He got to his feet. "You know, the Guild has a stake in this alien discovery. We may just find that we haven't seen the last of that valley after all, recruit."

He was gone and Vye, eager to have the past done with, and the future beginning, reached for the dictation mike.